COWBOY GAMES

DATE DUE

ILL 3-10-09 WRS	
ILL 4-20-09	
ILL 5-12-09	
ILL 7-17-09	
ILL 8-17-09	
ILL 10-28-09	
FEB 1 5 2010	
JAN 02 2013	
JAN 1 6 2013	
AUG 1 9 2014	
AUG 1 9 2014	

GAYLORD   PRINTED IN U.S.A.

A SIREN PUBLISHING BOOK
IMPRINT: Erotic Romance

COWBOY GAMES
Copyright © 2008 by Wendi Darlin
ISBN-10: 1-60601-084-0
ISBN-13: 978-1-60601-084-6

First Printing: August 2008

Cover design by Jinger Heaston
All cover art and logo copyright © 2008 by Siren Publishing, Inc.

Printed in the U.S.A.

PUBLISHER
Siren Publishing, Inc.
www.SirenPublishing.com

DEDICATION

For Mike, for a million reasons, and for my family and friends who support me no matter how long it takes! I love you all.

Chris and Neville, you are the best.

COWBOY GAMES

Wendi Darlin
Copyright © 2008

Prologue

"I'm sorry Mrs. Ryder, we did everything we could."

He couldn't be dead. Rebecca Ryder stood in the emergency room staring at the doctor, barely hearing anything beyond those first words.

"…aneurism…" the doctor said.

Todd couldn't be gone.

Her tears caught the fluorescent overhead light and held it, blurring everything but the pain. How could a man like Todd have an aneurism? He was thirty-four years old, healthy and strong as an ox. He worked out every day, ate right. He hadn't missed work for a legitimate sick day in over four years. The only time he had called into the office and said he was sick was when she refused to let him out of bed in the morning.

Ten years of marriage hadn't dampened her desire for him. Just this morning she had tried to keep him home, but he had a meeting he couldn't miss. He was up for a promotion and the last couple of weeks had been filled with meetings and training seminars. She joked with him that she'd had to take an imaginary boyfriend because he wasn't around enough.

"Who is this lucky man?" he asked her.

"A cowboy." Her voice was husky, the one she used to pull him back to bed. She draped his tie around his neck and clenched each side of it in her fists. "And he *never* takes his hat off."

"Never?" Todd's lips barely moved, the word coming out on his breath. The want in his eyes, obvious, spurring her on.

"Never." She ran her hands down his chest, teasing his nipples through the smooth fabric of his shirt.

"You like that do you?" He reached for her, pulled her hips against his.

"Uh huh," she said, hoping she could get him to cave, to crawl back into bed with her and make love until she screamed. "There's just something about that hat," she breathed.

Todd slipped his hands beneath her camisole and nuzzled the thick locks of dark hair that buried her ear. "I'd give you a cowboy if I could, but right now I've got to get to the office."

Her nipples tingled then tightened beneath his touch. She sighed. He couldn't stay, not today, and it only made her want him more.

"Maybe you could pick up a hat on the way home."

He brushed her hair back to kiss her high on her neck in the exact spot that drove her wild. "Anything else your cowboy does?" His mouth found her skin.

She gasped. "He calls me darlin'."

"Alright, darlin' tonight you get your cowboy." He kissed her again and pressed his hips into her, teasing her with how hard he'd grown.

"Can't you just be a little late?" she pleaded, running her hand over the front of his pants.

"Not today." He gripped her shoulders and held her away. "But I'll make it up to you tonight."

"Promise?" She knotted his tie and slid it into place.

"Promise." He kissed her goodbye, picked up his briefcase and headed for the door. "I love you, darlin'."

Rebecca wiped away a tear. He couldn't be gone. Not Todd.

Chapter 1

A year later

The line for baggage check-in at Charleston International Airport moved, and Rebecca wheeled her suitcase forward another foot. At six a.m. the line should be shorter, but apparently everybody and her sister got up at the crack of dawn on the first day of spring to jump on an airplane. She adjusted the shoulder strap of her carry-on and took a breath to quiet the butterflies in her stomach. It was a pretty safe bet not a person in line was going to the same place she was.

"Todd would think this is funny. Don't you think?" Rebecca asked.

"Who wouldn't? This is hysterical," Melinda said, her eyes glued to the full-color glossy brochure for Fantasy Ranch. "Listen to this: Are you ready for the ultimate ladies' vacation? Come on darlin', kick off your boots and stay awhile at Fantasy Ranch where the cowboy of your dreams is yours. That's right, for one romance-filled week on an authentic ranch with one of the most spectacular views in Wyoming, a real-life cowboy will be yours and yours alone. Not only can these boys wrestle steer to the ground, they will wine, dine and treat you like the lady you are."

"Can you imagine who comes up with this stuff?" Rebecca asked.

"If I didn't know you, I couldn't imagine who would actually go to this place." Melinda pushed the brochure over to offer her sister another look at the dozen cowboys seated on a fence. Hats, boots, rugged good looks and lazy smiles on every one of them. Snowcapped mountains stood in the distance behind them. "They're hot as hell, but you're still out of your mind," she said.

"Life's a game, might as well play it."

"Roulette's a game too, but you won't catch me playing that," Melinda said. "And this is the worst false advertising I've ever seen."

"What makes you so sure?"

"First of all, these guys have to be models," Melinda said. "There's no way they all work in one place, and second of all, Fantasy Ranch is probably a front for some perverted serial killer's garage."

"What kind of serial killer targets women who have a thing for cowboys?"

"One who always had to be the Indian when he was a little boy." Melinda's lips curved into a smile. "I have two psychology classes under my belt. I know what I'm talking about, and there is no way this place really exists. Not like this anyway."

"Have a little faith," Rebecca said. "You don't trust anyone or anything."

"With plenty of reason."

"I'm sorry. I didn't mean to bring that up." Rebecca placed her hand on her sister's shoulder and gave it a squeeze. "But seriously. It's not too late to get a ticket, and there's plenty to go around. Look at this one." She pointed to an olive-skinned hottie, with movie star eyes. "Says he likes riding bareback, sleeping under the stars and taming mustangs, but when it comes to the ladies he's got velvet hands."

They both laughed.

"It's probably another identity theft scam," Melinda said. "A creative one. I'll give them that."

"It's not."

"You have to give them all kinds of personal information for the required background check, don't you?" Melinda asked.

"Yeah, but I did my homework." Rebecca pulled her suitcase forward another couple of feet and closed the gap in the line. "I called the Canyon Creek, Wyoming Chamber of Commerce."

"And..."

"And," Rebecca continued. "The lady that answered the phone laughed, but she said Fantasy Ranch is owned by two local cowboys named Garrett and Gavin Carter, and they're very easy on the eyes."

"She say anything else?" Melinda asked with renewed interest.

"She said the staff changes regularly, but she's never received any complaints about them. They're running a legitimate operation with a steady stream of customers flying in from all over the place."

"Do they have their own little cowboy out there pointing out 'da planes' when they land?"

"Everybody left that island with what they came after," Rebecca reminded her.

"It says you can ride horses and picnic alongside 'a pristine mountain stream.'" Melinda twisted her lips, looking anything but convinced, and turned to the next page of the brochure. "At least you won't need to pay extra for the riding lessons."

Rebecca had been riding horses since she was five. Somewhere in her attic at least fifty ribbons from jumping competitions were collecting dust. She still spent weekends at the stables exercising the horses whose owners didn't make enough time for them.

"I already did." Rebecca's smile was purely wicked. "It ought to be fun having a cowboy show me how to do it his way."

"I'd pick that one." Melinda shoved the brochure toward her and pointed to a man with smoldering green eyes, an easy grin and jeans that lay nicely over the muscles beneath them. It was hard to tell with his hat on, but Rebecca guessed he was blond. "Which one did you pick?"

"I'll have to take whatever's left. I booked on short notice."

"It's like getting to the meat counter during the last hour of the sale," Melinda said.

A woman behind them in line chuckled.

"They all look beefy enough to give me what I'm after. Remember the real stuff will be up to me anyway." Rebecca laughed and lowered her voice. "Fantasy Ranch, rule number one: NO SEX."

After skimming past the legal gibberish, the contract was simple. A background check was required of all guests, and there were two stipulating clauses: 1) No sex; and 2) No contact or attempted contact after the week is up. Clause number two was accompanied by a clear warning: Any attempt at contact will be considered 'criminal stalking' and treated as such. A sure sign the cowboys were very good at making women think they had fallen in love.

"Whew, the price is hefty." Melinda scanned another page. "You didn't tell me it cost this much. You sure you don't want to go out with Ray first? Kind of ease back into the dating pool and keep some of your money in the bank?"

"He's not my type. None of Scott's friends are my type."

"Ray's not bad looking and at least he's not made out of plastic with a battery compartment."

Rebecca groaned. "I'd probably have better sex with my vibrator." The man in front of her took a quick glance over his shoulder, and Rebecca covered her mouth with her hand. "Sorry," she whispered.

"You're not going to find Todd in Wyoming or anywhere else." Melinda softened, and dropped the brochure to her side. "You need to at least open your eyes to other possibilities."

"I did." Rebecca gave her a weak smile. She pulled the brochure from Melinda's hand and flipped it open to the image of the green-eyed sex pot Melinda had already pointed out. "That one."

Melinda took the brochure back and studied the picture. "If you're going to go crazy, he's the one to go with," she said. "And for the record, you're definitely going crazy."

"You really should come. Go crazy with me for once."

"Scott and I need some time together." Melinda sighed and flipped over to the next page. "I don't think a cowboy would help matters."

"Might not hurt to give him a taste of his own medicine."

The man in front of Rebecca stepped up to the baggage clerk and another slot opened up. Rebecca handed over her bag, her tickets and her ID.

"One bag. Charleston to Dallas. Dallas to Yellowstone Regional Airport, Wyoming." The clerk attached the baggage labels and hefted Rebecca's suitcase onto the conveyor belt behind her.

Just before the security line, Rebecca pulled Melinda in for a hug. "Thanks for bringing me to the airport. Call me if you need to talk."

"I'll be fine," Melinda said. "But Becca, are you sure you're ready for this?"

The year since Todd passed away had eased the pain but the emptiness inside her had only grown. She still missed him everyday, his laugh, the light that flashed in his dark eyes, his undying love for her. She ached for his touch, the feel of his body, and the way they made love.

"It's time, Mel. I need to see what it's like to have other men around, and I know I'm not ready for a real one. I figure this will be easier, you know? It's just a game and I don't have to play any harder than I want to."

"I hope you have a good time." Melinda exhaled sharply. "But you call me if anything at all seems fishy and I will have you escorted away from that place by a S.W.A.T. team if I have to."

Rebecca adjusted the grip on her carry-on. "Todd would think this is funny, right?"

"You two would be playing cowboy 'til you had saddle sores," Melinda said softly.

Rebecca wiped the tears from her eyes and smiled.

"Well, if you're really going to do this, you better get in line."

"Don't worry about me." Rebecca hugged her again. "I'm going to go out there, do a little horseback riding, let some sexy cowboy wine and dine me, and when I come home, maybe I'll be ready for a real date."

* * * *

"What am I up against?" Gavin Carter kicked his Nike runners up on the broad pine desk across from his brother. He tilted his head back and ran his fingers through his dark blond hair, a little longer than was respectable on a cowboy, but the ladies liked it.

"Rebecca Ryder," Garrett read from the file in his hand. "Thirty-two, biotech consultant from South Carolina. Widowed."

"When did her husband die?"

"It's been a year," Garrett said, flipping over to the following page.

"Good." Gavin reached into his desk for a tennis ball. "An easy week."

The worst of the grief was behind her. What they did was a lot like therapy for many of the women who booked a vacation at the ranch. Most of them just needed a boost of confidence and a little attention from the opposite sex. A few needed to know men could act like gentlemen, even men who were strong enough to wrestle a steer to the ground.

For the most part the job was easy, the guest entertainment part of it, anyway. He was more than happy to be what a lady needed, as long as she only needed him for a week. In another year, he and Garrett would have too much on their plates to spend time entertaining guests, but for now it made business sense.

Fantasy Ranch was a business, a growing business, and there was plenty to be done to make sure it kept turning out a profit and continued to adjust to the changes necessary for it to grow. To lower overhead and maintain an authentic feel, the resort office was in the big house, and it was the only room other than the dining hall and downstairs bathroom that was open to guests and employees. Gavin and Garrett's bedrooms were upstairs, the same ones they'd grown up in. Aside from basic updates, the rest of the house hadn't changed since they were teenagers and they liked it that way.

"I'm glad it's your week," Garrett tossed across the desk at him. "Last widow I had cried every time I touched her, then cried when I didn't."

"That's because, big brother, you don't touch a woman like I do." A slow smile crept across Gavin's face. He bounced the ball off the pine timber walls and caught it when it ricocheted back.

"I'd rather not touch them at all," Garrett said with a grin.

"Lucky you." Gavin threw the ball again, not looking forward to another week without a soft, warm body beneath his. "I'm horny as a bull and I've been so busy around here lately I haven't had a chance to go out and even look for any relief."

"You can always join the boys in the bunkhouse." Garrett's grin erupted in a laugh.

"No thanks. You fellas are pretty, but not my type."

"Just don't so much as breathe on your guest this week," Garrett warned him. "I'm just waiting for the Sheriff's office to send out an undercover."

"Heard anything from the lawyers yet?" Gavin grabbed the ball out of the air as it shot toward him.

"Ms. Cardin recanted her story once she learned we have camera surveillance in the cabins. Travis will be cleared to come back to work as soon as the case is officially closed. If he still wants the job, and I don't blame him if he doesn't."

"Thank God she didn't read the fine print of the contract. If she'd known about the cameras, it would have been just as easy to say he attacked her in the barn or on the trails." Gavin ripped the ball against the wall again. "It's unbelievable what people will do to shove a buck in their pocket."

"A lawsuit like that would have shut us down." Garrett stacked Rebecca's file with the ones for the rest of the guests arriving the next day and lined up everything on his desk at right angles.

Gavin had to give his brother credit. He never would have believed that Fantasy Ranch would be as successful as it had turned out to be. Sure, he knew what women needed to hear, but he never thought so many of them would be willing to pay so much money to hear it. He was on his way to a very early retirement.

"Are the guest rooms ready?" Garrett asked as he turned off his computer and stood to leave.

"Fresh flowers, chocolates on the pillow, and wine in the chiller. Everything a lady might want when she doesn't have a cowboy wrapped around her pretty little finger," Gavin said.

"Good. I've got a theatre meeting. I'm going to need you to meet the last flight at the airport."

"How many are on it?"

"Two. Yours and Clayton's."

"If you don't have anything else for me this morning," Gavin said, dropping his feet to the floor and depositing the tennis ball back in his desk drawer. "I'm going for a run."

"Don't stay out too long," Garrett said. "The first group's coming in on an early flight. And they don't ever picture the cowboys in running shoes." He picked up his empty mug and carried it around the desk.

They left through the living room and crossed in front of the walk-in fireplace with the antique bison mounted above it. The glassy-eyed bull looked like it had charged the wall and gotten stuck at the base of its neck, with just the slightest bulge of shoulders breaking through. Gavin had plenty in common with the old beast, his head in one place, his body in another and his heart cut out completely. Work was the only thing that really mattered anyway, and maybe this would be a good week on the job.

At thirty-two, Rebecca Ryder was a lot younger than most of the guests. Maybe that meant she'd be up for some of the more physical stuff the ranch had to offer, and he wouldn't have to stand around taking square dance lessons for the umpteenth time.

* * * *

A green paisley duffel with the pink yarn pompom made another round on the baggage carousel at Yellowstone Regional Airport, but Rebecca's suitcase was nowhere in sight. Nearby, a young couple sat down on the floor and canoodled, seemingly content to make the most of their wait. Within seconds they were lost in a kiss. Rebecca shivered and goose bumps scampered across her bare shoulders. Probably just her body sending another sign that she had stone-cold lost her mind. The evidence was stacking up.

The thin cotton dress with spaghetti straps had seemed like a fine choice when she left South Carolina, but the Wyoming air was cooler than she had expected it to be. She cursed again for losing her jacket while running for her connection in the Dallas airport. This little getaway was off to a great start.

The same few pieces of luggage led by the pompom-adorned duffel made their way along the belt again, and not many people were left milling around the baggage claim area. A cowboy approached, probably back to check for his bags. The place was crawling with men in boots and belt buckles. Coming here was such a big mistake.

She rested her elbow on the carry-on slung over her shoulder and glanced at her watch. She'd better go out front to let the limo driver know she was waiting, or else she might miss her ride to the ranch.

Just what she needed. A week without all the clothes she'd packed, and worse, no vibrator. Rebecca swore under her breath. How hard is it to put a piece of luggage on the corresponding flight? Isn't that what all those obnoxious paper tags are for? She waited for the carousel to make one more round and tried to convince herself she wasn't stalling. She glanced again at the full-color glossy brochure for Fantasy Ranch gripped in her hand. She was out of her mind alright. And she was definitely stalling.

Maybe Melinda was right about the cowboys, and the ones on the website were just models used for advertising the place. The real ones probably had scraggly beards, three front teeth and hands so callused they'd tear a girl's skin to pieces.

"Where are you going?"

She didn't have to look up. The pointed toes of his boots and faded denim that traveled up from there gave the speaker away. A cowboy.

"Crazy apparently," Rebecca said without making eye contact, focusing again on the brochure. What in the hell had she been thinking spending a small fortune for such a load of crap? She was on her way to the nuthouse alright, and getting there fast.

"I'm headed there myself," Cowboy said in an obvious attempt at a joke. "I'll give you a ride."

He sounded friendly enough, but she didn't feel like being hit on. She glanced up to tell him so, but was too blindsided to remember what smart-alecky comeback she'd planned to use. Melinda had been right about one thing. If she had to go crazy, he'd definitely be the one to go with.

"Are you Rebecca?" His dark blond hair hung to his chin in silky strands that begged to have fingers dragged through them, and his eyes could melt a girl.

A flush crept over her. No false advertising there. He was even more gorgeous in person. Her stomach did a somersault. What had she been thinking? She couldn't go through with this. He was hot enough to sway a nun, and he was just the driver. How in the hell was she going to keep her horny hands to herself for a week? Or more to the point, how would she keep them off herself.

The cowboy held her stare and a slow easy smile spread across his face. Her head defogged enough to remember he'd asked her if she was Rebecca, and she hadn't had the whereabouts to answer him. He spoke before she could twist her tongue around an answer.

"I'll take that as a yes. I'm Gavin. Let me get this," he said, reaching for her carry-on and easily hoisting the bag over his shoulder. "You don't travel this light do you?"

"Gavin?" she managed. "Gavin Carter?"

"You did your homework," he said with a smile. "I did too. Rebecca Ryder, thirty-two, biotech consultant from South Carolina."

He summed her up like a bio off a dating site and his appearance was enough to shake her to the core, broad athletic shoulders v-ing down to narrow hips, long muscular legs and a rugged beauty that took her breath away. She forced air into her lungs. No man was going to take her breath away. That's not what she had flown across the country for.

"You forgot to mention I like riding bareback at sunset and hot ass cowboys," she said.

"I didn't know that about you. Like your temper, it wasn't in your reservation application."

His smirk nudged her irritation up another notch, but the light that danced in his eyes sent her animosity slithering away.

"Having second thoughts, or just hungry enough to bite my head off?" he asked.

"Both." She tilted her face to the ceiling and blew a heavy breath. The man was just doing his job - the job she had paid for him to do - nothing she needed to get so miffed about.

"Sorry," she said, "I'm not usually nasty. Or crazy. I don't know what I'm doing here. And it looks like they lost my suitcase."

"We'll get you settled in the truck and I'll go check on your luggage. You'll feel better when we get you to the ranch. I promise." He reached for her, his hand barely resting on her lower back.

A sizzling shiver shot down her spine and tripped over itself heading back up again. Holy hell, the devil couldn't have lit her hotter than Gavin Carter and they'd barely gotten past a rocky introduction. She had to get it together if she was going to survive an entire week out here.

He guided her toward the line of double doors that led out of the airport in a gait as sure and unhurried as the rest of his demeanor.

Maybe the cowboy she was assigned to would look good enough to keep things interesting, but not half as good as Gavin. That would make things a whole lot easier.

Parked at the curb was a stretched out Dodge truck with dual tires, a silver ram on the grill and windows tinted as dark as midnight. He held the door while she climbed in and slid across the cool leather seat. Ahhh, relief. The door shut between them, and her breathing resumed on its own. She wasn't chilled anymore, nope she was hotter than Hades, and considerably worried she might break into a sweat.

And she wasn't alone either.

"Hi, I'm Marge," said a middle-aged woman seated with her back to the front of the truck. Marge's jeans were new, and she had paired them with stylish but orthopedic shoes. Her body was soft and had settled into its current stage of life. She had to be someone's mother, maybe even someone's grandmother. Good for her. A woman's never too old to want a little love or to go after the attention she needs.

Rebecca smoothed the skirt of her cotton sundress and introduced herself. "You think they're all as hot as the driver?" she added.

"I don't know if my ticker can take it if they are." Marge choked on a nervous laugh and patted her chest. "I guess I really didn't know what I was in for out here."

"He does get your blood flowing, doesn't he?" Rebecca let go of her nerves. She wasn't the only one Gavin affected that way.

Marge sized up Rebecca's outfit. "Those are cute boots. I couldn't find any comfortable enough." She pulled a bottle of champagne from the door. "It's all just pretend anyway, probably won't even need them. You want a glass?"

"Sure," Rebecca said, "I'm parched." But she wasn't paying attention to Marge.

Gavin had stowed her carry-on in the truck and was headed back into the airport. He looked as good going as he did coming. A surge of pleasure overtook her, a sensation she hadn't felt since Todd was alive. At least when the man was that far away she could still breathe.

She was sipping champagne when he opened the door again. A steady fire fanned out from the pit of her stomach, and it had nothing to do with the alcohol. Damned traitorous body.

"Some bags were diverted to another flight, but they'll be coming in later tonight. Yours will be delivered to the ranch when it arrives," he said. "In the meantime, I'll be happy to provide anything you might need."

She was pretty sure he could provide exactly what she needed, if there wasn't that No Sex clause in her contract.

"Thanks." She was careful to keep her voice as natural as possible. "I have a change of clothes in my carry-on. I'll be fine until tomorrow."

"Alright then. I'll take you ladies home." Gavin's eyes lingered on her long enough to singe the hair on the back of her neck, then he shut the door and walked around the front of the truck.

"I hope there's plenty of water in here." She relaxed into the seat and took a deep breath. "You might have to hose me down before we get there."

Marge laughed. "If a man looked at me the way he just looked at you, I would have torn his clothes off and thrown him down on the curb." She looked down at the hand curling nervously in her lap. "I would've wanted to anyway."

"I think I'm going to like you," Rebecca said.

"No offense, but I hope I'm too busy with some little cowboy half my age to get to know you." Marge took a long pull and winked at Rebecca over the rim of her glass.

The women laughed again and Rebecca settled back to watch the landscape roll by. She dug her phone from her purse and dialed her sister's number.

"Hey, ridden one already?" Melinda answered.

"No." Rebecca rested her head back on the thick leather seat, sinking into it like a pillow. "But from what I've seen so far there wasn't any false advertising."

"Seriously?" Melinda's voice was missing its usual spunk. She was having a rough time dealing with Scott's latest affair, although by now she should be used to the heartache.

"Seriously," Rebecca said. Her sister needed distraction more than a lecture. "And the airlines didn't put my bag on the right flight. So I'm out here without my little friend."

Marge chuckled across from her and lifted her glass in the air. Usually Melinda would have laughed too, but instead she sighed, and the sound of a door slamming echoed from her end of the line.

"I'm sure you'll manage," Melinda said, her voice suddenly deflated.

"Mel, you okay?"

"I've got to go. Scott's home." Melinda dropped her voice to a whisper. "Call me when you get a chance."

Rebecca dropped her phone back into her purse and sipped her champagne while she watched the back of Gavin's head through the clear glass that separated him from them. He had taken his hat off and for the second time she imagined running her hands through his silky hair. He caught her eye in the rearview mirror and smiled. She should have had the decency to turn away, but she couldn't bring herself to stop staring at him.

His thumb tapped out a rhythm on the steering wheel, and the tendons in his forearm danced along. She hadn't even seen as far as his elbow, but the slight strain of the fabric against his bicep promised it only got better up there. He was golden, like he spent time in the sun, but not enough to turn himself to leather, and there was just the right amount of pale blond hair coating his masculine arms. The lady at the Chamber of Commerce had nailed it. Gavin Carter was easy on the eyes. Very easy on the eyes.

The truck eased to a stop, and beyond the windshield two massive gates swung forward in the standard Wyoming pace. Slow and steady. Scrollwork across the top of the gates spelled out the moniker: Fantasy Ranch. Beyond stood a massive ranch house and several outbuildings flanked by endless acres of natural countryside and the bluest sky in the world. Heaven couldn't be more beautiful. A woman could definitely lose herself here.

Rebecca raised her glass to Marge. "Let the cowboy games begin."

Chapter 2

Marge filled her lungs with the clean breeze that swept down from the mountains, so different from the stale, hot air that lay over the asphalt outside her Philadelphia apartment building. At Fantasy Ranch the quiet was almost nerve-shattering, and the colors of the landscape were literally a sight for sore eyes.

A lifetime of living in the city meant her senses had become accustomed to the never-ending barrage of horns, sirens, and engines. The constant awareness of her surroundings and guard of her personal safety had become instinctual. But here, there was peace, a sense of security she could almost taste.

Years of stress fell from her shoulders like bricks, with every step she traveled from the limo to her cabin. The soft grass beneath her feet reminded her of her grandmother's house in New Jersey, the one she hadn't been to in over twenty years. Her grandmother's house was where she'd always let down her guard, a place where she didn't need to hide from anyone or worry who might be watching.

Marge hugged herself. She was already in love. Not with a cowboy, though she could see where so many women might make that fall. The young man chattering away at her side was a dream, but too pretty to be anything more than that. His voice was soft, almost feminine, and his hands, clamped onto her luggage, were better manicured than hers.

"I hope you enjoy your stay," Clayton said as he climbed up the steps to her cabin and unlocked the door. "If there's anything I can do to make you more comfortable, all you have to do is ask."

"Just keep the horses away from me." She smiled but her lips faltered. "I'm afraid of horses. Terrified really." Her cheeks grew hot. "I know it's ridiculous."

"There's nothing ridiculous about facing your fears." He set her suitcase on a luggage rack at the foot of the bed and carried her smaller bag to the bathroom vanity.

"I'm not facing anything."

He moved about the room, turning on lights and pulling back the bedcovers. "You don't come to a ranch to avoid horses. Maybe you're braver than you think."

"I guess," she mumbled as she took inventory of the room. Five-star accoutrements were everywhere her eyes landed. Rustic elegance had never been so purely defined. It would be a shame to bring such a nice place down. This crazy world needed a little less reality and a few more resorts. Or maybe that's just what she needed.

"I couldn't imagine anywhere more perfect." She passed a folded bill toward Clayton.

"No, ma'am. Thank you, but we don't accept gratuities. Your comfort is my pleasure."

She tucked the money into the side of her purse and braced herself against a sharp twang of guilt. As he closed the door behind him, she dug a roll of antacid out of her purse. Deceiving people always upset her stomach, especially nice people.

If these cowboys were criminals they had better manners than any lawbreakers she could've ever imagined. This assignment wasn't going to be as easy as it had sounded.

* * * *

Damn. There were probably at least a thousand words to describe Rebecca Ryder, but 'damn' was the first one that popped into Gavin's head. His eyes followed the swell of breasts down to her narrow waist then over the curve of her hips. Giving her all his attention this week wouldn't be much of a problem. Either that or it would be a very big problem and he would be taking a hell of a lot of cold showers. Probably both were true, and he'd better start off with the shower.

"Office is in there, first door on the right," he said, going through the routine as they passed the big house on the way to her cabin. "Dining hall is to the left of the main staircase."

She followed the direction of his hand with those dark eyes that had swallowed him when he first saw her.

"The house is beautiful," she said. "I've always loved that rustic mountain lodge feel with all those rough timbers and stacked logs."

Every word lilted out of her in a soft southern way that made him want to just sit back and let her go on for a while. Even when she'd torn into him at the airport she sounded sexy enough to take a bite out of. A voice and a body like that would be one hell of a combination in bed. It figures she'd show up at the one place he couldn't lay a hand on her.

"You stayed in one before?"

"Once." She turned away from the house then, and he figured it was something she didn't want to tell him about. Either that or she would spill every detail about it on his shoulder before the week was up. Comforting her wasn't the worst thing he could think of.

A jaw-dropping beauty like Rebecca didn't need to waste money paying for male attention. Men must stalk her in the grocery store. He was close to certain she'd never dropped anything that she had to bend over and pick up herself. Her hair alone was enough to bog his mind with all kinds of ideas he shouldn't be having about a guest. That damned southern accent melted right into him, and her eyes. Don't even get started on her eyes.

Damn. She'd be one hell of a soft, warm body to fall into that's for sure. And she was smart to boot. She'd have to be to do what she did for a living. Unless, of course, she'd lied on the application. Garrett was thorough with his reference and background checks, so she probably hadn't lied.

Who would ever expect a biotech consultant to fill out a dress like that? Even boots looked sexy on her. He could only imagine what a pair of high heels would do for those legs, or what they'd feel like wrapped around him. He shook his head. He hadn't gotten laid in too long. Way too long.

"Over here we have the corral." He gestured to their right, trying to focus on the job instead of how bad he wanted to get his guest naked. "You signed on for riding lessons, so we'll start off with them there before we head out on the trails."

She smiled at him then, her full lips parting to reveal a heart-shattering smile. Yep, Rebecca Ryder could find plenty of men to whisper sweet nothings that she wouldn't have to pay for. He'd be the first in line. What was she doing here?

Experience warned him she was either some kind of psycho, one of those fatal attraction types, or she was a long way from over her husband. He caught her dark eyes again, searched for signs of crazy, and was thrown by the same feeling of momentary loss he'd experienced at the airport, like he'd tripped and fallen into her, without taking a single step.

This was a woman he was going to have to watch himself around. Too bad he hadn't met her at the grocery store. She turned her smile on him in a way that made him suspect she could tell what he was thinking. He chuckled at having been caught, and tipped his hat to her.

She didn't look like she was off her rocker. Most likely he'd need to go easy on her, let her tell him all about her husband, and make sure he kept a handkerchief in his pocket. That was the worst part of the job – watching them cry. Especially, he imagined, one as beautiful as the one walking alongside him right now.

"Over there behind the barn is a hot tub, or if you prefer there's a Jacuzzi in your cabin."

"Never pictured a hot tub behind a barn before." Her face contorted, sending one eyebrow higher than the other and carving lines into the smooth skin of her forehead. But it was her mouth that twisted something in his gut. Her full lips had settled into a smirk that plumped them in such a way he couldn't think of anything but taking them in his, to feel them against his skin, all over him soft and wet. A chill crept down his abdomen and met the flame that had sparked in lower regions. Shit. He needed to get a grip.

"It'd kind of take away the authentic ranch look if we put it out front where everybody could see it, but actually it's nice back there. Wide open view of the sky and private as long as nobody else decides to use it the same time you do."

"Where's the 'pristine mountain stream?'" Again with the smile. She had relaxed since her bout of nerves at the airport. And her humor did more for him than her temper. Not good.

"Over the first ridge there. Just under an hour on horseback, but don't worry, we'll have you riding well enough to make it over there if you want to go."

"Are you a real cowboy?" she asked.

That was a first. Most women came ready to play the game. They didn't need anything more than the hat and boots to convince them they'd gotten what they paid for. "Born and raised right here on this ranch," he said, glad it was true. "Ropin' steer before I could eat solid food."

Her smile was ready, a genuine smile, nothing practiced about it. He couldn't help smiling back. Yes, he was doing a lot of that.

"Here we are." He stepped onto a narrow porch and up to a door marked 'Darlin'. "You're Darlin'. Between Sugar and Honey."

"Cute." She glanced around summing up her surroundings, probably getting her bearings.

"We thought so." Gavin looked for that smile again but it was gone.

Her posture stiffened as he put the key in the door and pushed it open, but she entered without hesitation. Some women actually stood outside until after he left, like they were afraid he would throw them down on the bed and violate them. He had never considered lying in bed with any of them. Rebecca was another story, but he'd definitely never take advantage of any woman. And even if she wanted it as bad as he did, the business had to be put before his johnson. No woman was worth losing his livelihood for. He'd learned that the hard way.

He stowed her bag at the foot of the bed, opened a bottle of Pellegrino and poured it into a glass that he left on the table for her to take when she was ready for it.

"You should find everything you need," he said, "but, of course, if you want anything at all I'm at your service."

She studied him for a minute, like she wanted to say something, but didn't.

"There's a schedule of events on the night table, here," he said, moving across the room. "Of course you're free to pick and choose what you'd like to do. You're welcome to wander around the ranch, just please avoid the areas that are posted 'private,' and we don't suggest you venture off into the woods by yourself." He placed the room key in her hand. Something was definitely worrying her. "Most important thing to remember is, I'm all yours."

Surprise registered on her beautiful features.

"You're mine?" she asked raising her brows. Color rose to her cheeks and a nervous smile played on her lips. He had been right, her bite at the airport had more to do with nerves than anything else. Something had her scared half to death, and every gene in his body wanted to protect her.

"Yes, ma'am, all yours." There was more innuendo in his words than he'd intended. He would have felt like an idiot, but her smile grew and a light jumped in her dark eyes that sent a fusion of lust and regret surging through him. Why in the hell couldn't he have met her at the grocery store?

"Umm." Her face creased in worry again. "How do I find you?"

"I'll check on you here every hour. In the morning, I'll come by after breakfast. Around nine. You can either have that meal delivered to your room or you can come up to the dining hall. You're not obligated to spend any more time with me than you'd like to. On the other hand, if you don't want to wait, you can find me at the front desk." Since when had he told a guest she could come get him? Never. Not once. "Oh, and cowboys are not allowed in guest's rooms after ten thirty in the evening and all of the facilities close at that time."

She seemed genuinely uncertain. A good indication she had probably signed on for more than she was ready for. Yep, there'd be tears. Damn. She'd be fine though, once she realized nothing but sweet talk went on at the ranch.

He brushed a thick lock of hair from her shoulder and laid it down on her back. He wasn't sure why he did it. He definitely wasn't required to touch the guests any more than necessary and her hair had been perfectly fine right where it was. Her shoulder was nice though. Her naked skin fueled his imagination and threatened to pool more blood than he needed below the belt.

He looked up to find she had caught him again, and a look of amusement had replaced the worry on her face.

"I'll give you a chance to settle in," he said. This is where he would customarily take his leave, but he hesitated. Again, he wasn't sure why. There wasn't any other reason to stay, but his feet didn't seem to want to move.

She narrowed her eyes at him then, looking like everything had clicked into place.

"You're really good at this aren't you?" she asked.

"Good at what?" Getting turned on by gorgeous women?

"What you do. The cowboy, lover-boy thing."

"You make my job very easy," he said. So much for rule number two: Never stop playing the game. Guests don't want to be reminded that the cowboy's getting paid to make them feel special. "I better go. Don't worry though." He paused with his hand on the doorknob. "I won't go far. I'll see you in an hour." Before he closed the door he added, "And if you have a sweater or jacket, you'll want to wear it tonight, the temperature drops after the sun goes down."

"No luggage," she reminded him.

"I'll bring you something."

"You can keep me warm can't you?" she asked. There was a playful twinkle in her eye. Maybe she wasn't quite as delicate as he'd imagined. Damn. Damn. Damn.

"Yes ma'am, I can." He closed the door behind him and took a deep breath before he made his way back to the house. If he had half a brain he'd bow out now, ask Garrett to take care of Rebecca and go do something about what seemed to have become a permanent hard-on.

* * * *

Maybe if she ate more chocolate she wouldn't masturbate so much. Yeah, right. If she took up residence at the Godiva factory she would end up making chocolate dildos. Rebecca fell back on the bed and stared up at the exposed ceiling beams. She smoothed her hands over the front of her dress. Her panties had gone from damp to in need of a good wringing when Gavin brushed her hair off her shoulder and looked at her like he could've eaten her for dinner. He'd be more than a meal himself.

She closed her eyes. The way her mind drew her hot cowboy with nothing but his Stetson, flared the familiar and already raging need between her legs. How people could choose lives of celibacy was beyond her. She was on the verge of losing her mind to constant fantasies and there was no real sex for her anywhere on the radar. Not that she honestly thought she could handle anything real. An imaginary romp with a dreamy cowboy was always welcome though.

Her grief counselor assured her she was fine, but she wasn't under any delusion this constant consuming need could be healthy. Ignoring it didn't seem right either. She tugged her dress up her thighs and slipped her hand beneath the silk of her panties. She was so slick and swollen she probably could have gotten herself off just by walking across the room a couple of times. Had a complete stranger ever had that kind of effect on her before? No. Never. Not even Todd when she first met him. God, she needed to start having a sex life with somebody other than herself. But a girl's got to do what a girl's got to do.

* * * *

In the early evening light, Gavin looked showered. His hair was damp. No hat this time, but his jeans made up for it, not too tight but naturally accenting his athletic build. His smile was as ready as ever and he had a thick bundle folded beneath his arm.

"I apologize. This is the best I could come up with. It's probably still too big."

HARVARD was embroidered on the well-worn crimson hoodie he offered her.

"Is this yours?" she asked holding the sweatshirt by the shoulders.

"We don't have any women's clothes around the house." He looked genuinely apologetic. "Everything decent I have would swallow you."

"You don't mind if I wear it?" Wearing his shirt after imagined sex with him, blurred the line between fantasy and reality enough to bring a genuine smile to her face. This game promised to be even more fun than she expected.

"I don't mind at all," he said. "I'm sure it'll look better on you than it ever did on me." His voice was sincere, making it very hard to remember he wasn't treating her any differently than he treated every other guest he had been assigned to.

She slipped his shirt over her head. The soft jersey cotton smelled like him, clean, a touch of mountain air and something softer, like a hint of sandalwood. The warm scent trickled into her chest and raised her body temperature ever so slightly. He lifted her hair out of the hood and let it fall along her back.

"I was right," he said. "Looks much better on you."

"Does this mean you're not planning to keep me warm?" She looked him straight in the eye and added just a hint of challenge to her voice.

"It doesn't mean that at all," he said. "You want to go for a walk before dinner?"

Outside, the sky was filled with stars, and the nearly full moon shed more than enough light to guide them.

"There's a trail back here," he said, motioning toward a patch of towering trees in an otherwise open meadow. "It's not much as far as hiking goes, more for strolling." He draped his arm around her waist as they walked past the barn. The weight of his body against hers sent another surge of heat through her. He felt even better wrapped around her than she'd imagined.

"Do cowboys stroll?"

"Only if a pretty lady wants them to." He pulled her closer. "Do you want me to?"

"Is that line straight from the Fantasy Cowboy Handbook or did you come up with it on your own?" She put her arm around his waist, enjoying the movement of his body beneath her hand.

"Who do you think wrote the handbook?"

"There's not seriously a handbook?" She couldn't keep the laughter from her voice.

"There is." He squeezed her playfully. "My brother wrote most of it. The other guys have to use it, but I prefer to wing it. And I'm not supposed to be talking to you about that or any of our other trade secrets. You're supposed to be falling in love, remember."

"I think lust is all I can manage."

His brow creased. A question formed in his eyes, a question she didn't have any intention of answering. The man she married owned her heart, and his absence didn't leave a vacancy. Lust would work just fine. Although, she wasn't managing the lust nearly as much as it was managing her. And if she didn't get a firm hold on something besides Gavin's oblique she'd be back in bed with him again soon. Very soon.

The trail led them into the trees where candlelight danced in wrought-iron casings along the path, lending a resort-like feel to the otherwise natural landscape.

"Okay," she said, speaking before he could. "Tell me something about yourself that's not in the handbook."

"I prefer running and horseback riding to strolling," he said. "Sometimes I even do a little rock climbing. What about you, are you a stroller?"

"Only when a hot cowboy asks me to," she joked and earned herself another of his infectious smiles. All she had to do was keep the conversation flowing, keep things light and breezy, enjoy his company and have a good time. She had no intention of getting bogged down in the loneliness she carried around with her at home. This was a vacation, a reprieve. "I used to kayak and mountain bike a lot," she said. "I tried rock climbing once. But it's been a while." A chill crept up her arms and she shivered.

Gavin responded by tucking her in closer to his side. "How long's it been?"

"Over a year." The memories flooded back before she could stop them. She and Todd had spent almost every weekend outdoors, playing until they were physically exhausted and then making love until they collapsed in one another's arms. She hadn't done anything adventurous since he died. Until this week. And she could only imagine that he would laugh about where she was right now. If he couldn't comfort her, he'd want someone to. He was secure like that, and she had loved him for it. Insecure men usually had a reason to be.

"Maybe we can squeeze a little rock climbing in if you're up for it," Gavin said, interrupting her thoughts, forcing her out of the past, bringing her back to the fantasy.

An outing with a rock-climbing cowboy would kick the old imagination into second gear. Imaginary outdoor sex. This vacation was getting better by the minute.

"I'm definitely up for it," Rebecca said, unable to hide her grin, "but I didn't see that on the schedule."

"I'll toss it in. A complimentary outing for having to wear my old college sweatshirt."

The trail turned and the grade of the land rose. They were already headed back. Much too soon.

"Did you go to Harvard?" she asked.

"Undergraduate and graduate."

Her bullshit meter hadn't gone off yet, and it had a pretty sensitive trigger. He had to be one hell of an actor. A genuinely nice guy with brains underneath a frame as gorgeous as his was too much, even for a fantasy. If he wasn't lying, there was something about him that hadn't come out yet. Something that would explain why a man like him only let women pretend to fall in love.

"What are you doing here? I mean…no offense." She squeezed his side. The dense muscle beneath her hand would give her plenty to think about later. "You seem very good at your job and you definitely look the part, but after Harvard, why this?"

"It's home. My brother needed my help and I needed a career change."

His reasoning sounded feasible enough, even if the 'career change' bordered on evasive. Either way she really didn't want to believe he was a liar. That would ruin all the fantasies she had plans for him starring in. There was no room in her bed for dishonest men. No matter how good they looked.

Just before the trees opened onto the meadow again, he guided her over a thick root that lay across the path.

"The ladies don't have anything to do with why you're here?" she asked.

"This isn't my personal dating service," he said, stepping into the open field. "Even if I chose to use the ranch to spice up my personal life, most of the women who come through here aren't my type."

The wind picked up, bending the grasses. Rebecca swept her flyaway hair behind her ears and stopped to twist and knot it behind her head. She reached up to tuck a strand of Gavin's hair out of his eyes. His hair was a little longer than she usually went for, but it worked for him. Did it ever. The longest strands hung to his chin and she could imagine how it would fall forward when he was lying above her, brushing her cheek before his lips touched hers. Those lips were something else to dream about, full and curled into a wide smile. Her gaze rose to meet his again.

"What are you thinking?" His voice had a huskiness she hadn't heard in it before, a tone that entered her ears and exited much lower on a tide of liquid heat. His gaze bounced around her face like he couldn't decide where to focus and his chest moved beneath her hand. She stared at her fingers, not remembering how her hand had come to be there. It must have fallen on its own after she moved his hair, driven by her subconscious, no doubt. Her breath matched his and as he moved closer she stopped breathing altogether.

"Are you going to tell me what you're thinking or are you keeping that secretive little smile to yourself?" he asked.

"I was thinking about what it would be like to make love to you," she whispered.

Enough heat passed between them to edge the polar bears a little closer to extinction.

"That's not going to happen." He brushed his knuckles along her cheek.

"I don't really want it to," she said, loving the feel of his touch, wanting to roam his body with her hands, to feel a man who lived beyond the boundaries of her mind. "I just want to think about what it would be like. You don't mind do you?"

He laughed softly. "I definitely don't mind. Anything else I can do for you?"

"Be honest with me. I know that's not how this game is played, but it's the way I have to play it. No lies about anything. Don't even give me an empty compliment." She ran her finger along his bottom lip, indulging herself. He didn't seem to mind. "Can you do that? Can I believe everything that passes through this sexy mouth?"

"I can do that." He caught her finger between his teeth and brushed the tip of it with his tongue before she moaned and pulled it away. "If that's what you really want," he added. "But it won't make much of a fantasy."

"It's what I need." She smiled. "Among other things. But now it's time to talk about something else." If she didn't change the subject she was going to have to change her underwear and thanks to airline incompetence she only had one more pair.

"So Mr. Harvard Cowboy, what did you study?" she asked taking him by the arm and moving again toward the big house.

"Marketing."

"Oh." She laughed. "The winking cowboy is yours then."

The email response she'd gotten to her initial inquiry of the ranch had an animated cowboy winking as seductively as a computer-generated man could. "Hey darlin', wanna come back to my place," the cowboy drawled. The animation looped around again, wink after wink, invitation after invitation, and every time it dissolved Rebecca into a fit of laughter, much like the memory of it did now.

"Don't laugh too hard." He quieted her with a playful nudge. "He got you here."

Harvard Cowboy did have a point. What did she know about marketing anyway? Gavin Carter was probably good at everything he did. He acted like a man most things came easily for, and if he was driven enough to take on Harvard, he wasn't afraid of working either.

The dining hall in the big house was set up like a restaurant that only seated couples. The tables were draped in white. The lights and music were low. Candles flickered.

For the first time since she'd arrived and Marge's cowboy met them at the limo, she saw the other men at the ranch. Incredible-looking cowboys were coupled with women of varying ages and physical descriptions. There wasn't a man in the room whose looks didn't rank well above average, but Rebecca was convinced beyond doubt she had scored the hottest one on the payroll. Last minute reservations were definitely the way to go.

"Are you hungry?" Gavin asked.

"Starved."

"We could eat here," he said in a voice low enough that no one else could hear, "or I know somewhere a little more romantic."

"I like romantic."

"Come on," he said, taking her hand and leading her into the kitchen, past the brass plate that designated the area for employees only. On his way through the waiter's station, he scooped up enough silverware for the two of them and rolled it into a couple of napkins. In the kitchen he grabbed two ready plates off the chef's table, wrapped them in foil and balanced them on his arm. Just before they reached the back of the house, he stopped and motioned with his head for Rebecca to open a door off to the left.

"You mind grabbing a bottle? Anything on the right. And two glasses," he whispered.

The wine cellar was cool and organized. It was easy to find what he'd asked for, and within a couple of minutes she was following him back out into the night.

"Here's the tricky part." He bent his head toward the house. "That window right there is the office. My workaholic brother is in there at his desk and we don't want him to see us."

"But you're okay with this?" She raised her brows. His playfulness reminded her of Todd and her heart swelled. How could a man she just met, wreak such havoc on her?

"You want to eat in there with everybody else?" he asked.

She shook her head and followed him as he ducked beneath the window where Garrett sat with his back to them, a spreadsheet open on his computer.

Clear on the other side, Gavin stood up straight and led her to the barn. "Feels like high school doesn't it?" he asked.

Her cheeks sang in the cool night air. He had been right about the temperature and she was more grateful than ever to be wearing his shirt. Even more like high school, all she needed now was his class ring and a window steaming make-out session in his truck.

"And exactly why do we have to hide from your brother?" she asked once they were inside the barn.

"Because he likes to make rules, and he likes for everybody else to follow them. If he doesn't see me when I'm not, I don't have to listen to him crap about it."

Gavin's boots thumped against the soft wood. The scent of leather, horses, and hay infused the air. The familiarity of the smells was comforting, just like the horse stables back home. Pitchforks hung in the corners, hay was stacked and strewn on the floor and dust danced in the moonlight that filtered through the open doors and down from the loft.

"Are barns romantic?" Rebecca asked, her voice dripping with sarcasm.

"Don't you trust me?" He looked anything but wounded by her verbal jab.

"No."

"Good answer. Now, we're going to need to climb that ladder right there."

She held out her hands, stemware hung from her fingers on one hand and her other hand was wrapped around a bottle of wine.

"I'll go up first and you can pass me the rest of the stuff." He balanced the silverware and napkins in the crook of her arm.

She had a great view of his ascent and balancing act with the plates. He was possibly built even better than Todd, and that was saying something.

Once everything was deposited in the loft he hung his head over the edge, his hair falling just as she had imagined it would. The muscles between her thighs tensed in response.

"All that's missing is you," he said. "Want to come up?"

In the loft, moonlight poured through the open shutters. She tucked her legs under and wrapped her skirt around them as a barrier against the spiny straws that scattered the floor, then leaned back against a stack of hay bales.

Gavin reached for the wine.

"Damn," he muttered.

"You need one of these?" She pulled a corkscrew from the pocket of his sweatshirt.

"Where'd you get that?"

"Same place I got the wine."

"Ah, a lady who thinks ahead. I'll have to keep an eye on those sticky fingers though." He opened the bottle, poured each of them a glass, then held his in the air. "To our first romantic dinner."

Rebecca clinked her glass with his and sipped one of the best wines she'd ever tasted. She reached for the bottle to read the label.

"From Garrett's personal collection," he said. "And since you're the one who pilfered it, you definitely don't want him to catch us."

Pilfered wine had never tasted so good. But her throat closed tight around the chicken. This was the first meal she'd eaten alone with a man since she was married to Todd. She managed to swallow the food down, but her heart contracted. Strange how walking with Gavin earlier, arm in arm, hadn't made her miss Todd as much as this simple act of dining.

She sipped the wine a little more steadily than usual, but managed to swallow enough food to keep it from going to her head. Eventually the wine settled where she needed it most, around the ache in her chest.

"So how come your brother gets to make the rules?" she asked.

"He's older. He knows I'll break them, and it gives him something to worry about." He paused before adding, "I think he likes to worry." His eyes reflected the moonlight, as if they needed an accessory, and the way he held her gaze told her there were plenty of rules he would probably break.

"You bring all your ladies up here?" she asked.

He pulled a piece of hay from her hair and didn't so much as blink when he said, "Just you."

"Why me?" She couldn't wait to hear the next cheesy line that rolled off his silver tongue. It was a shame he hadn't taken her seriously about telling the truth though.

"I don't know." He shrugged his shoulders in that easy way of his. "It just seemed like the thing to do. Honestly, I didn't spend much time thinking about it."

Not what she had expected. She opened her mouth to ask him something else.

"My turn." He cut her off.

"Ask away." Rebecca drained her glass.

"Why did you come here?" He lifted the bottle of wine from the hay and refilled her glass.

"Same reason everyone else comes," she said automatically.

"You don't seem like any of the other women we've had here."

"What do mean?" Rebecca tried to gauge how different she could be. "My age?" Maybe she was younger than Marge and the other women she'd seen at dinner, but they seemed normal enough. She liked to think she was normal. If there is such an animal.

"That's part of it, but..." He shook his head and studied her. "You're different," he finished. "Tell me what convinced you to come."

"The cowboy love." She closed one eye in an exaggerated, oversexed wink. "One whole week of it." She tipped her glass to his. "I should give you more credit. You're a marketing genius."

"That's what I get for sharing personal information with you. And now I know why the handbook says to keep my mouth shut. Garrett's smarter than I give him credit for." He drank to the toast and narrowed his eyes at her over the rim of his glass. "I'm letting you off the hook for now," he said, "but before the week is up I'll figure out what brought you here."

His smile mixed with the wine and Rebecca grew warm from the top of her head to the bottom of her feet. He stacked her plate with his and slid over to put his arm around her. Stars twinkled in the sky. Clouds sailed by and the loft grew dark when one crossed the moon. He was right. Barns could be romantic, a great stage for a fantasy.

"If this was a real date, what would you do right now?" she asked.

He bent his head close. "I'd kiss you." His mouth was within inches of hers. She wondered how the wine would taste on his lips, his tongue. Would he take her mouth slowly, or be demanding, letting the passion that boiled beneath the surface lunge forward and consume them both? Would his lips demonstrate his strength or his gentleness, or a delicious blend of the two? How much more fire would his mouth pour into her than his hands already had? It would be so easy to eliminate the distance between them, to bring this fantasy to life, to know the answers to all those questions.

"Why do you and Garrett run the ranch the way you do, instead of the traditional way?" she asked, sitting back against the hay and bringing her glass to her lips. She hoped he couldn't see how her hand was trembling.

"Daddy got sick and was too proud to let anybody know it. The property was on the verge of foreclosure, and we had to step in fast or let the bank take it." He set his glass down and crossed one ankle over the other. "Neither of us wanted to spend our lives rounding up steer, but our father worked too hard for this land for us to just let it go."

"But how did you come up with the fantasy idea?" She tried to maintain eye contact, hoping he'd never know how the hint of a kiss could shake her.

"Garrett came up with it," Gavin said, easing back next to her. He seemed happy to change the subject himself. "He's always understood women, what they really want."

"What about you? Don't you understand what women want?"

"I can usually keep them happy for a week."

That sounded honest enough. She leaned into him and rested her head against his chest. The way his body felt against hers was worth every penny she had spent to be there. "A whole week, huh?"

"Usually. You're not giving me much of a chance to work my magic though. We're not supposed to be talking about other women, or my job, or my brother, or anything but you, and how beautiful you are, and how lucky I am to be right here with you right now." He rested his chin on the top of her head and rubbed his hand along the sleeve of his shirt she was wearing.

Maybe it was because she was paying him to hold her, or maybe because she saw something she trusted in his eyes the minute she met him, whatever the reason, she was completely comfortable in his arms. And she really didn't want to try and rationalize anything. She wanted to just live the fantasy, pretend to love the fantasy cowboy, play his game, and let a few more days of her life slip by.

"Are you cowboys required to cuddle?" she asked.

"Purely optional. We discourage it, actually. And trust me there are plenty of ways to avoid it."

"You're not avoiding it now," she said.

"That's the last thing on my mind."

"What's the first?" She tilted her head so she could see his reaction. His lips spread slowly across his face and lit his eyes. His hand cupped the side of her face and his thumb teased her bottom lip.

"Your body next to mine," he said.

"I like the way you think," she murmured into his shirt and closed her eyes.

After a few minutes, she relaxed, almost completely. In the calm, she thought about his question. Why was she here? She told Melinda the fantasy cowboy game was a step toward dating, that she was ready to move on. But even now that Gavin had proven a man's touch wouldn't send her over the nearest cliff, moving on was a theory, something she agreed to so people wouldn't worry about her, not something she was convinced could actually be done. Finding physical relief again would be enough. Maybe friendship. Friendship with benefits. More than that was out of the realm of possibility. There was only room for one man in her heart, and he'd live there forever.

"Hey," Gavin said, his voice soft. "You asleep?"

"Uh uh."

"I better get you back to your room." He pulled her to her feet and started toward the ladder.

"What about the mess?" she asked.

"I'll come back for it. We'll go by the office first to see if your luggage made it in."

He held her close as they walked to the big house. Garrett looked up from his computer as they stood in the doorway of the office.

"Garrett, this is Rebecca. Rebecca, Garrett."

"Nice to meet you," she said. "Has my luggage arrived?"

Garrett's eyes flickered to Gavin's arm around her, or maybe his shirt that she was wearing, and then to Gavin. Something passed between them, but the exchange was too brief for Rebecca to grasp what it might be.

"I'm sorry Ms. Ryder. It hasn't. I did call about an hour ago, and they said the next flight we could expect it on won't arrive until tomorrow morning. Of course, if you need anything at all before then, we'll continue to do our best to accommodate you."

Outside again, Rebecca asked, "Is lending your clothes against the rules?"

"Garrett's not very subtle sometimes," Gavin said apologetically. "We usually keep a strict division between business and personal matters."

"This is kind of a personal business isn't it?"

"Less than you'd think. But we're not going to talk about that are we?"

At her cabin, he waited while she slipped her key in the door. "You have anything to sleep in?" he asked.

"Your shirt if that's okay."

"Keep it, it's yours." He reached for her waist and held it long enough to make her forget for a minute that what they'd shared wasn't real. "Sweet dreams," he said.

"You'll be in them." She winked and backed inside.

"Gavin?" she called out to him as he walked away. "Is it against the rules for me to leave my room? To use the hot tub while everyone else is asleep."

"I won't tell Garrett if you don't."

* * * *

Marge stretched her legs, sending the porch rocker back toward the cabin wall. Clayton had draped himself over the steps and tilted his hat low on the back of his head.

"I know how we can help you over your fear of horses," he said.

She laughed. "Sweet thought, but I couldn't even read Black Beauty without having nightmares."

He sat up straighter. "We've got a foal. They're like puppies and kittens, you can't help but love them."

Marge patted her chest where her heart was pounding. "I don't know."

"Big brown eyes. Little bitty body." He laughed. "We'll keep a fence between him and us. What do you say?"

"I don't know."

"Alright. You sleep on it and you can let me know tomorrow." Clayton stood to take his leave as Gavin walked by and lifted his hand in a wave.

"Good evening, Ms. Owen," Gavin said.

Marge returned the pleasantries and headed inside. She was ready for bed, but she had to call her nephew first.

"What have you got?" Chet said. "I'm ready to nail these scumbags once and for all."

He was just like his father, more ambitious than he had a right to be. And the only route he could find to the top had him stepping on people along the way. He was her sister's son though, the only family she had left.

"I haven't got anything yet. My cowboy is a nice young man. He tells me every pretty word he can think of, but he hasn't tried to lay a hand on me."

"What does he say? Does he make any invitations, offer himself in anyway? He doesn't have to touch you. An attempt to solicit is all we need."

"I don't think this is going to work. I'm old enough to be his mother."

Chet snorted. "You think that matters?"

"They seem nice. Maybe it's not what you think here."

"It's exactly what I think, and I'm going to prove it. Call me tomorrow night, and keep your eyes open. I want to know everything you see."

* * * *

Rebecca curled up on the bed, dialed Melinda's cell phone for the third time in less than twenty minutes, and wrapped her arms around herself. Tonight was no different than when she was younger and went out with some boy she really liked for the first time. Her body was alive and tingling everywhere he'd touched her and soon it would start tingling everywhere he hadn't. Maybe the dating game wouldn't be as hard to get back into as she had thought. As long as she could meet more men like Gavin.

Five rings and no answer. She resigned to hang up when Melinda picked up the phone without saying hello.

"Go ahead, tell me how hot he is." Melinda sounded tired. It figures, tonight would be the one night Melinda had gone to bed at a decent hour.

"You wouldn't believe me if I told you, but if you were asleep I can give you all the juicy details tomorrow."

"I wasn't asleep."

Rebecca recognized the lack of energy in her sister's voice for what it was. Melinda had been crying. The hot cowboy stories would have to wait.

"Are you okay?"

Melinda was slow to answer. "I should have come with you."

"Call them up. See if you can still get a reservation. Have I mentioned they really are hot? And the ranch is amazing."

Melinda was silent on the other end of the line. This was more than a little spat with Scott.

"Mel?"

Melinda sniffled.

"I'm sorry," Rebecca said quickly. "What happened?"

"Scott left."

"What do you mean *he* left?"

Melinda's husband, Scott, had gotten caught having an affair again, this time it was his secretary. Last time it was a stripper. The time before that it was either the cashier at the dry cleaners or the waitress from Chili's, Rebecca couldn't keep them straight anymore. It didn't matter anyway because Melinda had forgiven him *again*.

How could that jerk have the nerve to walk out after crying for years that he couldn't live without her and swearing he would change if she'd just give him another chance, and then when he blew that chance, another? A man that dishonest should never be trusted with a badge and a gun. Apparently the city of Charleston didn't feel the same.

"Says he's in love with Sheryl." Melinda's voice cracked and she failed to muffle her sobs.

"His fricken' partner?" Rebecca exploded. The man should arrest himself. He was worse than half the people he put behind bars.

Melinda lost her battle with the tears and cried openly.

"So where did he go?" Rebecca took a deep breath and calmed herself. Melinda didn't need to hear her anger.

"Her place, I guess. I don't really give a damn." She said the right words, but the way she said them didn't hide her lie.

"I'm sorry I'm not there." Rebecca loosened the knot at the back of her head and leaned back against the birch headboard.

"You're in a better place." Melinda attempted a laugh.

"There are so many men who would actually treat you right." Rebecca said. "I just wish you could see that."

"There was only one Todd in the world," Melinda said evenly. "The rest of them are lying, cheating assholes. Now go have fun with your cowboy. Real men aren't worth the effort."

"Love you. Call me if you need to," Rebecca said before hanging up. She pulled Gavin's sweatshirt over her head, stepped out of her dress and put on a robe she found hanging in the bathroom. Nothing dampened her sexual appetite faster than the heartbreak in her sister's voice. She'd be fine without her luggage tonight, unless she started thinking about Todd.

* * * *

Gavin deposited the plates, glasses and the rest of their dinner implements into a basket. The loft was cleaned, but he wasn't ready to leave. He sat back against the stacked hay and stared off into the sky.

He'd been a walking hard-on since he picked Rebecca Ryder up at the airport. It was a wonder he had enough blood flowing to his brain to speak coherently. He had to get it together. He'd almost kissed her. What in the hell was he thinking? Thank God she had the sense to back off.

Tomorrow would be better. She would be more settled in. He could use his standard pattern of flattery and questions and more flattery, let her do most of the talking. Find out just how screwed up she was. Whatever happened, he'd keep his personal life to himself. There were reasons they didn't talk about themselves. Good reasons. He'd just shut up and try like hell to keep his hands off of her. At least she didn't seem to mind that he was pawing her. She didn't seem to mind his hands at all, and he definitely didn't mind hers. She touched him like it was the most natural thing in the world, like he had wrapped her in his arms a thousand times. That alone should have been enough to scare some sense into him.

She undoubtedly just missed her husband, not enough to cry about him yet, but that would come. She'd loved the guy enough to marry him, memories of him had to still hurt sometimes. Marriage and memories were not always a good combination. He didn't need the women who came to the ranch to teach him that.

Footsteps on the deck surrounding the hot tub carried up to the loft. Gavin immediately formed an image of Rebecca stepping into the water, and his hard-on sprang up even faster than the picture in his mind. He should just be glad the damned thing worked as well as it did, but that wasn't going to make this week any easier. He threw his head back on the hay and stayed there until he was sure she'd had plenty of time to submerge herself. Then he crawled forward and peered down from the open shutters to say hello.

"What are you doing up there?" Garrett asked. His head was back against the side of the tub, his eyes open wide.

"Thinking."

"Not about your job, I hope," Garrett said.

His not-so-subtle hint hit home. Gavin held his tongue and waited. There would be more to come.

"I didn't see you at dinner."

"We dined al fresco. My guest needed the air." She had, hadn't she? Or was it him who needed the air, or needed to be alone with her?

"I noticed she needed your clothes too." Garrett adjusted himself in the water and closed his eyes.

"Would you rather let her wear yours?"

"You could have given her one of the souvenir logo shirts."

Gavin didn't have a ready answer. He had gone straight to his closet. It never crossed his mind to go anywhere else.

"What's going on here, Gav?" Garrett opened his eyes and stared up at his brother.

"Just another week at the office."

"You sure?"

"What else would it be?" Gavin rubbed the back of his neck.

"That's a good question. Especially with the eggshells we're walking on right now."

"Well, when you figure out the answer, I'm sure you'll let me know." He wasn't kidding Garrett anymore than he was kidding himself, but maybe he could figure his way around this attraction to Rebecca before he did anything too stupid. It didn't help that she curled into him like she belonged there. Or that he wanted to keep her as close to him as he could.

Garrett sighed. "We've got a problem."

"Rebecca's not a problem."

"Don't bet on it. I ran into Alvie at the theatre. He's got it on pretty good authority there's an undercover out here this week."

"Let them send out the whole damn department. There's nothing to uncover."

Garrett grunted and trailed his fingers over the surface of the roiling water. "The camera repairman didn't make it out today. He's coming tomorrow afternoon. You probably should take Ms. Ryder out on a ride so she won't see him. I don't want to take any chances. And watch yourself." Garrett closed his eyes again. "You looked a little cozy."

The surveillance system in Rebecca's cabin was only recording intermittently. It had seemed like a smart decision to put his guest in the cabin that wasn't adequately monitored. That was before he had initiated the 'bring your dick to work' policy.

Chapter 3

Rebecca sipped her coffee on the porch and watched Gavin leave the big house and head over to her cabin. Before he was within three feet of her, she had almost completely forgotten he could possibly be like every other man her sister had described. A lying, cheating asshole. A gorgeous, lying, cheating asshole. The worst kind.

"You're up early," he said.

"Couldn't sleep." She dipped her face in the steam of her coffee. The warmth soothed her tired eyes almost as much as the sight of him did.

"Must be contagious." Gavin sat down on the porch rail facing her.

"What keeps a cowboy up at night?"

"Don't you watch the movies?" His smile came to life at its usual speed. "It's a lonely life out on the range, coyotes howling, a hard ground to sleep on."

"Your range has a bed."

"It's still lonely."

Rebecca sipped from her mug and wondered if that was a come on or a simple admission of truth. Whatever it was, it painted a picture in her head that didn't have him very lonely at all. He was dangerous. That beautiful façade and smooth tongue could have a woman naked and doing his bidding faster than he could change his underwear. Another visual. Shit.

"I'm glad to see you in jeans," he said. "Ready for a riding lesson?"

She followed him to the corral where a dark brown horse with an even darker mane was saddled and waiting.

"This is Pilgrim. He's a good starter horse. Nothing to be worried about. If you're comfortable enough we can go on a trail ride after lunch," he said.

"I'd be up for that." She rubbed Pilgrim's jaw and patted him on the neck.

"A lady with confidence. I like that, and I'm glad you're not afraid. A horse can sense fear."

"Pilgrim's gentle as a lamb. You can see it in his eyes."

"Lesson number one and you're already the horse whisperer." Gavin laughed and took Pilgrim's reins.

"Just like with people," she said. "Eyes don't lie."

"I'll bet some do." He led Pilgrim in a half-turn, bringing the saddle alongside Rebecca. The smell of horse and damp leather blended with the morning air.

"Do yours?" She tilted her chin to get a better look at him.

"What do you think?" He turned them on her then, green as the sage blowing in the meadow, and warm as the morning sun.

Her stomach twisted like a pretzel, but she let his stare sink into her, wanting to hold it for as long as she could. "I think you and Pilgrim have a lot in common," she said when her body screamed uncle.

His eyes creased in the corners. "You ready to learn how to ride?"

She listened patiently while he explained the importance of approaching and mounting a horse only on its left side. He demonstrated how to put one foot in the stirrup, grab hold of the saddle horn and swing her right leg over the saddle. Rebecca watched him rather than the technique and kept her smile under wraps as much as possible. He was a good teacher, patient, thorough and pumping every instruction full of smooth confidence that would rub off on even the most timid student.

She was careful who she surrounded herself with, but he was someone she could see in her life. He was a good guy. Probably a loyal friend, someone who could be counted on. The gentleness wasn't an act. Eyes don't lie.

And if it was possible for a man to become more attractive by the minute, Gavin Carter had that gift. Everything about him sent her nerve endings into overdrive, his deep melodic voice, his perfect backside. She was getting turned on by the roundness of his wrist bone. The man was impossibly gorgeous, but he had a way of setting her at ease, even when he was completely stirring her up. She hadn't had to remind herself to breathe all morning. Well, maybe once. He lowered himself to the ground.

"Ready?" he asked.

"Ready as ever."

He held the stirrup in place until her foot was securely inside then put his hands on her hips to guide her up and over Pilgrim's back. The ripples of his touch traveled all the way to her toes.

"Not bad," he said as she held herself in the saddle.

He stood ready to catch her when she dismounted. She stood in the stirrup and moved her leg slowly over the saddle, then just so he wouldn't have to stand around empty handed, she stumbled when she hit the ground. She could have melted into his arms, and probably would have if he hadn't dropped them to his sides and gotten back to the business at hand.

"You did great. Want to try again?" he asked.

"Like this?" She stepped up and seated herself effortlessly in the saddle.

"Either you're a natural..." He took his hat off and set it back down on his head. "Or you've done this before."

She shrugged, not committing either way. "So what do we do now?"

"We can round the corral a couple of times, until you're comfortable up there."

"You're the cowboy. Whatever you say."

He led the horse twice around the corral, walking close enough to her side that his shoulder brushed against her leg, which made it very hard to concentrate on anything else. Good thing she didn't need to. Just breathe.

"When you want to stop," he said. "You just pull straight back on the reins, like this. Think you've got it?"

"I think so." Rebecca bit her lip in contrived worry.

"Want to give it a try on your own?"

"You sure I'm ready?" She really just wanted to keep him talking, keep those lips moving, so she could watch them.

"Only one way to find out." He patted her thigh, sending another wave of heat through her.

"Where will you be?"

"I'll wait for you right over here." He motioned to the fence.

"Alright, I'll try." She sat motionless and watched him cross the corral. Jeans had never fit a man that well before, and she was starting to really like that slow Western gait that gave her even more time to enjoy the view.

He hefted himself onto the fence and balanced his heels on the crossbeam, his arms relaxed at his sides.

"When you're ready, just loosen up on the reins, and shift your weight forward a little. The horse will do the rest."

"Like this?" She repositioned herself in the saddle and nudged Pilgrim with her heel. The horse took off at a trot. Gavin jumped off the fence and started after her, then stopped, a look of recognition crossed his features. Obviously, he knew the posture of an experienced rider and if he hadn't, the grin on Rebecca's face would have given her away. She rounded the corral twice and reined the horse in next to where he stood.

"I'm thinking maybe you've done this before." He stared up at her, light dancing in his green eyes and a smile playing on his lips.

"Maybe."

"I don't suppose you need me to help you down."

"No, but I'll let you," she said.

He caught her at the waist as soon as her boots hit the dirt.

"Now what?" she asked twisting her head to look up at him. His hands didn't move and she didn't either, nor did she break eye contact, wondering what he would do next, if anything. Finally, he cleared his throat.

"There's somewhere I want to take you," he said.

* * * *

"Look how cute he is." Clayton was kneeling with his arm stuck between the fence beams. "All innocence and expectation."

Marge's hands were clenched in fists at her sides, she was trembling like a leaf, but the cowboy had a point. The dark brown foal licked feed out of his hand and stared up at them with trusting eyes.

"Go ahead," Clayton said. "He won't bite. He's practically been hand raised."

Her fingers uncurled slowly, but her arm wouldn't move. "I can't. I want to, but I just can't."

He rubbed the horse and smiled up at her. "Ever been this close to a horse before?"

She shook her head, and the realization of how much she had accomplished spread across her face in a smile.

"I'm proud of you," he said.

She gauged the two feet between her and the animal. "I am really close aren't I?"

"Within reach." He squeezed her hand. "What part scares you the most?"

"The hooves."

"Makes sense." He reached for the young horse's leg and gave it a gentle tug. The animal bent his knee and danced to keep his balance. Clayton ran his hand over the hoof then back up the leg as the horse settled back on all fours.

"And the teeth." She grimaced. "Long and yellow and big enough to hurt."

He nodded. "Some horses bite. Hard." He stood and leaned against the fence next to her. "The animals we keep around here have pretty good manners. Garrett and Gavin don't take chances when it comes to safety."

Marge shifted. Her bunion had started to ache and as much as she wanted to overcome her fear the horse was making her nervous.

"Want to sit down for a while?" He gestured toward a bench tucked into the shade of the barn.

"Good morning." A nice-looking man who resembled Gavin hefted himself over the fence. The foal loped over to him.

Clayton's response held a note of something that had Marge turning to catch his expression. The young man's emotions were written clearly across his face.

She cleared her throat. "Very handsome isn't he?"

"Garrett? Yeah." He turned away quickly, taking her arm as he led her toward the bench.

For several minutes neither of them spoke. They both watched Garrett with the young horse. It was no wonder the animal was gentle, he was handled with such affection and respect.

"I dated the same man for thirty years," she said, surprised at how easily the words had rolled off her tongue.

Clayton shifted next to her. "You never got married?"

She shook her head. "He was my boss."

"There's got to be more to it than that." He had turned most of his attention to her, but glimpsed one last time at Garrett before he turned his back to him completely.

She released a heavy breath. "He was already married."

Clayton whistled. "This sounds juicy. You *have* to spill it now." Then as if catching himself, he grinned. "I mean, do you want to tell me about it?"

She laughed at his eagerness and her own nerves. "I've never told anyone. Not even my priest." She twisted her hands in her lap. "I kind of figured maybe forgiveness wasn't something I should ask for if I wasn't willing to give him up, and if all I planned to do was wait until I could have him all to myself."

"Thirty years? That's a long time to wait. Why did you finally end it?"

"It hasn't ended. He'd be more than a little jealous if he knew I was here. I told him I was visiting my nephew." She frowned. "Which isn't entirely untrue. I'll see him before I go home."

"Why are you telling me?"

"I guess it's the horse. The two things I've always been most afraid of are horses and someone finding out my secret."

"So now you've faced both fears. All in a matter of minutes."

"Thanks to you." She squeezed his wrist. "Turnabout's fair play. What are you most afraid of?"

He glanced over his shoulder. "Same as you. Someone finding out my secret." He grinned from ear to ear. "We're a lot alike, you and me. Let's go get some iced tea before we discover we're soul mates and the stars have conspired against us."

"I always wanted to meet somebody who wouldn't bat an eye when I said I was the other woman," she said as they made their way toward the big house.

"Love defies reason," he said. "Always has. Always will." He looped his arm in hers. "You love him don't you?"

"I do, and I don't want to stop."

"I understand." He squeezed her arm. "You have no idea how well I understand."

She smiled. "His name is Harold." God, it felt wonderful to say that so freely. "I love Harold." She laughed. "I wish I had a son like you."

"I'm available. Especially if you're looking to pass down any antique Biedermeier. I eat off a card table at my house."

As they passed the corral, Rebecca was holding the reins of two horses while Gavin walked the gate closed. Clayton steered a wide berth, keeping Marge as far from the horses as he could.

"What do think about those two?" she asked.

"The horses?"

"No, the lovebirds."

"Gavin and his guest?" He chuckled. "I've only got eyes for you, but of course you've broken my heart since you confessed to loving someone else."

"I'm serious. Look at them."

He looked back. "They make a great-looking couple."

"A real couple, don't you think?"

"Honey, this is Fantasy Ranch. The only thing that's real is the fantasy."

* * * *

A half-hour later, Rebecca and Gavin slowed Pilgrim and Gavin's horse, Silver, to a walk. Gavin's eyes searched the sky, studying both directions. "We can't stay out too long, it's going to rain."

"How can you tell?" She examined the clouds, trying to see what he had seen.

"The weather channel." He grinned.

"Cute," she said, but couldn't keep herself from laughing.

At the lip of a gorge, dizzying in its depth, Gavin dismounted and came over to help her down. He was in no bigger hurry to let her go than he'd been the last time.

"I like this game," she said, putting her hands over his and leaning her back into his chest.

"What do you want to happen next?"

She turned herself around to face him. "This is your ranch. You're the cowboy. As long as you keep your hat on and call me darlin' I'll let you take the lead." She tipped his hat back just enough to raise the shadow of it above his eyes. "Provided, of course, we don't do anything I'll regret in the morning."

"We wouldn't want to do that." His eyes danced with humor.

She stepped back so he could unbuckle a saddlebag and let the horses wander off to graze nearby. Together they spread a flannel blanket on the ground and divided the sandwich and potato salad he'd packed.

"This is breathtaking." She sat looking out over the gorge, while he faced her. The sun was warm overhead, and there was no sign of the rain to come. "Makes you feel small and bigger than life all at once."

He passed her a bottle of water. "I thought you might like it."

"Do you bring all the ladies out here or did you break the rules again?"

"I've never brought any of the ranch guests out here."

"You bring your real dates here?" She studied him. Any idea she'd had of flying across the country to play with a warm-blooded blow-up doll had been completely misguided. Gavin Carter was someone she wanted to know, someone who held her interest longer than any of the pretty pictures on the Fantasy Ranch brochure. But she wasn't even allowed to contact him after she left. There'd be no lasting friendship, nothing more than a single week of make-believe. The rules of this game were more complicated than she had imagined them to be.

"I don't like to date."

"Don't you have...needs?" she asked.

"Of course I have needs." He narrowed his eyes, and added, "I go out and pick up a nice young lady when I need to, but I wouldn't exactly call that dating."

"How often do you need to?" She bit her lip, curious how honest he would be about his appetite. She couldn't imagine he didn't get laid anytime he wanted to.

"A lot more often than I do, unfortunately." He shook his head and lifted his eyes to hers. "I don't know why I'm telling you this. Or why you're asking."

"Because it tells me a lot about you." She bit into her sandwich. "And sex just happens to be my favorite subject. Speaking of..." She grinned. "I'm sure the casual sex is fine, but don't you ever want more than that?"

"Don't you ever run out of questions?" He wiped the corner of her mouth with his napkin.

"Sorry for being nosy. I'm just wondering what I've got ahead of me. I'm not exactly a pro at dating anymore." She tipped her bottle to his and tapped the plastic together. "And for the record, a man like you shouldn't be lonely, unless of course you like it that way. So I'm guessing you must."

"I could say the same thing about you."

"I hate being lonely," she said. "I have to ask one more question."

"I give up. Shoot."

"Are you really treating me differently, or just telling me that you are? Remember, no lies."

He laid his sandwich down on the blanket, and reached for her hand. "Don't you want the fantasy?"

"I came here didn't I?" She put her sandwich next to his and spread his hand open, brushing the rough skin of his palm with hers. It was masculine, but not overly callused, or abrasive. She liked the feel of it. She liked it very much. She rested her hand on his, palm to palm, and met his eyes. "I can play any game you would ever want to play. I just need to understand what parts of this game are real."

"If it's a fantasy," he asked, "how can it be real?"

"Fantasy and reality can blend together very nicely when you want them to. Haven't you tried that yet?"

"Not so much."

"Here's an example." She turned around to sit next to him and placed his hand around her waist. "Now you lie down."

He raised his brows and shook his head. "I don't think that's a good idea."

"Don't worry. This is a PG example. I'm not going to seduce you." She winked. "I'll save that for later, when you're not around."

He laughed and let her push him back onto the blanket. She rested her head on his shoulder, wrapped her arm around his chest, and relaxed into the rhythm that his breath and his heart played beneath her arm. He stroked her hair and held her.

"See?" she asked.

"No."

"You're a fantasy, this whole week is a fantasy, but you're really holding me. I really feel you." She snuggled closer. "And I really like it."

After a few minutes of silence, he took a deep breath.

"I don't bring guests out here," he said. "We stick to specific parts of the property when we're entertaining. And I haven't tried to make you believe anything that isn't true."

"So why aren't you entertaining me where you're supposed to be?" She didn't lift her face to see his expression. She didn't want to move.

"I guess because I wanted to bring you here." His hand slid along her side, but not far enough in either direction to cross any kind of sexual line. "I don't want to treat you like anybody else."

"You haven't called me darlin' yet."

"Darlin'," he said in a smooth drawl, "is the fantasy the only reason you're here?"

"I can fantasize at home. I flew to Wyoming for this." She ran her hand along his arm. "I miss this. To touch someone. To be touched."

He shifted his body and pulled her in even closer. She closed her eyes and held onto what she had been longing for since the day fate took her husband away. Lying there like that, it was easy to remember Todd, to imagine it was him she was holding, to believe for a moment that she had him back again and that she would never have to let him go.

"Why exactly did you sign up for a riding lesson?" he asked.

"This week is about living my fantasy, isn't it?"

"And you fantasize about riding lessons?"

"I might after today." She gave him a wicked grin. "What's your fantasy?" She flattened her palm over the curve of his shoulder and followed the slope of his arm.

"You're not allowed to ask anymore questions, remember?"

"Just tell me one of them, the tamest one, if you're chicken." She stopped and waited for him to answer.

"A biotech consultant with a southern drawl and a thing for cowboys."

"That was too easy."

"And too true." His lips brushed her cheek. "Way too true."

The sleeplessness of the previous night caught up to both of them. The afternoon became evening, and the first drops of rain hit like ice pellets jolting them awake.

The sky had grown dark, darker than it should have been. Pilgrim and Silver had wandered at least a hundred yards away. Thunder rolled toward the mountains.

"I'll get the horses," he said as raindrops the size of dimes began a steady descent.

Rebecca rolled up the blanket, gathered the trash and stuffed everything back into the saddlebag before she ran to help him. The rain came down too fast for the ground to absorb it and puddles dotted the meadow. Her boots splashed mud onto her jeans and her blouse clung to her in a thin transparent layer.

Lightning sliced the sky and rain pounded harder by the minute. By the time she reached him, Gavin was as soaked as she was, but he had both horses by the reins.

They rode back as fast as the horses could carry them on the slippery ground.

In her cabin, water ran off their clothes leaving a puddle on the floor. Her jeans were splattered with mud and her blouse wouldn't have been wetter if she had gone swimming in it.

"If my luggage didn't come today, I might have to run around naked tomorrow."

"Give me your clothes," he said.

"Isn't that against the rules?" With her hands on her hips, she sized him up, tempted to hand every stitch over to him and demand his in return. "And not a very smooth come on, for a man with a natural talent for such things."

"Unless Garrett has added a No Laundry clause to the handbook we'll be okay." The way his smile lit his eyes was enough to kill a woman. Literally kill her, or at least make her think she was going to die from cardiac arrest, she was sure of it.

"Does your fantasy start anything like this?" She pulled her blouse over her head and laid it in his hand. The paper-thin shirt had already revealed as much as he was openly admiring, but the man obviously had an appreciation for skin. And her skin had an appreciation for his laser-hot eyes. She could feel the burn spread like a flame across her chest.

Before he could answer, she picked his Harvard sweatshirt off the back of a chair and carried it to the bathroom. Rebecca rested her back against the door and closed her eyes. Damn the No Sex clause. At some point she was going to have sex with someone, and that man probably wouldn't get her blood pumping half as fast as Gavin could. Damn it, damn it, damn it.

She toweled off, and came out with the rest of her clothes in her hands and his sweatshirt hanging to her thighs. She unloaded the dripping articles into his arm. She should have kept her underwear to hand wash them in the sink, but she had shamelessly folded them into her jeans.

"Have I mentioned how good you look in that shirt?" he asked.

"Not today."

He brushed a strand of hair from her face. For a minute she thought he was going to kiss her, and she was surprised when she leaned toward him. The angle of her stance was so awkward she grabbed his arm for balance. She was ready. Ready to taste his lips, feel the warmth of his tongue. The nerves were gone. He moved closer, rested his hand against her neck, his fingertips brushed the top of her spine, shooting life into her every nerve. He inched closer, then froze, his stiff arm holding her at a distance. After a lightning-quick glance toward the corner of the room, he moved to leave so quickly she almost toppled after him.

The cold rain blew in through the open door prickling her skin and cooling her overheated neurons, finally allowing her brain to make strong enough connections with her nerves to shut them down to a manageable level.

"I'll bring you something to eat." His voice was unsteady. Almost embarrassed.

Lightning lit the ranch, and crashed in a ball of thunder close enough to vibrate the cabin walls. Enough electricity surged through the air to send the soft down at the back of her neck on end and a tickle zipping toward the base of her spine.

"I'm not hungry, but thanks." She was an idiot, brushing away a chance to have him back. "You shouldn't be running around in a storm like this. I'd ask you to stay, but…" He needed to get out of his clothes and he definitely couldn't do that in her cabin without serious repercussions.

"I can't stay." The look he gave her suggested his thoughts weren't that different from hers. "If your luggage is in the office, do you need it tonight?"

"It'll be hard, but I think I can live without it." Hard was an understatement. Fantasies wouldn't be difficult to come by tonight.

"Sweet dreams then." He ducked his hat into the deluge and headed for home.

* * * *

In the mudroom, Gavin hung his hat on a peg, stripped and wrapped a towel around his waist. Garrett came in as Gavin was dropping his and Rebecca's clothes into the washer. Her blouse was in his hand and the strap of her bra hung beneath it.

Gavin read his brother's irritation and intercepted him. "You want her running around here naked, or in more of my clothes?"

"We should probably install laundry facilities in the little cabin." Garrett's shoulders relaxed. "We never use it anyway."

"Probably wouldn't hurt." He shook detergent into the machine and closed the lid. Garrett was still standing there, watching him.

Gavin didn't feel like talking business, didn't feel like talking at all. He should have been freezing, but he wasn't, he was hotter than hell. The entire day had been one big exercise in self-control, and he was more than a little tense from it all. Too many thoughts floated around in his mind. Every single one of them had something to do with Rebecca and not many of them involved clothes. And they'd all been amped up a notch by that little peep show she had given him through her oh so wet and oh so thin bra.

"Rebecca Ryder seems to like your company," Garrett said.

"Isn't that the idea?" The muscles between his shoulder blades tightened. A two-year-old could have picked up on what Garrett was getting at. He was spending too much time with her, and none of it where they were supposed to be. And yes, the ranch was under enough scrutiny right now.

"Yeah, that's the idea," Garrett told him. "As long as we're on the same page."

"I'm not going to fuck her," Gavin said through clenched teeth. He was madder than he should have been, but he had restrained himself more in one day than he had in his entire life, and he was still catching hell for it. He wouldn't risk the business or their home for sexual gratification. He could go to Trucker's, the local night club, for that kind of comfort any night of the week and not risk a thing.

He rubbed a dry towel over his head, knowing full well when he was done, Garrett would still be standing there. His brother had hit on a nerve, and he wasn't going to go away until he settled it. Gavin dropped the towel around his shoulders.

"You seem a little on edge," Garrett said. "But her luggage still hasn't come in, so I'm glad you're washing her clothes. Just try not to let her catch pneumonia either."

"Are the cameras in her cabin working yet?" It wouldn't be good to have documentation of her peeling off her clothes and handing them to him. Especially since he hadn't had sense enough to do anything but stand there and gawk like he'd never seen a woman in a bra before. He got another boner just thinking about it. She had his dick on a string she didn't even know she was pulling.

"No," Garrett said. "They didn't have the right something or other. They'll be back tomorrow. Maybe you can keep her away from the cabin again. It's going to take at least an hour."

Gavin exhaled. He shouldn't be thinking about how easy it would be to go back to her cabin, fold her in his arms, and feel the warmth of her body next to his, especially on a night like tonight with the rain pouring down. And if she wanted that too, there were no cameras to see anything they did. Since when did cameras matter? They weren't running an escort business and his services sure as hell weren't a part of the guest package. He'd be happy to extend them to her for free though. Any night of the week.

Damn. He couldn't remember the last time a woman got under his skin like that.

"Anything else or can I go to bed?" he asked.

"I need you to take my guest next week. I'll take yours the week after."

"Why?" Normally it wouldn't have mattered. Neither of them ever ventured far from the ranch anyway. They had worked it out early on that they would alternate weeks in the office. One week Garrett took care of a guest while Gavin focused on his part of the business and managed the little things that always popped up, the next week they switched. For the most part it kept them both busy and out of each other's hair. They never had to spend too many hours holed up in one room together, getting on each other's nerves with their polar personalities.

"I need to run up to Cody for a couple of days." Garrett smiled and Gavin recognized the look in his eyes immediately.

"John's in town?"

"He will be. You don't mind do you?"

"Fine." Gavin carried himself upstairs to take a shower. He didn't want to take Garrett's guest, and he couldn't come up with one logical reason why.

Chapter 4

"You don't know me," Chet warned. "If you see me at the ranch, don't even make eye contact."

Marge's breath trembled from her lips. Her knuckles burned from the vise grip she had on the phone. "You're coming today?"

"It's better if you don't know the details of the investigation. Just tell me what you know about the other guests."

"Not much. Everybody's on different schedules except for meals."

"See if you can find out who Rebecca Ryder is. I need you to watch her like a hawk."

Marge's heart galloped in her chest. "Why? What's important about her?"

"Let me worry about that. You just report back to me if you see anything that looks suspicious between her and her cowboy."

"Okay."

"Anything at all. You understand?"

"Alright."

Marge jumped as a knock sounded at her door. "I have to go," she whispered, glad to have an excuse to key her phone off. Her nephew's intimidation tactics were too much for her nerves. This investigation was key to his promotion to detective, and he wasn't about to let her or anyone else screw it up for him. He'd placed his badge on the line sticking a civilian into a surveillance position, but that was their little secret. After he'd gathered enough evidence to shut down the ranch, she'd sign a statement saying that she was nothing more than a guest and after fearing for her own safety, she called her nephew and told him everything she'd witnessed.

She rubbed her hands down the hips of her jeans and took a deep breath. She could do this. She didn't have a choice. Chet was the only family she had left, and she'd probably have to rely on him someday. Harold would never be able to sign papers on her behalf or take care of her interests. His wife had already begun demanding more of his time and threatened him with everything under the sun if he wasn't at her beck and call. No. Harold had his priorities, and she wasn't one of them.

"Good morning, my equinophobic friend. Are we braving the hooves of horses or square dancers today?" Clayton asked with a grin as he stepped in through the door she held open.

"I think I'm going to read a book. Here. In my room." She gestured with her hand and realized too late, she was still trembling.

"My lord! You're scared to death. Is it the horses?"

"Yes." Even as she lied she shook her head.

"Yes? No? Maybe so?" He walked her over to the little table by the window and pulled out a chair for her to sit down. "I didn't traumatize you with that foal, did I?"

"No, no you...you were fine. It's family stuff. Nothing really."

"Nothing? You're shaking worse than Shakira. You need some wine."

"It's nine o'clock in the morning."

"And it'll be the same time at the hospital it is here, if you have a heart attack on me."

She wrung her hands while he pulled a bottle of red from the chiller. This is why she didn't have close friends. Lying was too hard. The secrets never fully belonged to her. Someone else always had something at stake.

* * * *

Rebecca dumped a full pot of coffee down the drain. This morning she didn't need as much stimulation as usual. She had woken full of energy even after another nearly sleepless night.

She washed her face and was hanging the towel next to the vanity when the sound she'd been waiting for arrived. Her smile came to life on its own and her heart quickened.

She answered the door in Gavin's sweatshirt, her hair pulled back and her feet bare. The morning sun bounced off his broad shoulders and shone gold through his hair. "Good morning. Thought you might want these," he said. Her clothes were laundered and folded neatly with her bra and panties on top.

"Thank you for doing that." She took them from him and laid them on the bed.

"I'll wait outside until you're ready."

"You can wait here." She picked up the panties, slipped her feet in and slid them up to her hips before he had time to turn away. She followed suit with the jeans, then crossed her arms to grab the bottom of the sweatshirt at each side.

His face was easy to read. She gave him a wink as exaggerated as his animated cowboy's then turned around before pulling the sweatshirt over her head. She covered her breasts with one arm and reached over to pick up her bra from the bed. She didn't turn around again until after her blouse was on.

"See, no harm, no foul, and you didn't have to stand around outside twiddling your thumbs."

He grinned. "You're not shy are you?"

She went to the mirror to brush her hair out. "Did it hurt you any to watch me get dressed?"

"No, ma'am."

"Did you see anything you wouldn't have seen if I was in a bikini?"

"No, ma'am."

"Then what's there to be shy about?" There. If he got to drive her crazy all week it was only fair he got played with a little, too. She grabbed her hair from underneath and drew it up into a ponytail.

"Leave it down," Gavin said. She eyed him in the mirror. He shrugged. "I like it down."

She let her hair fall around her shoulders, and turned around. "I guess we're ready then." Just knowing he had an opinion about her hair sparked something warm in her. She made a mental note to find out what else he liked.

Her boots were still wet, but she put them on over a dry pair of socks and followed him out the door. Pilgrim and Silver were saddled and waiting in the corral when they got there.

"We're riding again?" she asked.

"You wanted to see that pristine mountain stream didn't you?"

"I did."

"Do you mind riding Pilgrim?" he asked as she took the reins and grabbed the saddle horn. "We've got horses with a little more spunk."

"I like Pilgrim." She seated herself and leaned forward to rub the horse's neck. "I trust him." Pilgrim blew his appreciation through his lips.

"I think he likes you, too," Gavin said as he walked the gate open.

"How often do you ride?" she asked as the horses plodded alongside one another across the open field. Todd had never loved horses. He would ride with her occasionally, but she didn't ask him often. It was more fun to do things they both enjoyed.

"Every chance I get. What about you?"

"The same, usually on weekends. I've been riding a lot more than usual lately."

"You should come to the ranch more often," he said. "We've got some of the best riding I've ever come across."

"When I get home you can send me another winking cowboy. We'll see if your ingenious marketing is good enough to work a second time."

Gavin laughed. "You ever going to give it a rest?"

"Nope." The warm air soaked into her, the rhythm of the horses rocked her, and the easy conversation left a smile on her face. And to think she would never have owned this experience if life hadn't spun around on her. Laughter follows every tear. Her father taught her that. And Gavin Carter was proving it true.

"What's the best thing your father ever taught you?" Rebecca asked.

"If you love a woman enough, she's always right." He grinned. "He taught me other stuff too, but I thought you'd like that one."

"He should have a written a book. The man's a genius." Rebecca gave him an animated cowboy wink. "Must run in the family."

"That's it. I'm not telling you anything else. Ever." He nudged Silver to a trot and left Rebecca laughing alone. Pilgrim caught up easily and they rode the rest of the way in a comfortable silence. The stream was just over the nearest ridge and as pristine as promised. From the bank she could see every rock on the bottom. The crystal clear water hurried away from the mountain, but schools of fish remained relatively still in the center.

"Is it cold?" she asked, stepping down from Pilgrim.

"Freezing."

"I'll bet you're hot enough to warm it up."

"You can go in if you want to," he said as his feet hit the ground. "I'm not."

She walked around Silver and came to stand directly in front of Gavin. "There's nothing I could do to persuade you?"

"Not one thing." He caught her hands before she reached him. "And you better stop flirting with me."

"Why should I do that?" As if she *could* stop. She could eat the man with a spoon he was so delicious and it was easy to see he enjoyed her flirting as much as she did.

"Because," he said, squeezing her wrists, "I could out-flirt you with my eyes closed, and we'd both end up in a hell of a lot of trouble."

"And here I was, starting to think you were fun." She held his gaze. "But keep your eyes open. I like them." The man obviously didn't know who he was playing with. If he was up for a flirting contest, she was so ready to win.

She stepped away, slipped her boots and socks off and stuck her toe in the stream. He was right, it was a wonder there weren't ice cubes floating by. "So, I guess this is on the list of approved areas to bring guests."

"Yes, ma'am."

"Tell me how this works." She faced him and wrapped her arms around his back. He had either given up trying to stop her or he had changed his mind. His body was hard beneath his shirt and she loved the strength of his arms around her. The fire he ignited in her chest crept lower and settled between her legs, but she forced herself to focus on something besides her raging *need*. "There were probably a dozen fantasy cowboys in the dining room the other night, but I've barely seen anybody but you since I got here. Where do they all go?"

"Did you come here to learn the business or to fall in love with me?"

"Neither," she said, "but I like the way you hold me."

His arms tightened the slightest bit, pressing her close enough to him that her breasts brushed the front of his shirt and her nipples hardened.

Breathe.

"We sign out timeslots for different places around the ranch to keep you ladies separate. Now will you let me talk to you about something besides work?"

"It's all work isn't it?" She ran her hands over his chest. The thin fabric of his shirt wasn't enough to shield what he hid beneath it.

"Doesn't feel like work when you do that," he said.

She was standing close enough to feel him harden and she stepped back just enough to avoid the contact. "How long do we have here?"

"An hour and a half."

"What would you do if I wasn't ready to leave when the time was up?"

"I'd have to persuade you."

"How would you persuade me?" She moved her hands from the broadness of his chest, down his sides to the relative narrowness of his waist. He was firm and warm beneath her touch, his skin taunt across his muscular frame.

"Since you've demystified the entire process, I'd probably have to tell you we were about to have company, and that it was against the rules to be here when they arrived."

"I'm no fun either, am I?" She laughed and stepped out of his embrace.

"I didn't say that. You just make the job a little more challenging than I'm used to."

"Plenty of men would kill for your job," she said. "Women flirting with them all the time."

"This week they would."

He said all the right words, and said them in such a way that she wanted to believe every one of them, but she knew better. Still, it was nice to hear him talk. Very nice.

She plopped down on a grassy spot a few yards away, and tugged his hand for him to join her. He followed her down and sat back on his elbows. Rebecca repositioned herself and lay on her back with her head resting on his stomach.

"You don't mind if I use you as a pillow, do you?"

"There aren't many things I'd mind you using me for," he said.

She caught the twinkle in his eye and rolled over onto her side so she could see him better. She should be at least a little ashamed of wallowing all over him, but she couldn't find it in herself to care. "How many women have you brought to this stream?"

"We started the business four years ago, so however many that makes."

Her heart fell a little. This game was turning out to be a lot like chess. Knowing the rules didn't make it easy to play.

"Which ladies are your favorites? Besides me, of course."

"Of course." He grinned. "The older widows. I remember how lonely my mom was after Daddy died, and I like to think I can take some of that away from them for a minute." He gave her shoulder a nudge. "I don't let them grope me like you do though."

Rebecca laughed. "I do kind of make myself at home, don't I?"

"I hadn't noticed." His smirk was almost enough to send her crawling up on him to see if his lips tasted as good as they looked. It should be a crime for a man as eligible as Gavin Carter to spend so much of his time with women he wouldn't ever have anything real with.

"Why do you do this?" She searched his eyes. "Is it a commitment thing, are you afraid to commit?"

"No, I'm not afraid to commit." An unfamiliar edge sharpened his voice.

She had hit a nerve. Might as well get to the bottom of it. "What's the longest relationship you've ever had?"

"I was married for five years." Rebecca's mouth opened in surprise before she could stop it. "And before you ask," he added, "I'm not going to talk about it."

"Fair enough." She ran her hand through her hair and let it fall back into place. "Tell me something you've never told another guest at this ranch."

"I don't usually talk about myself any more than I have to. So pretty much everything I've told you falls into that category."

There he was making her feel special again. Special equated to tingly. Tingly was nice. Very, very nice. "Why me?"

"Because you refuse to just shut up and fall in love with me." His smile crept across his face and Rebecca caught herself smiling back.

"You want to play the game?" she asked.

"Anytime you're ready."

"I'm ready."

"Does that mean you want me to call you darlin' now?"

"First let's find out if you're a cowboy I can fall in love with." She sat up and swung one leg over him, positioning herself with a knee on either side of his hips. He lay back and his hands went to her waist. She fought to keep her eyes open, to dampen the desire his touch sent deep into her. "Tell me exactly how you'd make love to me."

His grip tightened sending another shot of pleasure through her. "I'd have to show you," he said, "and not only could I get arrested for that, but we wouldn't have nearly enough time here."

Her chest grew warm and she reached for a strand of hair that fell just below his ear. "Don't you like to talk about sex?"

"You didn't say sex. You said make love."

"There's a difference to you?" she asked.

"Isn't there for you?"

She swallowed the uncertainty and forced a smile. "I want you to tell me what you think the difference between sex and making love is. And make it good, I want something to think about later."

His grin widened until a dimple she hadn't seen before sank into his left cheek. "Sex is sex. It's great, it feels nice, and when it's over, it's over. Hopefully everyone walks away with a smile and a little spring to their step." His fingertips grazed her stomach, traveled up just below her breasts and made their way back down again. "Making love is exploring another person's body because your souls need to meet, letting yourself be completely vulnerable, and pleasing someone because there's nothing else you'd rather do."

Rebecca leaned forward and braced her arms at either side of his head. "Wow, did you come up with that on your own?"

"Not bad for a cowboy, huh?" His voice was low, and the way he looked at her made it impossible to breathe through her nose, made it difficult to breathe at all.

"Well, you did go to Harvard." She swallowed the lump in her throat. "Is that really the difference? Between sex and making love." She licked her lips and watched the confusion settle into his features. "I'm not sure what to expect," she whispered.

"You've never just had sex for the hell of it?"

She could tell he found that hard to believe. "I've always been one for relationships." She bit her lip and tried not to think about the stiff ridge of man that had risen between them and was setting off fireworks in her veins. "I always seemed to have a boyfriend. Then a husband. I'm embarking on a new venture, I guess." She forced herself to maintain eye contact, although the confession was one she'd never shared. "I'm sure I'll manage. I guess the first time will be the hardest." She rubbed herself against him. Her body trembled from the waves that ripped through her and she gasped.

He rolled her over onto the grass, and held himself above her, close enough to raise her temperature even higher, but far enough away to keep her from tearing his clothes off. His shirt gapped open enough to give her a view of what lay beneath it. Hell couldn't have been hotter than the flame that licked between her legs as he continued to tease her, his erection pressing through the double layer of denim between them.

"Your husband was a lucky man," he said. His thighs were between hers, moving slowly, deliberately, spinning all kind of ideas in her head. "Every man you choose to be with will be luckier than he deserves. I can promise you that."

"And I thought I was horny before I got here," she said, reaching for his hips to pull him closer. "I'm going to have a forked tongue before I leave." She loved the way he played, giving her exactly what she wanted, teasing her as much as she teased him. And my God what he could do to her, what he'd be able to do to her if this was real.

"So now the truth comes out." He looked down at her with a sexy glint in his eye. "You're here because you have needs."

"I have so many needs. But I know you aren't in any position to take care of them, so don't worry. I'll handle them myself. I don't mind if you get me worked up though."

His gaze drifted lower. "I'm in a very good position to take care of your *needs*." His laugh settled over her like a blanket. His lips brushed her ear. "Maybe I can give you something to think about," he said softly, grazing his tongue against her skin.

The low moan that escaped her throat was full of desperation. "You've already given me plenty to think about." She curled her legs around his back. "Do you want me to give you something to think about?"

"You've got my thoughts pretty wrapped up." His chest was hard against her breasts, her nipples strained toward him, pressing through her thin blouse.

"I was worried it would be hard for me to touch another man," she admitted, staring over his shoulder into the pale blue sky.

"It's not?" He planted kisses along her jaw.

She ran her hands over his arms trailing the muscular slopes and planes beneath his shirt. "It's not hard the way I thought it would be. Stopping is the hard part." She laughed and bumped his hips with hers. "One of the hard parts."

"We're going to have to get up from here," he said. "Before our *needs* overpower our brains."

"My needs overpower my brain every time you get near me, but I guess that's what makes this business of yours work as well as it does."

He took her chin in his hand and forced her to meet his eyes. "First of all, the business doesn't work this way. I'd fire my men in a second if I caught any of them in this position." He shoved his hair back, in a useless attempt. It fell right back where it had been. His brow furrowed. "What if I made arrangements for you to stay at another ranch this week, and I came by to take you to dinner or see the sights while you're here."

She dropped her hands to the ground and took a deep breath to relieve the tension that had clasped her lungs. "I didn't come here to date," she said steadily. "I came for the game. If you want me to leave, I'll go back home and go out with one of the men my sister's trying to shove down my throat."

"I don't want you to leave," he said. "But we can't roll around on the grass and dry hump all day either. And…" He paused to brush a strand of hair off her cheek. "I don't think you're being honest with yourself."

"I'm honest to a fault," she said quickly.

"Alright then, if you're so determined to have the fantasy, why do you do your best to make me forget my job, but constantly remind yourself this a business?"

She tore her eyes away from his and found distraction in an odd-shaped cloud drifting overhead. A frog with wings. Or a cape. Super Frog. Anything but the man poised above her.

"Tell me why you won't really play the game," he said, bringing her back, urging an answer she didn't want to admit.

Because he had her on a slippery slope. If she didn't remind herself of exactly who he was and why he did what he did to her, she'd slide down in a heartbeat and fall headfirst into him. She'd lose every rational thought in her head, and Todd deserved more than that from her. She wasn't about to give a piece of her heart to a man she'd paid to take it. Or to some pseudo-cowboy who made women pay him to let them fall in love. But aside from that one little detail - the way he sold his body but wouldn't give his heart away - she liked the man beneath the hat. Little detail. Ha.

"I love games, and fantasies are my specialty." She rolled the fabric of his sleeve between her fingers and tried to play it safe. Honest, but safe. "I just have to trust the person I'm playing with."

"And you don't trust me?"

"I trust you enough to lie beneath you out here in the middle of nowhere, but you're just doing your job right? Whatever it takes to make me fall in love, short of boffing my brains out. I can't exactly trust you with my heart. And I don't know how to fake that."

He studied her for a long while, then settled down beside her, propped on his elbow, his other hand on her stomach.

"Tell me what you're going to look for in a man, when you're ready."

"His hand has to feel as good as yours does every time it lands on me." She smiled, relieved he seemed to be backing down and not calling bullshit on her dance around the question. "But more than that," she said, "he has to be honest, someone I can trust completely."

"Anything else?" His fingers crept beneath the hem of her blouse and traced a fiery pattern on her stomach. Her breath caught as the sensations ripped through her.

"I want someone who'll play with me, and I don't mean just in the bedroom. But he would have to be an insatiable lover who let me have my way with him almost every time I wanted to." She ran her hand over the back of his arm. "And it won't hurt if he's strong as an ox and easy on the eyes."

"You don't ask for much do you?" She hadn't seen him move, but suddenly he was closer, his breath warm on her lips, his nose almost touching hers. His eyes were so close she could see the flecks of brown scattered like patches of earth on the prairie and the spark that lit his soul.

"My husband was all those things," she whispered, barely allowing her lips to move, afraid they might touch his. Afraid of how much she wanted to feel his mouth against hers.

"Will any man ever be able to compete with the memory of your husband?" The light in his eyes faded as he waited for her answer, still so close she could almost taste him. The scent of him filled her senses, making her want to forget about everything else. Her chest contracted. This was so wrong. She couldn't forget about Todd. She wouldn't.

Gavin's eyes were soft, searching her with caution but loaded with sincere curiosity. He waited for an answer.

"Why?" she managed.

"I want to know what it takes to be with a woman like you, and to keep her in love for so long."

Something in his need to know told her he'd been burned and he was far from healed. Maybe he was one of those men who would never heal, never let a woman close enough to hurt him again.

"I already told you. He was my best friend and the most incredible lover I'll ever know."

"You can't tell a man that another man's better in bed than he could ever hope to be." His brows lowered in disbelief. His lips were still dangerously close.

"You're serious aren't you?" she asked. His hand slid to her hip. Her heart pounded at the firmness of his hold on her, the directness of his stare.

"Of course, I'm serious. And any other guy would tell you the same thing, if he didn't turn tail and run."

Rebecca studied him, the tension in his forehead, and the firm set of his jaw.

"Why do you feel threatened?" she asked. He was so close his hair caressed her cheek. The slightest movement and she would be wrapped up in him. Lost in him.

"I'm not threatened." He visibly relaxed a little and his voice dropped lower. "Apparently, I just have a lot to prove."

"You're legally and contractually restricted from being my lover," she challenged him. "So why do you care? What difference could it possibly make?"

Without giving another thought to the consequences Gavin took her lips in his. It was ridiculous to think he should deny what they both were so obviously feeling. They were adults, consenting adults. With needs. Excruciating, overpowering *needs*.

She welcomed him more ferociously than he'd expected, like a spring coiled tight inside her had been sprung. She clung to him, her fingers sharp in his back, her body anything but still beneath him as her tongue slid against his. His stomach clenched then flipped.

He dug his hands into her hair. Her tongue was like a cool drink of water after he had spent his life in the desert searching for something that would quench his thirst. A moan poured between them, urging him deeper. In that moment, her body beneath his became his world. Nothing else mattered. Her heat radiated through her clothes. She flowed around him as if he was sinking into a sun-warmed oasis. She molded to every line of his frame. He could only imagine how much better she would feel naked. How good they would be together. He needed Rebecca. He needed to be in her, on her, all over her at once. All this from a kiss. Making love to her would be the end of him.

Her nails dug through his shirt, every nerve ending he had stood on high alert. And for some unfathomable reason his damn brain had to kick into gear. He had to stop. He couldn't do this. Sex with a guest was illegal. Prostitution. He could lose the ranch. Go to jail. One more minute he told himself, taking her mouth harder. Tasting her tongue like he might never sample it again. He would stop. In one more minute. Her legs tightened around his waist and he thrust his hips to hers. The double layer of denim between them left him far from satisfied, but his dick got harder with every stroke and every muffled cry that slipped from her mouth.

He slid his hand beneath her shirt and over the thin silk barrier of her bra. Her breast filled his palm, soft and hard. He ran his fingers over the pillow of flesh and caught her rigid nipple between his knuckles. The contrast shuffled his mind. He had to taste her skin, every warm intoxicating inch of it, then bury himself deep inside her. Just like he'd known the first time her eyes met his. There was something more between them than mild attraction. He could feel it now in the way she trembled and clung to him, and in his own irrepressible need to give her all that he had to give. He may not be able to offer her more than she'd already known, but he'd be damned if he was going to let her go back home to some equally deserving jerk without giving her all he could.

Lightning couldn't have sent a stronger jolt through Rebecca than the need she saw in Gavin's eyes as he broke the kiss and held his face above hers. The scent of him filled her, made her dizzy. She had to part her lips to breathe. She was weak and powerful all at once, and for the first time in way too long she was alive, her body rejoiced with life. She needed to tell him to stop before she lost her senses altogether. But she didn't want him to stop. She didn't want to stop touching him, tasting him, feeling his weight distributed over her like a blanket she could curl up in. Still, she couldn't do this.

Before she could speak, his mouth opened against hers in another kiss. One that was both gentle and too powerful for her to take ownership of. He was in command, and she was helpless to do anything but follow his lead. She would follow him anywhere. His pull on her was stronger than any half-hearted resistance she could muster.

His lips were so much softer than they had been only a minute before, his desire so much more than she had been prepared for. Every movement of his tongue swirled cravings in her strong enough to wipe her mind blank of everything but him. He explored her slowly. His hands moved along her sides pulling her into him as his tongue delved deeper.

She reached for his neck, grasping at the strong tendons that tightened beneath his skin. His control was intoxicating, but just as she started to get drunk from it, he pulled away.

Her breasts rose and fell with each exaggerated breath that stumbled in and out of her. Seconds passed before she trusted herself to speak.

"Those shouldn't be allowed." Her voice was thick, her mind and body too scrambled to make sense of anything.

"They're not." He was so close the breath of his words rushed over her. The subtle scent of his cologne drew her in, made her want more, but her thoughts finally converged and screamed logic she didn't want to hear.

"A rule you've broken before?"

"No." His eyes never left hers.

Longing rose in her like a balloon but it was soon followed by something else, something far heavier, and much harder to carry.

Guilt.

This man wasn't her husband. He wasn't Todd, but that kiss had dipped beyond sexual need. He had stirred emotions in her that she swore another man would never touch. Tears pricked the backs of her eyes. She looked away before Gavin could see what was happening and wiped her face with the back of her hand.

"I'm sorry." He rolled to his side and hugged her to him. He was breathing hard. The length of his body against hers was more comfort than she'd had in a year, and at the very same time it was completely disconcerting. "I shouldn't have done that," he said.

"Don't apologize." His heart pounded in her ear. Her back remained stiff, and her arms hung rigid from her sides. "I was all over you. Teasing you. I should've expected it."

"You didn't do anything I didn't want you to do," he said softly, "and I'm the one who's supposed to keep things in line here."

"I wanted to kiss you." Her voice was so low she wasn't sure he heard her. His only response was to reach for her hand and lace her fingers with his.

A horse snorted, signaling someone's approach.

"If I didn't own half the company I'd have lost my job already," he said, sitting up. "I've broken nearly every rule in the book, and I can't get you to fall in love with me to save my life."

She squeezed his arm and swallowed the rock that had lodged itself in her throat. "You've put me in a healthy state of lust though." She hated wanting him. She hated what she had done, but if she could go back to before the guilt hit and do it again, she would jump at the chance with both feet and arms flailing through the air.

She was terrible. And terribly stupid to think she was getting anything from Gavin Carter that he wouldn't give to a million other women. Or to think she could ever experience sex casually.

"Come on," he said and helped her to her feet. His generous lips spread into an easy smile. "It's time to get you back." He started to pull her in for a hug, but the snapping of a branch and the sound of horses jerked him back.

Three men in saddles emerged from the tree line. Garrett was in the lead. The other two were unfamiliar, and not nearly attractive enough to be fantasy cowboys. Badges on their chests caught the glint of sunlight and their putty-colored polyester button-downs told Rebecca everything she needed to know about them. In Podunk, Wyoming even the local law enforcement wore Wranglers, boots, and cowboy hats.

Gavin swore under his breath and turned his back to the trio as he led Rebecca to Pilgrim and Silver.

"Friends of yours?" she asked.

"Wouldn't need enemies if they were." His smile was tight.

"Working hard today Gavin?" The thinner of the two donut-holes called out.

"I do everything harder than you, Chet," Gavin jabbed back.

Garrett cleared his throat, and Rebecca mounted Pilgrim with a thinly concealed smirk on her face.

"Catch you next time," Chet called out as Rebecca and Gavin heeled their horses and trotted off.

* * * *

Sex isn't love. Sex is sex. Every person on the planet seemed able to compartmentalize the two, separate them conveniently. Rebecca wanted to. She would have to, but they had been so tangled together in her life for so long what if she couldn't?

Gavin's fingers were intertwined with hers, but he hadn't said much as they made their way back to her cabin. He probably thought she was an emotional train wreck. He wouldn't be far off track. His thumb traced the top of her hand, but his eyes were distant. He probably didn't even realize he was touching her that way. He definitely didn't understand what his touch did to her.

When they kissed at the spring, she had wanted to pull him so far into her it would be impossible to tell where he ended and she began. Her heart raced. Her lungs fought to breathe, but she almost believed as long as he was kissing her she didn't really need air at all. Was that lust? Just lust?

His ultra-sexy body and those fricken' green eyes that could equally reflect gentleness and fire were enough to inspire a bucket of lustful thoughts. But what about his humor, his intelligence? That spark of recognition when their eyes met? What about her incessant need to question him, and the gnawing realization at the back of her brain that she would probably never meet another man who she'd want to know nearly as much? Was that just lust too?

"I'm sorry," Rebecca whispered at the door to her cabin. "I'm really screwed up. More than I thought."

"You don't have anything to be sorry for." He wiped away another tear that had begun to slide down her face. "I really shouldn't have kissed you. No matter how much I wanted to."

The gentleness in his voice was too much. She couldn't hold back anymore. "You're the first. Since Todd. You're the…"

"It was just a kiss." He pulled her back out onto the porch and held her while she cried. "But it won't happen again."

She sobbed into his chest and clung to him like she would collapse if she didn't. Just a kiss she told herself, a mind-scrambling, body-rocking kiss that only felt that way because it had been so long since she'd had any male affection at all. Gavin's hold on her was comforting, his whispers reassuring. She eventually calmed enough to stop crying. She had to take a page from his book. It was nothing to him. Nothing. Just a kiss.

"You must think I'm crazy," she said with her face still buried in his shirt, embarrassed to have broken down so completely. She was stronger than that. So much stronger. The tears would have to stop. She would not permit another single drop to fall.

"I don't think you're crazy." His arms were as gentle as his voice, and if she could have melted into him she would have gladly surrendered, but she straightened her shoulders instead and filled her lungs with the warm scent of his chest.

"I'm crawling all over you one minute and bawling because you kissed me like I wanted you to the next." She snorted a laugh. "I think I'm crazy."

"Just tell me what you need from me." He smoothed her hair and pulled it away from her face. The gentleness had spread to his eyes and it made her want him as much as the fire. Maybe more.

"A handkerchief." She sniffed.

"I have one of those." His voice held a tinge of laughter. He shook open a neatly folded square of cotton before he handed it to her.

She wiped her eyes and nose and leaned into him as far as she could. His hands moved slowly over her back, protective, reassuring, everything she needed him to be.

"Tell me what you really need," he said.

"I don't know. Maybe I just need to go home."

"How about this." He pushed her shoulders back so she could see his face. "Stay the rest of the week. Treat it like any other vacation. Consider me your personal concierge. Or a friend. Or whatever you want me to be."

She smiled and blinked away the threat of more tears. "What if I want you to be my cowboy?"

"That's my specialty." He grinned back at her. "And I'll keep my hands off of you."

"Really?" He had meant to make her feel better, but something inside her sank.

"If you keep yours off me." His smile was genuine, meant to reassure her. "The way you touch me clouds my brain. Makes me forget everything but my name." He squeezed her shoulders. "I'm not looking for those kinds of emotions any more than you are. And the ranch isn't the place to explore them even if that is what we wanted."

The scars of his marriage must run deep. No wonder he wouldn't talk about it. Either that or he was just a consummate playboy, happy with his lot in life. Without a doubt he could find plenty of women ready to play with him. Women who wouldn't cry until after he left.

"I'll try to keep my hands to myself." She bit her lip and smiled. "But you're really hot. And have I mentioned all those needs I have?"

His soft laughter filled the space between them. He lifted her chin and forced her eyes to meet his. "So you're okay?"

She nodded. Okay. She assured Gavin just like she assured her parents, her sister and her friends. She was okay. There was nothing else she could be. She didn't have a choice. She plastered a perfect smile on her face, proof to the world she was as okay as she said she was.

* * * *

Gavin crumpled another piece of paper and tossed it into the wastebasket beside his desk where wads of discarded attempts already filled the lower half. He had the kitchen send over Rebecca's lunch, though he doubted she'd want it. She was more shaken than she would admit. He could tell she'd held back a lot more tears than she had shed.

Her pain ate at him. He couldn't imagine losing someone like she had and still having enough heart left to laugh. She was like a kid trying to play, desperate to play. She really did make him feel like he was in high school, following rules, abiding by curfews, restricted from going farther than he physically wanted to go.

He shook the fog out of his head. He wasn't fifteen, sneaking off to play backseat baseball when his parents weren't looking. He wasn't dating her. He was catering to her, making sure she got the vacation she had purchased from the company he owned. He was a man, not a kid, and if he wanted to get laid he knew how to do it. He didn't have to makeout and cuddle and talk for hours on end just to get to the payout. There were plenty of available women who didn't need more than a pleasant invitation.

So why did he feel like he had let her down? It was that damn front she put up, that brick wall that was nothing more than carefully constructed ash, ready to crumble in the slightest wind. Her tears were nothing compared to what he'd seen behind them. He was a colossal ass for not realizing how fragile she was. For hounding in on her because she was the sexiest woman he'd ever laid eyes on.

"What are you working on?" Garrett asked from the doorway.

"Thought I'd try a new mascot." His intention had been to lose himself in work. Not an easy thing to do when he couldn't think about anything but Rebecca. And not a bit easier when he was still shaken by their kiss. Had a kiss ever hit him that hard? Her first response had been as heated as his, more heated. Maybe that's why the tears felt like such a sucker punch. Or maybe she hadn't punched him half as hard as he'd kicked himself. There was no room in his life for those kinds of feelings. No way in hell he would make himself that vulnerable to a woman again.

"I like the winking cowboy." Garrett moved around to his side of the desk and sat down with his back to the window.

"It's a little amateur." The winking cowboy had always been amateur, purposely amateur. It was comedic relief to put potential clients at ease, and let them know it was okay not to take the ranch too seriously. Fantasy Ranch was meant to be a good time, a place to come play a game that could never be real.

"He works," Garrett said. "We're booked for the next two weeks and filling up fast for the next two months."

Gavin sketched a cowboy with a lady on his arm, a lady that looked remarkably like Rebecca Ryder.

"How's this week going?" Garrett asked.

"Fine." Fine, my ass. He could still taste Rebecca's lips, smell the soft floral scent she wore. His body was still hot from the way she had his heart pumping. There was nothing fine about the way she had rocked him. He knew better. Even if she wasn't a guest. Even if she wasn't broken. A woman who could do that to him was a woman to stay the hell away from.

Garrett set his elbows on the desk and scratched the back of his head. A sign Gavin knew too well.

"I appeased Chet Bening by taking him down to the spring after I thought you would have already left with Rebecca. I was ahead of them coming through the woods."

"And?" Gavin didn't look up from what he was doing.

"And I saw you."

"It was nothing." That was the understatement of the year. Probably the biggest bald-faced lie he'd ever told.

"To you it was nothing. To her —"

Gavin cut him off. "I know what it was to her."

"Look, Gav. All I'm trying to say is her husband died, if she was dating other men, she wouldn't be here. You're just supposed to make her feel like it's okay to fall in love again. You're not supposed to actually let her do it. Not to mention if Chet…"

"Don't mention it. And she's not falling in love with me. She's still very much in love with him." The lead in Gavin's pencil snapped against the paper. He flung the pencil into the trash and reached for another one.

"Sometimes it doesn't take much to make a heart change direction," Garrett said.

"A lesson I've already learned." That would shut him up. Garrett wasn't about to delve into the Taryn issue. "Any other sage advice? I need to shower before I check on my guest."

"I don't know, little brother. You're not yourself this week. And you've definitely got more on your mind than this business. We're in enough shit if you haven't noticed."

"This business is just as much mine as it is yours, and my interest in it is just as vested." Gavin pushed his chair back and stood up. "I know what I'm doing."

"What are you doing?"

"Just playing the game." Gavin tossed the picture of the cowboy and Rebecca in the trash and walked out the door, letting Garrett have the office to himself.

"Where's your lovely opponent?" Garrett called after him.

"Rebecca's in her cabin, and for the record, we're on the same team," he shouted back.

Damn it. Garrett had made his point. Gavin headed up the stairs reminding himself he was thirty-five years old. A grown man who needed to start acting like it again. Garrett's remark really got under his skin, though. He'd never felt camaraderie with a guest before. It was always him against whatever brought her to the ranch. Him against her low self-esteem, him against her broken heart, him against her loneliness, him against her man-sized libido. He'd never felt like he was playing the game with any of them before. He always played it against whatever baggage they brought.

Rebecca had stepped off the airplane without any visible baggage at all. Maybe that's what threw him. He forgot to worry about all the stuff he couldn't see. And all he could focus on was how they could play this charade together. How far they could push the rules before the game started pushing back. Well, now he knew. The kiss was too much, one step too many. Time to go back three spaces and roll again.

He would put everything back on track, prove to her that men weren't supposed to make her cry. She deserved that. She deserved a hell of a lot more than he could give, but he could give her what she needed this week. Maybe that would be enough for both of them.

* * * *

"He kissed you?" Melinda's voice rose an octave and Rebecca held the phone out a few inches from her ear. "What a slut. He'd probably tongue his own grandmother if she signed on for a week out there."

"I'm not that old," Rebecca said. Melinda's words were like cold water on the fire that had started a slow burn beneath her skin.

"He's lucky to kiss you," Melinda said. "But, can you imagine some of the women he must have to kiss? He can't be attracted to all of them. How can anyone do that?"

"He says he's never kissed another guest." The words sounded stupid the minute she said them.

"And he says he went to Harvard, yeah right. He probably did an internship in Nevada at the Bunny Ranch. You don't actually believe the things this guy says do you?"

"He can be convincing." Rebecca buried her hand in her hair and closed her eyes.

"Becca, you put a significant dent in your savings account to spend a week out there. He better tell you anything he thinks you want to hear."

"I know."

"That kills me. This guy would rather lie to lonely women every day than get a real job. What was he doing before he came up with this grand idea, giving foot massages at a convalescent center?"

Lonely women. God, the truth could sting. "He's got a graduate degree in marketing." Her voice was too weak to be convincing, and she braced herself for Melinda's next blow.

"They don't offer those at the Bunny Ranch." Melinda's tone was as full of bite as she'd expected.

Rebecca threw herself back on the bed with a groan. She focused on the ceiling beams and waited for her sister to tell her what she so obviously needed to hear.

"You weren't really buying into any of that crap were you?" Melinda asked.

"I guess I got caught up in the experience for a minute. It's so beautiful out here, and so quiet." The only scenery that held enough intrigue to shuffle her mind was the rugged beefcake she'd wrapped herself around. "With a man as sexy as Gavin, I guess it's hard to keep a firm grip on reality."

"Keep a firm grip on his ass if you want to. Treat him like what he is. Just don't let him treat you that way."

Rebecca's embarrassment slipped into sadness. It was hard to hear her vivacious, optimistic, usually lovesick sister worn down to such a cynical shell. "You're angry Mel, very, very angry."

"I am." Melinda sighed. "And I'm sick. I've been throwing up all day." Her breath was heavy against the phone. "I'm pregnant."

Rebecca shot off the bed. "What did you say?"

Her sobs came before her words. "I'm pregnant."

"Oh, Mel." A child on the way and a husband out the door. Rebecca felt sick, as sick as if it had happened to her. "When did you find out?" She clutched her stomach, willing it to settle and paced in a tight circle.

"After I dropped you off at the airport, I had a doctor's appointment."

"Why didn't you tell me?" A fresh wave of guilt crashed into her before Melinda said a word. Her little sister was still protecting her, the way she and everyone else in the family had been doing since Todd died.

"You were already worried about me. I didn't want to screw up your vacation."

"I wish you had told me," she said quietly. "How far along are you?"

"Eight weeks." Melinda's voice had dropped so low, Rebecca had to press the phone closer to her ear.

"Does Scott know?"

"No. I was planning to tell him over dinner the other night, but he told me he was leaving before I had a chance."

Rebecca cleared her lungs in one fiery breath and dug her toes into the floor planks. Nothing could have shaken her out of la-la land and sent her plummeting to the ground harder than Melinda's situation. "What a bastard. How did you ever end up married to him?"

"He sounded a lot like the cowboy." Melinda sniffed.

Melinda had said goodbye, but Rebecca was still holding the phone when Gavin knocked for her. She swung the door open ready to hate him, ready to show him how much patience she had for men like Scott, because he probably wasn't all that different. He stood on the porch, showered, shaved and in a fresh pair of tingle inspiring jeans. When had her body decided to so completely buck her brain? Despite everything Melinda had said to steer her straight and all the tears she'd shed since she last saw him, Gavin Carter still made her heart beat faster.

"Hey, you feel any better?" He looked almost as concerned as he did gorgeous. His hand started toward her, but he paused mid-air and dropped it back to his side.

She was ready to close the door between them, give herself a chance to regroup, take a shower, pack her bag. Something. Anything. Apparently her muscles were as rebellious as her heart and lungs, because she couldn't move.

"These are for you." He pulled his other hand from behind his back and held out a can of peas. The label was worn, and rust crept around the rim of the lid. He laughed at the expression on her face. "I know it's silly," he said, "but my dad used to give these to my mom whenever he screwed up. It's a peas-offering."

"Sounds like your dad had a good sense of humor," she said unable to tame her smile.

"He made her laugh. That's all that really mattered."

"Thank you." She took the peas from him and stepped out of the doorway. "Want to come in? I can't offer you anything as nice as these peas, but there's wine in the chiller."

He hooked his hat on the wall and grabbed two glasses off the shelf above the wet bar while Rebecca opened the wine. They sat down across from one another at the small table next to the window. Even the distance between them wasn't enough to squelch the way her body reacted to him or the thoughts that refused to stop racing through her mind. She wanted him to be the one who taught her the difference, to show her how to have worthwhile sex without emotional strings.

He lifted his glass to hers. "To the winking cowboy, and whatever he did to bring you here," he said.

Rebecca took a deep breath and set her glass down on the table. "Can I be honest with you?" Maybe if she told him the truth, the burden wouldn't be so hard to carry.

"I'd like that."

"I came because of Todd." She glanced over to make sure Gavin was at least half interested in hearing what she needed to tell him. His eyes were fixed on her, waiting for her to continue. He hadn't taken a drink from his glass either.

"He used to…we used to play these games. Role playing. He'd pretend to be whoever was turning me on at the moment, and I'd do the same for him."

Gavin didn't say anything, just kept watching her, waiting.

She drew the wine glass to her lips for a little liquid courage and set it back down. "The morning…the last time I saw him…" Tears welled in her eyes and she wiped them away. "I'm sorry. I just want you to understand. So you won't think I'm crazy."

Gavin reached across the table and took her hand. "I want to know."

She drew in her breath. His touch gave her the courage she needed, connected her to him in a way that made her want to remove the last vestiges of this wall between them. "He was going to be my cowboy that night, but he never made it home." Silent tears slid down her face.

Gavin cleared his throat. His grip on her hand loosened.

"I thought coming out here might help me remember. I don't know, maybe I thought it would give me one more chance to be with him before I tried to go out with someone else. I didn't expect this all to be so … real."

"It's not real." He drained more than half his glass and set it back on the table between them. "This place is as fabricated as Disneyland. That's what it's supposed to be. Just a bunch of windup toys, spitting out whatever the guests want to hear. Most of the guys don't even use their real names. They're actors. This is a chance to hone their craft, and to make a little money while they're doing it."

Anger crept up on her. Irrational anger. He wasn't telling her anything she didn't know, or shouldn't have been able to figure out, but she felt betrayed, stupid that she could have felt anything for him. "Are you an actor?"

"No, just a business man. For now, Garrett and I can save a lot of money if we entertain guests ourselves, and usually it's a good way to keep some quality control. Although, after this week, I should fire myself." He twisted the stem of his glass on the table. "I need to know something."

She covered her roiling emotions as best she could and nodded for him to continue.

"When I'm holding you, do you pretend it's him?"

Rebecca couldn't meet his eyes, her heart quickened, but she refused to lie. There was power in truth; lies were a coward's tools. "Most of the time I've been too overwhelmed by the sensations of you touching me to think about anyone but you. But sometimes when I closed my eyes…when your touch felt almost familiar…I could see him in my mind. I could remember the way he loved me." She paused to wipe a tear. "And when you kissed me…"

Gavin let go of her hand and adjusted himself in his seat. "What happened when I kissed you?" His voice had a sharpness she hadn't expected.

"Nothing should have happened." Heat crept in prickles up her neck and across her cheeks. "If you knew half the things I've thought about doing with you, a kiss definitely shouldn't have sent me over the edge. Even that kiss." She ran her finger over the curve of her glass until she had the courage to meet his eyes. "I didn't know anyone else could get me going like that. Like you said, it was just a kiss. But for me it felt so…like so much more. And I felt like I betrayed my husband."

"Do you still think you betrayed him?" Something she said had taken the edge from his voice. The gentleness was back, and it stirred something in the depths of her abdomen.

"A little." She steadied herself, not sure what had caused the shift in him and equally confused by the way her body responded to his slightest nuances. "Does it bother you that I've thought of him when we were together like that?"

"Yeah." He didn't look at her when he responded. "It shouldn't, but it does."

Was his ego so massive he couldn't handle the thought of another man anywhere near the fantasy he was meant to create, or was there something more to his aversion of her thinking about her husband? "Why does it bother you?"

He sipped his wine and made eye contact again. "Because I'd like to be the only man on your mind. This week."

"And then you'll forget all about me and move on to your next guest. That's not exactly fair to me." The anger she expected didn't come. Instead, her heart was consumed with the hollowness of loss, and her body was doused with a cold splash of reality. "So, do you think I'm going to get any better at this? I mean when I get back home, do you think I'm going to cry every time a man kisses me?"

He rounded the table and coaxed her to her feet. Standing so close to him unnerved her, made her want to be closer. Even with tears of regret still fresh in her eyes, she wanted to feel his lips, taste his tongue, lose herself in his arms again.

"I think," he said, "when you're with the right man, you won't think about Todd or anyone else at all." He moved toward the door, and already Rebecca knew if any man could do that for her it was the one walking away. The one who wasn't supposed to be real.

"What if that man is you?" The words slipped out of her, barely audible, and she prayed he hadn't heard them.

"I'm not that man." He pulled his hat off the wall and opened the door. "I'll have the kitchen send your dinner out here."

"Don't you want to have dinner with me?" The way she had understood the game she was supposed to be calling the shots, deciding when to spend time with him.

"Can I be honest with you now?" He thumped his hat against his thigh and looked toward the big house. "I told you I'd be whatever you needed me to be." He brought his eyes back to her. "But I won't be Todd, and nobody else is going to either."

"I know you're not Todd." She unleashed an unsteady breath and squared her shoulders. The rules had changed too quickly for her liking, and the sting of his words fired her defenses. "But I paid you to make me fall in love, not to dismiss me."

"You're not going to fall in love with me." His tone was hard, certain. The muscles in his neck tensed. "Don't worry, I know my job. I'll come by in the morning like you're *paying* me to do. If I don't, you can have your money back."

He closed the door and left her more alone than she'd ever felt before.

* * * *

Gavin tied his shoes and left through the garage to avoid being seen by any of the guests. He ran along the fence line that bordered the highway and poured over the last conversation with Rebecca. He didn't have any right to get so pissed off at her. His brain didn't seem to be connected to his blood pressure, though. This week, his brain seemed to have disconnected itself from the rest of his body altogether.

His chest was heavy. He knew where he was going, and he didn't want to go there. His mind didn't care what he wanted. It took him back anyway, back to the day Taryn left. The day she told him she was in love with someone else. Relating that day to what had happened with Rebecca was ridiculous. Of course she loved her husband. Why would he care if she thought about the guy when he had her in his arms? He shouldn't give a damn. He shouldn't have her in his arms.

His feet pounded the trail he'd run into the grass over the years. The fenceposts zipped by faster than usual, his lungs pulled in more air than he needed, weighing him down, making it hard to let go and let the run take him away from everything he wanted to escape from. An all too familiar conversation replayed itself, a conversation he didn't need to hear again.

"Don't you even want to try and make this work?" he had asked her.

"I can't." Taryn laid her wedding band on the kitchen table and crossed her arms. "I'm sorry," she said.

"How do you know we can't get past this?" They had been arguing over stupid stuff more than usual, but he hadn't been prepared for the reasons she was so unhappy. Her admission blindsided him.

"When I'm in bed with you, or kissing you, every time you touch me, I wish it was him. I pretend it's him," she said. "I'm in love."

"Who is this guy?" His head spun. He hadn't even suspected she was having an affair. "How well can you possibly even know him?"

"I'm really sorry," she said and wiped a tear from her eye. A fucking crocodile tear. A heart could change direction alright. It could spin the fuck around in one beat.

"Why won't you tell me who he is? How you met him? What it is about him that's worth our marriage?" His hands had trembled, and he remembered looking at them as if they belonged to someone else. His wedding band was still on his left hand because he hadn't accepted what she had told him. Hadn't even had time to process it. Her bags had already been hauled away when he came home from work, but she had stayed to tell him she was leaving. How noble of her. A truck pulled into the driveway in front of their house and Ron, his oldest friend and business partner, got out.

"He needs me to sign off on a contract we worked up today. I'll tell him to leave," Gavin said. She reached for his arm, stopping him before he'd taken a step.

"He wanted to be here. To tell you with me." Her hand tightened around his arm. "Don't lose your temper."

"Why would I?" He looked through the glass door at the man walking toward the house and then back at his wife, reading the expression on both their faces. He had never felt so stupid in his life. So betrayed. "You're fucking *Ron*?" His teeth clamped down so hard he could taste the blood from the inside of his cheek. He jerked out of her grasp and started for the door.

"Gavin don't!"

Gavin stopped running and bent over at the waist. His chest heaved. His heart pounded. Sweat poured from his face into the sand of the trail. He reached for a fencepost for support and pulled himself over to the railing until he could catch his breath. Fuck. They had really screwed him up. And Rebecca didn't have anything to do with why he couldn't pretend to be another man for her. Or why he could never give her what she needed.

* * * *

Rebecca washed the remnants of a long nap from her face. Her stomach growled. She probably shouldn't have refused the dinner Gavin had sent over, but all she'd wanted to do was sleep. She ignored the familiar knock that came later. She probably shouldn't have done that either, but she was going to play this game on her terms. Or not at all.

She ran a brush through her hair, and pulled Gavin's sweatshirt over her head before she went outside and crossed the damp grass to the big house. The office light was on. It wasn't ten thirty yet, so even if Garrett was still in there working, she could ask for Gavin without causing a stir.

At the window her heart stilled, then resumed with a pounding that vibrated her chest wall. Gavin was bent over his desk. His hair fell around his face. His features were drawn in concentration. He was so damned good looking her lungs burned and the last drop of irritation with him drained out of her. Not good. Really not good.

She raised her fist to the window. Just before her knuckles tapped the glass, he glanced up, saw her and smiled. Obviously the time apart had been good for him, too.

Breathe. She wiggled her fingers in a wave that brought him around the desk. He slid the window up and sat on his heels. She didn't let her eyes linger on the denim stretched across his thighs, but every other part of him was just as appealing. Her body responded with a need that heated her through the bone.

"I have an idea," she said, speaking before he could, determined to put things right again.

"And what would that be?" His voice was soft, his eyes softer.

"Maybe tomorrow you could treat me like every other guest. Do whatever you'd normally do, and I won't cry or cling to you, or act psycho in any way. I promise."

"I don't know. I was sorta getting used to your kind of crazy." His hand covered hers on the windowsill, reminding her how big her promises were. "I missed it so much, I came by your cabin. Guess you didn't want to see me. Not that I blame you. I—"

"No more apologies, the peas have you covered for today." Her heart hammered away, while her brain screamed how stupid she was for letting her body go on like that. Her peripheral caught Garrett before he stopped next to Gavin at the edge of the desk.

"Goodnight, Garrett," she said both relieved and disappointed at the interruption. "I was just leaving." Then to Gavin, "Want to meet me for breakfast?"

"Eight thirty?" He released her. The cool air swallowed the heat from where his hand had been.

"Okay," she said. "Well, 'til then, sweet dreams."

She walked back to the cabin with her hands in the pocket of his sweatshirt, and her heart in her throat. She was lucky to have met him at the ranch. In the real world, she would have been screwed, and not in a good way.

* * * *

Gavin had time to close the window but hadn't completely made it to his feet before Garrett confronted him.

"You gave her the peas?"

"I fucked up. I had to do something." The kiss had been the least of his mistakes, but he wouldn't make another one.

"Must've been a pretty big fuck up." Garrett's voice had a bite to it. "I hope it happened before the camera in her cabin was fixed."

"Look," Gavin said, running his hand through his hair. "Let's just get this out in the open." It was time to try being honest with Garrett and himself. He could never give himself to a woman like Rebecca, not one he could lose himself in so completely. He wasn't a man who made the same mistake twice.

Garrett tapped his fingers on the corner of the desk and waited.

"I didn't do anything more than what you saw, the one time. I know enough to keep my pants on. Even if I didn't, she's not ready for me or anybody else. So I apologized, and we're good. Tomorrow's a new day. Business as usual."

"That easy, huh?" Deep lines carved Garrett's brow.

"Doesn't matter. That's the way it is." At least he had met her at the ranch. In the real world he would have been screwed. Royally.

"What are you going to do tomorrow to put everything back on track?" Garrett asked.

"Exactly what she asked me to do, and…"

"And what?"

"And nothing. That's all I have to do. Pretend she's someone I have next to nothing in common with, who doesn't make me hard every time I look at her, and treat her like every other woman that comes through here." The absurdity of what he said was laughable, not that he could laugh about it. He was in way over his head and despite everything he tried to convince himself of, he'd dive in even deeper if she gave him half a chance. Dumb ass. He had to get his act together. And fast.

"You've got it bad little brother," Garrett said, taking a seat at his desk.

Through the window he could still see her, making her way back to the cabin. "She'll be gone in four days and everything will be back to normal," he said.

"And that's the way you want things?"

"That's exactly the way I want things." He didn't take his eyes from her until she disappeared inside her cabin.

"I haven't seen you look at a woman this way since Taryn. Maybe there's something to be said about that," Garrett said as Gavin turned away from the window.

"Yeah, like I should be glad to wave her off at the end of the week and thank my thick head I was smarter this time." He had a hard time believing Rebecca would be a mistake, but he would have said the same thing about his wife. He wouldn't be that wrong again. Ever. All he needed from women he could get any time he wanted to. Marriage, love and family was a bigger fantasy than what they offered at the ranch.

"Every woman you meet shouldn't have to pay for what Taryn did," Garrett said.

"I can't believe you're telling me to make a move on a guest. You read another romance didn't you?"

"No." Garrett flung a pen at him. "But maybe you should read one. And I'm not telling you to do anything while she's here. You shouldn't even step foot in her room the way things are right now. I'm just saying she won't be a guest forever."

"I'm not picking that up." Gavin motioned toward the pen on the floor. He hadn't made it back to his side of the desk before Garrett rolled his chair across the floor and picked up the pen.

"You could see if it would be okay to contact her after she leaves."

"No." Gavin said automatically. "Make that *hell* no."

Garrett picked up a file. "Fine. Just don't let Taryn keep screwing everything up for you. She's already done more of that than anyone should be allowed."

Gavin sat down, picked up his pencil and tried to concentrate. Like that was going to happen. He held his head in his hands and closed his eyes. Less than a week ago everything had seemed so simple. He had a job to do. He told women what they wanted to hear, padded his bank account and didn't think beyond the next seven days. Then Rebecca showed up wanting him to do what he did all the time, and he couldn't do it. He couldn't distance himself enough to let her have her husband back, to let another man take the credit for the way he made her feel. He'd done enough of that when he was married.

He had done it again, compared her to Taryn. She was nothing like Taryn, but she scared the hell out of him anyway. At least she was smart enough to figure out what he needed to do, just get through the next four days. He could go through the motions, keep himself locked down like always. She wouldn't have to know anything more than that.

"I'm turning in," he said.

"Sweet dreams," Garrett called after him in a high-pitched southern drawl.

Gavin raised his middle finger before disappearing completely through the door.

Chapter 5

Rebecca laid her knife across her plate. The neckline of her blouse dipped low, exposing inches of lush cleavage. The silky skin of her breasts probably tasted even better than it looked. He'd love to find out, but it sure as hell wouldn't get him out of the mess he was in.

"Are you staring at my boobs?" Her words brought his eyes back to where they were supposed to be and jerked him out of the testosterone haze he'd gotten lost in.

"Yes, ma'am." He set his coffee mug on the table, less embarrassed than he should have been. "I forgot for a second that you're just a guest."

She hooked her fingers in the front of her blouse and tugged it higher, completely covering the tempting valley between her breasts. "Does this help?"

"Immensely." He smiled. "But in all honesty I liked it better the other way."

The dining room chimed with clinking silverware, soft laughter and hushed conversation. All the cowboys were in attendance for breakfast with their ladies, and for the first time all week everyone was where they were supposed to be.

"What are we doing after this?" she asked. At least one of them had sense enough to change the subject.

"Since you haven't officially signed up for any of the activities, I thought I'd give you a roping lesson this morning, and join everyone for the afternoon group dance class. Then after dinner, if being a regular guest hasn't put you to sleep, we'll join everybody around the campfire for some cowboy poetry."

"Sounds like a rigid schedule."

"Of course, you're welcome to spend as much time alone as you'd like." He smiled at her over the rim of his cup, hoping she wouldn't take him up on that offer even if it would make his promise to stick to the game a hell of a lot easier. He had woken up almost giddy this morning, probably from the orgasms she'd given him in his sleep. He liked being around her, looked forward to it. He could admit that much. He could admit more if he was pushed, but nobody was pushing.

"I didn't come all the way to Wyoming to be alone," she said.

"Good, because I kind of like your company." Her blouse shifted back into its previous position and derailed his thoughts again. Her smile was sweet, less flirtatious than before. She was working to make this easy and all he could do was mentally undress her. Was he really that much of an ass hound? Apparently.

"What would you do if you didn't like my company?" she asked.

"I'd try to fake it." He cut into his omelet. Lying to her would make more sense, paint a prettier picture of who he was, but he didn't care to. Maybe it was better if she saw how much more importance he placed on the job than on anything real. Maybe that's how he could do his part to make this easy between them. "Now tell me something about you that isn't on your background check or in your reference file," he said.

Rebecca held a speared slice of strawberry in the air. "I never fake it." She slipped her fork into her mouth and raised one brow.

Damn. She wasn't going to make this as easy as he'd thought. "Tell me something else."

"I'm a total nerd with a post-graduate degree in molecular biology to prove it."

He put his fork down and lifted his elbows to the table. He gauged her, searching for the truth.

"I'm not making that up, but don't tell anybody else." Her smile lit her eyes. "I've got an image to uphold."

"And what about your future plans, personal goals I mean. Do you want to have a family?" Where in the hell had that come from? She was curvy and smart, so suddenly he was ready to mate. What was he, a fricken' caveman?

She didn't miss a beat. "Three kids, two dogs and a place in the country big enough for at least a couple of horses. But I'm not going to drive a mini-van, not even to soccer games."

He raised his brows. He had pegged her for a career woman, never thought she'd have family in mind. Not that it was a bad thing. Family was the most important thing in the world. The only thing that mattered in the end. Maybe he could club her in the head and have one. Somebody needed to club *him*. Club him hard. That happily ever after bullshit was an illusion for everyone except his parents. The success of the ranch was proved that theory.

"Not that I've given much thought to all that," she added with a smile that didn't do anything to tame his inner caveman.

"Obviously." He loved her mouth. Her lips were as soft as he'd imagined they would be before he kissed her, but he shouldn't be thinking about that. Or what it would be like to unleash his caveman on her, but he was thinking about it alright. He had to adjust himself to relieve some of the pressure in his jeans.

"I don't know if I'll ever have children," she said, bringing him back, "but it's the way I always pictured things when I was little. So I still hold onto the dream, I guess."

"So you do think you might marry again?" Maybe he'd had her wrong. Maybe she was ready to move on, just scared, not sure how to go about it. Who wouldn't be?

"I don't give remarrying a lot of thought. I guess I'm afraid of what it takes to get from where I am now to a place where I could even consider taking that step again." She set her fork down and leaned forward, giving him a much better view than he deserved. In a lower voice she said, "There was this one guy. A cowboy. Kind of. Anyway, he was the first man since my husband who kissed me. You should have seen what I did to him."

"What'd you do to the poor jerk?" Gavin played along, glad she didn't hate him for what he'd done.

"I cried all over him, made him feel so bad he brought me a can of peas."

"Sounds like you worked him over pretty good," he said, struck again by how absolutely beautiful she was. How much he wanted to feel her body around his.

"I did. I think he would have left me alone completely, if I hadn't hired him to spend time with me."

"I doubt it." He raked his teeth over his bottom lip, wondering how much of the truth he should let her know, and how much he should just keep to himself. He'd better keep his mouth shut. He couldn't give her what she deserved, and he wouldn't take anything from her he couldn't give back. "I bet he would have hung around for free."

"You think?"

"I'm pretty sure about that." He laid his napkin beside his plate. She hadn't started eating again, and this conversation could easily go to a place where it would be easier to lie than to tell her the truth. "You ready to learn how to rope a calf?"

"A real one?" she asked, obviously not sure she'd want to, but putting her napkin on the table anyway.

"No." He could have kissed her for going along with the routine, or for a thousand other reasons, but that was another mistake he wouldn't repeat.

"If I learn how to rope livestock, does that make me a cowgirl?"

"Come on." He slid his chair away from the table and offered her his hand. "You can be whatever you want. I'll be the one in the loin cloth." He laughed at the confusion on her face. "Never mind. We'd better just forget I said it."

* * * *

Gavin sat on the fence while Rebecca twirled the rope over her head, moving her wrist like he'd shown her. The calf dummy stood at the end of the corral about six feet from her, and the rope hadn't landed anywhere near it.

"You can do this," he called to her. "I have faith in you." She looked good trying, but she was the worst rope handler he'd ever laid eyes on. And she was getting madder about it by the minute.

The rope twirled over her head, she released, and the loop landed around her shoulders. "Ugghh!" She stomped her boot in the dirt, sending up a cloud of dust.

He couldn't help but laugh as she fanned the area around her face and coughed.

"Don't laugh at me!" Her cheeks were red and streaked with dirt, her hair was damp against her skin, and she hadn't held back any of her frustration throughout the entire lesson. "Why can't I do this?" she yelled.

He liked this side of her as much as the rest, this unabashed display of frustration and determination. The last thing he needed was to find something else about her that turned him on. "You're a little competitive aren't you?"

"No!" she yelled. "I just like to be good at...everything." She jerked the rope off her and got it going again.

"We can stop anytime you want to." He'd told her that already, more than once, and he had a feeling her answer would be the same one she'd given him before.

"I don't quit!" she repeated.

He pushed back his impulse to haul her off to the nearest bed, or cave, or half-private place he could find and take every drop of tension out of her. "Want me to show you again?"

"No! I'm doing what you showed me, and it doesn't work." He could almost see the smoke coming out her ears.

"Nobody's ever complained about my teaching before," he said, knowing it would rile her even more.

"Well, I'm complaining. And if I'd paid extra for this lesson I'd want my money back."

A woman yelling at him had never been something that turned him on before, but today was another story altogether.

"Try again," he encouraged her, doing his best to keep the laughter out of his voice and his butt glued to the fence. "This is the one."

"You actually think I'm going to make it this time?" One hand was on her hip, the other strangled the rope she had stopped spinning.

"No. But it's a hell of a lot of fun watching you try. Please don't stop now."

Her mouth set in a firm line, her eyes glared at him and she lifted her arm again. He cleared his throat in another effort to stop laughing. She spun around and sent the rope sailing through the air. Her mouth dropped open at the same time the rope settled over his shoulders and fell into place around his arms.

Gavin was too stunned to react before she jerked it, pulling it tight around him, pinning his arms to his sides. He jumped to the ground before he lost his balance and landed on his face.

"You been laughing at me cowboy?" She marched toward him, moving hand over hand along the rope.

"No, ma'am."

She hadn't hesitated for a second, before flipping the situation around on him. She was fighting mad one minute and ready to play the next. And for some reason that did even more for him than the yelling. More indeed. As if he needed her to do anything else.

She kicked up a cloud of dust. "You lying to me cowboy?"

"Yes, ma'am."

"I don't like liars." Her voice was firm, but her eyes were full of mischief.

"I'll never lie to you again," he said, glad she had him in a position that kept him in check, even if his zipper was about to pop.

"Now that I've figured out this damned rope, you'd better not lie to me."

"You planning to let me go?"

"I haven't decided yet." She lowered her eyes and brought them up him again. "You seem to like it." A smile played on her lips. "Are you finished laughing?"

"Are you finished ropin'?"

She jerked the rope again. The bristles bit through his cotton shirt.

"Okay." He held his hands up as far as they would go. "I'm done laughing."

She threw her head back and yelled. "Ugghhh! Sorry, I just needed to get the rest of it out."

The need to get his hands on her overrode every rational thought he could have had. "You want to untie me now?"

"I haven't decided yet." The smile was still there, but so was the attitude.

"Anything I can do to persuade you one way or the other? Anything at all?"

She raised her brows and looked him head to toe and back up again. "I do kind of have the advantage here don't I?"

Wherever she was going with this, he was going to like it.

"Don't I?" She lifted the rope, her hand wound around it, ready to yank it again.

"I am completely at your mercy." His focus fell between her breasts. The top button of her blouse had come loose and revealed a deeper valley of silky skin than the one that had already fried his brain. "Anything you say, but if you don't fix your shirt I won't be able to concentrate on a damn thing."

"Say uncle," she said, reaching for the button below the one that was already undone.

"Uncle." Uncle. Uncle. Uncle.

"Say 'you're the best darned rope slinger out of South Carolina.'"

He laughed.

"Say it!" She slid the button halfway through the hole and held her thumb behind it.

"You're the best darned rope slinger out of South Carolina." He cocked his brow at her. "And if you take that shirt off again I *will* wrestle you to the ground and show you just how dirty a cowboy can get."

Rebecca turned her back to him and glanced over her shoulder. "I'll let you go this time."

Instead of loosening the rope, she dropped it and sauntered away. With his first few strides, the rope grew slack enough for him to throw it over his head. He ran the next couple of steps, grabbed her from behind, spun her around. Before she had time to react, he slung her over his shoulder. With every stride her hands bumped the pocket of his jeans.

"Watch what you're playing with back there," he said, his voice not gruff enough to be convincing. Next he knew, she had two-handed grip on one of his butt cheeks. He bent over and planted her feet on the ground. She gave him a half-hearted shove and a whole-hearted grin, her blouse open to the bottom of her ribs.

"You're kind of fun," she said, every trace of anger gone except for the color in her cheeks.

"So are you and sexy as hell, but I don't think I ever want to make you mad."

"Let's go back to my place, get some water and sit in the shade for a while," she said, taking him by the arm.

He stopped her, holding her wrist in one hand and tracing a line down her chest with the other. Her heart beat hard beneath his fingers, as he dipped into the valley between her breasts. Color rose beneath her silky skin and the faint scent of perfume rose from the heat of her. He longed to cover her with his mouth, feel her burn beneath his tongue. Her breasts rose on her staggered breath and his groin tightened. "I can't keep my hands off you, if you're going to play with me like this," he said, dipping his lips to her collarbone. "You know that."

"Yesterday I had a weak moment. A couple of weak moments." She licked her lips and stepped closer. "I think yelling at you today made me feel a little stronger, and I like it much better when your hands are on me."

The caveman in him was already swinging his club, but the man his mother raised couldn't help but believe this was her real moment of weakness. One that would bring more tears than the last.

"As much as I want to believe you, I think you're overheated," he said softly, pulling her blouse together and slipping the buttons into place. He brushed her lips with his but backed away when she responded.

"Come to my cabin?" she asked.

"Tell you what, I'll meet you there in a little while." He hoped the finger he ran beneath her chin would soften the blow, but the way her spine stiffened told him it hadn't.

"Women actually pay to be treated this way?" She crossed her arms over her chest. "And you think they like it?" She marched away. "This sucks donkey dong," she threw over her shoulder.

Gavin would have laughed if he didn't so wholeheartedly feel her frustration.

* * * *

"What do you make of that?" Marge moved far enough away from her window that Clayton could see outside. Rebecca stormed toward her cabin, her blouse open to the waist. Gavin stood at the corral, hands on his hips.

He laughed. "There's some unadulterated frustration. They both look ready to blow."

"You think he'll have sex with her?"

Clayton shook his head. "No way. He may as well deed this place to the county. Now, you and I have some secrets to spill."

"You're not serious about this are you?"

"I'm beyond serious. Truth or Truth. I'll go first."

"Isn't it Truth or Dare?"

"Dares are for people too chicken to tell the truth. You and I are brave souls, and nothing we share will leave this room. He held out his little finger. Come on, pinky swear."

She hooked her pinky with his and followed him over to the loveseat. Her heart pumped heat to her skin and perspiration sprang from her armpits. The truth was something she could never tell, not in its entirety, anyway. But maybe this was just the opportunity she needed to dig up the dirt Chet wanted her to find.

"Have you ever done anything sexual with anyone here at the ranch?" Flames practically leapt from her skin, she'd never asked a man a question as personal as that. Not even Harold. She made love to Harold in near silence. His secrets were his, and she didn't really want to know anything he did when he wasn't with her.

Clayton's grin spread across his face and lit his eyes. "Going for the good stuff right off the bat, are you? Okay, yes."

"You have?" She hadn't expected him to be that honest with her.

"What? You want details?" He threw his head back and laughed. "I don't kiss and tell, at least not without changing names to protect the not-so-innocent."

"How many guests have you," she steadied her breath, "slept with?"

"Guests?" He put his hand on her arm. "Sweetheart, I've never touched a guest. Women aren't exactly my type."

Her cheeks felt as if they'd been scalded, and she clamped a hand over her mouth. "Oh."

Clayton laughed. "My lord! You've never been around a gay man before have you?"

She could only shake her head. She had been shocked to learn Elton John was going to marry a man. Her mind just didn't register the possibility. Even with men who were decidedly feminine, she didn't make assumptions.

"I thought you had me pegged. After you told me about Harold, I didn't even try to pretend you were here to fall in love. Oh, girlfriend. Have I shocked your panties off or what? Look at you!"

She shook her head again, remembering the way he'd looked at Garrett when she'd met the foal. "I just didn't...I didn't think about it."

"Well, now that my cat's out of the bag, you've got some major spilling to do. I want the dirtiest dirt you've got."

* * * *

Every member of the band at the back of the barn was wearing a checkered shirt, the same getup they wore every week. Playing the same music. Teaching the same calls. Gavin focused on Rebecca instead.

Walking away from her had been the last thing he wanted to do, but it wouldn't have done any good to combine her moment of weakness with one of his own. He didn't want to be the man who proved to her what his species was capable of. There would be plenty lining up to do that.

The thought of a bunch of horn dogs getting their hands on her body without giving a damn about the woman inside pissed him off. But who she slept with would be her decision. She was smart enough to know what she was doing, or she would be once she got her head in the game. It wasn't his job to protect her anyway.

"Now when you do-si-do, the caller instructed, you'll move forward, pass your partner's right shoulder, slide back to back, then step back to pass left shoulders. Then face to face again. Ladies, both hands on your skirt, swing it back and forth. Move your right hand forward when you pass the cowboy's right shoulder, then left for left. Everybody ready to give it a try?"

The fiddler slid his bow across the strings and the band started up.

"This is kind of hokey," Rebecca said, leaning toward his ear. "No offense."

"It's meant to be hokey." He answered. "I told you everything here is fabricated, and generally tailored for an older crowd. See what I've been saving you from?"

She looped her arm through his. "Can you save me now?"

"Come on." He led her out of the barn and into the fading late afternoon light. "What would you like to do?"

"I don't know." She wrinkled her nose. "But I'd rather ride a mechanical bull than square dance."

"We have one of those." Not one that was available to the guests, but she'd asked for it. Almost. And he didn't give a damn. He'd rather hear Garrett bitch for a month than stand in on another square dance lesson.

"You do not!" The glimmer in her eye made her even more beautiful, and he loved the way it caught him off guard every time, surprising him with how she could go from gorgeous to off the charts with that one little spark.

"It's in the employee rec room," he said. "We have to keep them busy so they don't slip off the ranch every night and show up late for work the next morning."

"Can we ride it?" Her voice rose in excitement, her Southern accent more apparent and just as sexy as ever.

"You know I'm not supposed to take you there." Garrett was going to have a cow. They kept guests as far away from the bunkhouses as possible. If they didn't, the fantasy would be shot to hell and back. Then again, Rebecca had never gone for the fantasy crap anyway. He was trying to rationalize the irrational and he knew it.

"When's a little rule ever stopped you before?" she asked.

"You're a wagonload of trouble, but you make a good point," he said. Besides, it was probably better to take her there than anywhere else he could think of.

The rec room was decorated like a country-western saloon, a very nice one thanks to Garrett's eye for detail and authenticity. A full bar lined the back wall, and the rest of the place housed a jukebox, pool tables, dartboards, worn leather club chairs, and right in the middle of the floor, a mechanical bull with a deep pool of straw spread around its base.

"Yee Haa!" Rebecca squealed, running over to climb on it. "I've never done this before, and I hate to admit it, but I'm dying to try." Her excitement was infectious.

"The idea is to get a good grip," Gavin explained. "Keep your right hand in front of your face. When the bull goes forward you go back. Find your rhythm and stay centered on the animal. Once you start to slide to either side, you're in trouble."

"Stick a quarter in this bad boy and let's go!" She was revved up, an amplified version of the woman he'd met at the airport and spent two days rolling in the grass with.

He pushed a button on the side of the ride and stepped back. This had to be what she was really like, or maybe the way she had been before life gave her a swift kick in the ass. He wanted to see more of this side of her. Much more.

The bull eased forward then rose back up. Rebecca's face was a study in concentration, her movements were carefully calculated, and she did fine until the pace picked up to a buck and her butt shifted to the left.

"Aaaahhhhh!" she screamed as she landed in a pile of straw on the floor.

"Not bad," he said, giving her a hand up. Before he could brush the straw off her back she'd thrown her leg over the machine again.

"I'm staying on this thing. Start it again, please."

"We're going to be here a while aren't we?" he asked as he pushed the button.

She grinned but didn't answer. There were worse traits than determination, he figured, and stepped back ready to stay until she'd ridden the machine into submission. She stayed on longer this time. The bull worked up to a fervor that had her body flailing back and forth like a rag doll. Her bottom slid again, and her balance became a struggle. She held on, desperate to keep the ride from kicking her off, but in the end the bull won and Rebecca lay in a heap laughing.

He helped her to her feet. "You like getting thrown around don't you?"

She dusted herself off and grinned. "I think I needed that," she said. "Especially after all that damned rope business. But I'm done now."

"You want a drink?" He didn't have her figured out as well as he thought.

"Got any soda?"

Gavin rounded the mahogany bar and filled two glasses with ice. "What do you like?"

"Diet Coke," Rebecca said, sliding onto a barstool directly in front of him. He dropped a straw into her drink and skated the glass across the bar.

"You're pretty good to your employees," she said, catching the glass in her palm like she had a habit of bellying up to bars. "This place is nice."

"They live here, so we try to make it somewhere they like to be."

"You must not have much of a turnover."

"About every six months we have a few new faces. They rotate weeks like Garrett and I do, so it makes life a little more challenging. They've got homes they leave behind for seven days at a time." He picked up his drink and came around to take the stool next to hers.

"Is it hard to find cowboys?"

"We've got a pretty good reputation, and a drawer full of applicants." Her questions made it easier to keep off more precarious topics, at least that's what he told himself. And he didn't mind that she was interested in the business. It was flattering in a way. "What about you?" he asked. "Do you like where you work?"

"I work out of my house for the most part. The company I'm contracted through is in Wisconsin, so I fly up there a few times a year for meetings, but most everything I do can be handled through email and overnight courier."

"Must get kind of boring sometimes." That would explain why none of the men at the office had been knocking down her door.

"My sister doesn't let that happen. She pops in at least three times a day. I'm lucky I get any work done at all." She smiled at him again and he wished like hell he could be the man who gave her what she needed.

"How many times has your sister called to check up on you here?"

"None. She's got some stuff going on right now. She's kind of married to a jerk."

"Kind of?"

"No." Rebecca swirled her straw. "And jerk's not the right word either. I'm being nice. He doesn't treat her anywhere close to the way she should be treated."

"You should tell her to come out to the ranch for a week." He breathed a little easier. At least Rebecca had high expectations and wouldn't likely put up with all the dickheads who were certain to beat a trail to her door. Of course, it was none of his business who she put up with. If he cared that much, he'd pony up to the plate and take a swing at being the kind of man she deserved.

"Are you trying to hit on my sister?" She narrowed her eyes at him again, a look he didn't mind that he was getting used to. There was plenty about her he wouldn't mind getting used to.

"I wouldn't dare hit on your sister. I've already got my hands full with you." He spun her stool around facing her body to his. Every promise he'd made to himself since his marriage ended crumbled to dust. There was one woman he was willing to take a chance on and denying it wouldn't make it any less true. "Would you go out to dinner with me tomorrow night?" he asked.

She cocked her head at the question.

"Off the ranch," he said, "there's somewhere I'd like to take you."

"Are you trying to treat me special again?"

"Yes, ma'am."

Her smile sent a wave of heat through his chest. "I was wrong about the regular guest thing. I like being treated special." She put a hand on each of his shoulders and stared him in the eye. "Especially by you."

"Does that mean you'll go out with me?"

She nodded. "What does that mean to you? What are your expectations?"

"We're going to take this slowly," he said, pressing his mouth to hers in a lip only kiss that left him wanting more, but that he hoped would prove his restraint, his determination not to push her for anything she didn't wholeheartedly want. "As slow as you need to go. Even if it kills me. Okay?"

Chapter 6

Marge followed Clayton along a trail behind the cabins. To one side of a dirt clearing, logs circled a crackling campfire. On the other side, tables were spread with traditional red and white tablecloths and most of the ranch guests were already seated with their cowboys. A smoke pit sent the delicious aroma of barbecue into the air, and gray smoke curled toward the blue black sky.

She was a million miles from reality and nothing had ever felt more genuine. Something clicked inside her soul, like the cog of a wheel had just fallen into place. Home. That was the feeling. This was a place she belonged. Not here at the resort, but here in this open country, in this unpretentious world where she felt safe and respected. Where she could fill her lungs with air and not breathe in someone else's opinion of her or take up anyone else's space.

With that emotional overload came longing, a need to give herself something that would make her feel as complete as she felt in this moment.

"Come on, honey. This isn't a funeral it's a barbecue." Clayton handed her a plate loaded with pulled pork, baked beans, corn on the cob and Western rolls. He led her to an empty spot at the end of one of the tables. Rebecca winked as they passed, but turned her full attention back Gavin.

Marge spread butter over her corn and leaned in close enough that only Clayton could hear. "Have you ever been loved?"

He shot her a look and shook his head. "Not nearly enough."

She lifted her corn. "Harold won't eat corn on the cob since he got his dentures."

Clayton twisted around until he faced her. "And why do we care if Harold eats corn on the cob?"

"He's got dentures."

Clayton waited, brows raised.

"He's old." She turned the corn, letting the butter slip around the cob. "If I don't hear from him for a couple of days, I read the obituaries."

His hand closed around her wrist.

"I used to think he would leave her, that I'd be the one at his side when he took his last breath." She set the corn down and pushed her plate away. "I won't even know if he dies unless I read it in the paper."

"Why are you so committed to someone who gives you so little in return?"

"In his own way he loves me."

Clayton pulled her in for a hug. "He doesn't love you nearly enough."

"What am I supposed to do?" she whispered, hoping he had a better answer to that question than anything she could come up with herself.

"Decide what you really want. And then go get it."

Over his shoulder, she saw Rebecca pierce a piece of meat with her fork, dip it in barbecue sauce, and offer it to Gavin. His lips closed around the bite, but it was Rebecca that he looked like he was ready to devour. Emptiness engulfed Marge's heart. Had Harold ever looked at her that way? Had any man?

* * * *

As Gavin's mouth closed around her fork, the back of Rebecca's neck grew warm as if he'd wrapped his lips around her directly.

"You're right," he said. "I might have to get to work on a new marketing campaign. Fantasy Ranch sauces, even hotter than the cowboys."

"You think you're hot?"

He shook his head. "Hot to me has a lot less facial hair, softer curves. Something more like you."

"So you think I'm hot?" She lifted her tea glass to her lips to cover the broadness of her smile.

"Yes, ma'am, I do."

"I can live with that."

She stacked her plate with his and tilted her head toward the campfire. "You think we should head over?"

He squeezed her fingers and escorted her to the circle of logs that surrounded a crackling blaze. Above, stars were scattered around a nearly full moon. Three cowboys had a log to themselves, the firelight danced across their features. One had his mouth and hands around a harmonica, the other two picked out a rhythm on guitars. Their song was full of prairies and storms and cattle and work. Real cowboy life.

Gavin sat down in the dirt with his back propped against a log, knees bent. Rebecca fit comfortably in the cocoon of his body, her back against his chest.

Around the fire, fantasy cowboys and guests were lined up along the logs. Most weren't sitting close enough together to touch, and the ones who were barely brushed shoulders. She tilted her head and looked back at Gavin. He met her eyes with a smile, and his arms settled around her. She could get so used to this man. So used to him.

She kissed her finger and pressed it to his lips. He caught her gently with his teeth, his tongue grazed her skin. The firelight that burned in his eyes sparked something deep inside. She settled back against him and let the night fall in around her.

A familiar pair of comfortable shoes sank into the dirt a few feet away. Marge's cowboy held the back of her arm as she lowered herself to the log.

"That's what I want," Rebecca heard Marge say. She looked over in time to see Marge's cowboy avert his eyes from her and Gavin. He draped his arm around Marge's shoulder and gave her a reassuring squeeze.

* * * *

"Did Rebecca's luggage show up yet?" Gavin asked from the door of the office.

Garrett flipped off his computer, shook his head and turned his attention to Rebecca. "I'm afraid not. Ms. Ryder is there anything we can do?"

"It'd be great if I could wash my clothes again." Her jeans and blouse were covered in dust and smelled like campfire smoke.

"Absolutely," Garrett said. "Gavin will show you where everything is."

"He's not so bad," Rebecca whispered as soon as they'd gotten beyond earshot of the office.

"He likes you," Gavin told her. He opened the door to the mudroom and pulled one of the signature ranch robes from a cabinet. "Everything else is right up here." He opened a cabinet stocked with detergent and fabric softener. "I'll wait for you in the kitchen." He closed the door behind him.

Rebecca tossed her clothes into the wash, knotted the robe around her waist and followed the smell of popcorn. With an oversized island and wide counter spaces the kitchen was large enough for the ranch chef and his staff to whip up dozens of meals, but the décor maintained a homey vibe. The stainless appliances were offset with custom maple cabinetry with detailed moldings, and the warm tones in the stone floors and countertops matched the exposed ceiling beams. Gavin set a bowl on the granite counter and pulled a puffed up bag out of the microwave.

"Up for a movie?" he asked. The scene was so domestic, so warm and unassuming. So unprofessional.

"Isn't it getting close to curfew?"

"Now that you've won Garrett over you can get away with murder around here." He pulled open the drawer to the beverage cooler. "Diet Coke?"

"Thanks." Rebecca clasped the cold soda and shivered. Standing this close to Gavin with nothing but a robe on kicked her tingle cells into overdrive. "Why does he like me?"

"He doesn't know you stole his wine."

"I was set up." His smile was so irresistible, the urge to kiss him was involuntary, but just as quickly her stomach clenched tight. Thank God he was willing to move at a snail's pace. To give her the time she needed to get used to sharing herself with someone other than Todd. Would men in the real world be as patient? Did she even want to find out? She knew she couldn't really have Gavin, but she also knew the attraction they shared wasn't going to happen with most of the men she'd meet back home. It may not happen with any of them.

He emptied the popcorn into the bowl and led her into the family room. The room was so different from any other part of the ranch she'd seen, less polished but every bit as comfortable. This wasn't part of the resort, it was Gavin's home. Family photos and old trophies filled the shelves. The walls held more photos and a collection of Western artwork. The rectangular pine coffee table was made for kicking your feet up on and the wood floor had worn footpaths and well-used rugs.

"Why don't you choose the movie, and I'll run upstairs and get out of these dirty jeans," he said. "Garrett owns every chick flick ever made, so I'm sure you'll find something." He swung open a door on the wall-to-wall armoire to reveal a top-to-bottom stack of DVDs. "They're in alphabetical order," he said.

Alone in the room, she selected a movie quickly and made herself comfortable on the distressed leather sofa. Somewhere above her, Gavin was getting naked, not an image she minded. The room was cool, but the memory of his arms around her kept her warm until he returned looking comfortable and hotter than ever in a t-shirt and loose sweats. The easy fit of the soft fabrics made her want to just curl into him and stay awhile. The cowboy getup was way overrated. He didn't need it.

He took the movie from her hand and grinned. "Finally, a woman with taste."

He put the DVD in the player and settled down next to her with the remote in his hand. Seconds later, the television screen filled with a carload of people traveling along a dark rural road. Fog hung within inches of the ground.

"My guess is everybody but the driver will be dead before this is over," she said, reaching for the popcorn.

"You haven't seen it?"

"Uh uh. I love these hack 'em up movies, but I can't watch them by myself."

The car hit something in the road. The driver stomped the brakes. "What was that?" squealed an overly dramatic girl in the backseat.

"She's the first to go," Rebecca whispered.

Gavin smiled and reached for a handful of popcorn.

On screen, a stranger materialized at the driver's window, blood dripping from his temple. Rebecca's knee jerk reaction sent a wave of popcorn over the edge of the bowl.

Gavin wrapped his arm around her. "I thought you liked this.

"I do," she said, peering out through her fingers.

He moved the popcorn off her lap and wrestled her wrist away from her face. "You're cheating," he said.

The music hit climatic notes and she buried her face in his chest. His warm clean scent wound around her. There was a reason she loved these movies, and it had nothing to do with watching stupid people get killed.

"Watch," he said.

She opened one eye and shifted enough to see the television. "I am watching. Oh my God! Why are they getting out of the car? Idiots!" She buried her head again.

"You're not going to watch this are you?" His voice was filled with laughter.

"This is how I watch. I'm not complaining about how you watch."

"I'm not complaining either." He gathered her hair in his hand and held it at the base of her neck. The brush of his fingers sprinkled magic down her spine.

"What are you doing?" Garrett stood in the doorway, his back straight as an arrow, his mouth drawn in a firm line making it hard to believe he really liked her as much as Gavin said he did.

Gavin glanced at his brother then back at the screen. "Waiting for Rebecca's laundry. You can join us if you want."

Garrett sat down and picked up the popcorn. "You look like you're trying to scare her half to death."

"She picked the movie."

"Jees!" Rebecca shut her eyes as screams echoed through the speakers behind them.

"She may be the most talented guest we've ever had," Gavin joked. "She's capable of watching a movie with her eyes closed, her head buried, and her hands over her face."

"We don't usually offer movies for ranch guests." Garrett's voice was tight.

Gavin stiffened. The tensing of his body was so subtle, Rebecca could almost ignore it. Almost.

"I'm sorry," she said, sitting up. "You probably look forward to having your house to yourself after a long day of work. I can get my clothes in the morning."

She stood. Gavin grabbed her hand. "You don't have to leave."

"Garrett's right. I'm a guest, and you've already gone out of your way. I'll see you in the morning." Just as easily as Gavin could make her forget this week wasn't real, Garrett could remind her of exactly what it was.

Gavin followed her through the house to the mudroom. The washing machine had stopped, so she threw her clothes in the dryer, not worried about delicates, or colors. "Do you mind bringing them to me in the morning?" she asked.

"I apologize for my brother." He reached for her hand. "You're welcome to stay and finish the movie. I'd like for you to."

"Don't apologize. He's right. I tend to make myself at home wherever I go. And I should call and check on my sister tonight anyway."

"If you really don't want to stay I'll make it up to you at dinner tomorrow night." He gave her hand a squeeze and let it go.

"You don't have anything to make up for, but you can walk me back to my cabin if you want."

Their feet didn't make a sound in the damp grass. Rebecca held her boots in one hand and Gavin's arm in the other. At her door, he pulled her in for a hug. She closed her eyes and wrapped her arms around his back. He pressed his lips into her hair. There was so much more she could experience with him, if she could just let herself go, let herself believe that everything would be okay if she did. He made her want to do that.

"Thanks for everything this week," she said into his chest.

"Don't thank me, it's…"

She braced herself. It was his job. She knew it was his job.

"…been the best week I've had in a long time," he finished. "Sweet dreams," he said before backing away.

"Gavin?"

He waited for her to speak, but no other words came. Her mouth had jumped ahead of her brain.

"What?" he prompted her.

"I'm really not a prude or a tease." She fumbled for the words. "I mean, sex is very important to me. Something I need a lot of."

"It's important to me, too." His eyes were laughing at her. "What are you trying to say?"

"I was thinking it would be fun to play a game." She licked the dryness from her lips hoping he would go along.

"What kind of game?"

"Wait here." She went inside and scribbled on a piece of ranch stationery.

"In fifteen minutes, dial this number."

He studied the paper and folded it into his palm. "What kind of game is this?"

"One I think you'll like."

* * * *

"What the hell was that for?" Gavin asked from the doorway of the family room. Garrett had written the book on customer service, he should know how to treat a guest. At the very least he should have the courtesy to respect anyone Gavin brought into their home. And he didn't need a book to tell him how. He was raised better than that.

Garrett looked up from the movie. "I think you need to ask her to leave," he said.

What the—

"One minute you're telling me not to let Taryn fuck up the rest of my life, and now you're telling me to get rid of the first woman I've even considered getting involved with in years."

"I think you should ask her to leave the ranch, then pursue whatever you want to pursue with her. I wrote out a refund check for her today. It's on your desk."

The movie score reached a crescendo and another scream zipped through the surround sound in the room.

"I'm not asking her to leave." What was he supposed to do, send her back across the country and flirt with her over the phone while some other man kept her warm at night? Long distance relationships might work fine for Garrett, but that wasn't the way to love somebody. Not the way Gavin could love somebody, if he could love somebody again.

"I got a call today from a Detective Scott Evans in Charleston, South Carolina," Garrett said. "He was asking questions about our standard operating procedures, and insinuating he didn't believe we were running anything short of a brothel."

"Why would a detective in South Carolina give a damn about us?"

"He's her brother-in-law." Garrett set the popcorn bowl on the table and dropped his feet to the floor.

"According to Rebecca, the man's a jerk. You didn't have to take it out on her."

"A jerk with a badge, the best kind."

"I haven't done anything illegal," Gavin reminded him.

"For how much longer?" Garrett swept the popcorn Rebecca had spilled into his hand.

"It won't happen this week." He gripped the paper Rebecca had given him.

Garrett dumped the mess into the bowl, and pushed on the remote. The screen went black and the room fell quiet. "I think she's the undercover." He put his hand up before Gavin could argue. "Has she been asking a lot of questions? Or snooping around anywhere she shouldn't be?"

"She's not the undercover," Gavin said, but even as he said it, his stomach twisted. "And even if she was, she'd have nothing more than a kiss to use as evidence. I expect you to trust me more than this."

"I do trust you. Just don't let your emotions get ahead of your brain." He held his hand up again anticipating Gavin's argument. "The last time we talked about this, you said it would be business as usual from here on out. But what I saw in here tonight didn't have anything to do with business. And now I'm not the only one worried about it."

"You don't have anything to worry about."

"Fine. But while she's here, play by the rules. If you don't, I'll ask her to leave myself."

"You'd better not even put the idea in her head," Gavin said before heading to his room. He'd be willing to bet the ranch Rebecca wasn't a cop, and he wasn't a betting man.

* * * *

"I might have seen something." Marge chewed on her bottom lip and rolled the stem of her wine glass between her fingers. "Earlier today, one of the guests came back to her cabin with her shirt unbuttoned, and she didn't look too happy about it."

"You know her name, or the name of the man she was with?" Excitement was evident in Chet's voice. There was no doubt he'd be at the ranch, sirens blaring, if he thought he'd have half a shot at making an arrest. "Please tell me it was Rebecca Ryder."

"Why?"

"Her brother-in-law's a detective. He called the department before she even stepped off the plane. He'll do whatever it takes to nab any bastard that lays a hand on her."

Marge couldn't help but remember the look in Gavin's eyes and the peaceful contentment on Rebecca's face at dinner. They looked like they had found everything she'd ever wanted. And she had the power to take it all away. Giving Chet the means to destroy a budding relationship didn't do much to raise her worth. "I don't think it was what it looked like though."

"You let me decide what it was! Just tell me exactly what you saw."

"That's all. She…she came back with her shirt undone and mad. But tonight at dinner she was with her cowboy. They looked like they were having a good time. She seemed happy." Marge raised the glass to her lips. "Maybe she fell off a horse or something. Anything could've happened. I don't think the cowboy did anything."

"You don't know either of their names?"

Marge gulped a mouthful of wine. Then another. "I haven't gotten a chance to meet most of the other guests or the cowboys."

"Dammit! It's your job to find out what the hell's going on there. Now quit acting like you're on vacation. If I don't get promoted to detective, I'll hang onto every dime of the money Mama left you, and you'll shrivel up in a nursing home sucking green Jell-o through a straw! Don't think for a minute I owe *you* anything. I promised Mama I'd look after you, but if she knew the kind of person you were she'd roll over in her grave!"

Marge shook so violently the glass fell from her hand and shattered to the floor. Chet had met Harold, caught them, so to speak. He'd come to Philadelphia unexpected, saw Harold, saw the ring on his finger, and did an investigation into her private life that reaped more information than she'd ever shared with anyone. She begged him not to tell, and he hadn't, but he held the secret over her head like a bell jar. Ready to imprison her with it unless she did what he wanted her to do.

"Call me tomorrow. And give me something I can use!" He slammed phone down. The dial tone hummed in her ear, but she didn't move.

* * * *

Melinda didn't answer her cell phone, so Rebecca tried her home number.

"Hello?" Scott answered.

Shit. "I thought you had a new residence."

"I still pay the mortgage here." He was as cocky as ever. She could picture his smug smile. He was probably strutting around in his t-shirt and socks with his gun still holstered under his arm. Looks had never been more wasted on a man. He thought just because he turned heads, he had an obligation to sleep with everything that moved.

"Is my sister there, or did you put her on the street and move your girlfriend into her house?"

"You just missed her." Nothing fazed the man. He would act cool as Kojak if the bowels of the earth opened up and sucked him inside. "By the way," he said. "I checked up on your little pay-by-the-hour boyfriend, today. His brother's a real ass."

"I'm sure you left a fine impression on him, too." At least she knew why Garrett was pissed at her. She could only imagine the kind of not-so-subtle intimidation techniques Scott had used.

"Come on back home before you get any more mixed up in that mess out there. I know a skunk when I smell one."

"Worry about your own mess. I can take care of myself."

"I always told Todd I'd keep an eye on you, and I mean to do it. They've been in a little bit of trouble out there lately. The local cops don't think too highly of them. You call me if any of them so much as brushes up against your ass, and keep your door locked."

"Spend some time worrying about your wife."

Obviously he and Melinda had been talking or he wouldn't have had all the information on Gavin and the ranch, like the two of them didn't have more important things to discuss.

"We're still family. You and me," he said.

"Go talk to your wife about family." Rebecca snapped her phone shut and fell back on the bed. Creep.

Maybe she was just as wrong about men as Melinda, and maybe Gavin was more like Scott than she wanted to admit. He definitely capitalized on his looks, spent day after day pouring out charm on women he didn't care anything about. Maybe his marriage failed for the very same reason Melinda's was falling apart.

What made her think she could believe everything he said? Because she did. She believed him, ate up everything she thought she saw in his eyes, and lived for the moments their bodies so much as brushed one another. God, she couldn't let herself be that stupid. He had a job to do, and this week she was that job, even if he was attracted to her. No matter how much she was attracted to him.

Friday morning she'd be back on a plane, and Gavin Carter would just be one sweet memory. She could do whatever she wanted with him, as long as she didn't forget that. Her phone rattled on the tabletop. She turned off the lights and placed it to her ear.

"Hello?"

"Rebecca?" Gavin's voice was low.

"Is that who you wanted to call?" She pulled the comforter down on the bed and plumped her pillows into place.

"It sounds like I got the right number." His voice was sexier than ever in the darkness of the room.

"Are you in bed?" she asked, licking the dryness from her lips, hoping he was calling her from some place private, that he hadn't misinterpreted the game.

"Yeah. Are you?"

"Not yet. I need to undress first." Her stomach tensed. This was the moment of truth. Was he going to play along? He was silent, not giving her any indication he was onboard yet. She swallowed the lump in her throat and lowered her voice to just more than a whisper. "What do you sleep in?"

"Nothing." His laughter was soft, deep in his throat. "What about you?"

"Usually more than that, but tonight I think I'll try it your way."

"I bet you'd look great in nothing." His voice spurred her on, made her want to please him, to let him please her.

"Close your eyes and picture me. I just untied the robe and now I'm slipping it over my shoulder." She switched the phone to her other ear. "And my other shoulder."

"Where is it now?" The urgency in his voice heated her.

"On the floor around my feet." She could tell by the way he exhaled he had painted a nice image of her in his mind. "Where's your hand?" she asked.

"On the phone."

He was going to make her work every step of the way, but that was fine, she didn't want to rush. "Your other hand?"

"Around my cock."

Oh yes, he was ready to play this game and the abandon of his words spooled her. She moaned softly, letting him know how much she liked the image he gave her. "If I was in your bed that's where I'd be. That's exactly where I'd be."

"Around my cock?" He wasn't finished with her yet, not ready to let her hurry past this, or get away with vagueness, and she didn't have any intention of letting him down.

"I'd be all around your cock. Warm and wet. My whole body so soft against the hardness of yours. I love how strong you are, how safe that makes me feel, like I can fall apart and you'll hold me together." Her voice was husky full of breath, the same tone that used to melt Todd. "I want to please you, make you need me as much as I need you."

"You're so sexy, so wild," he said. "I'll make you come so hard. Are you ready for that? Will you let me do that for you?"

"I'm so ready. I'll do anything you want me to do."

"Where's your hand?" he asked.

"On my stomach. Waiting for you to tell me which way to go with it."

"Are you in bed yet?"

She lay back on the mattress, made herself comfortable. "Now I am."

"Take your hand to your breast. I love the feel of your breasts."

"Umm." He wanted control and she wanted to give it to him, to let him take her where she wanted to go. "How would you touch my breast right now?" she asked.

"I'd cradle it. Feel every curve. The weight of it. The softness. It's so soft, so tempting I can't resist a taste. I have to taste your nipple. Do you like that?"

"I do like that," she said, wetting her fingers with her mouth then circling the hardened peak. She brought her knees up. "I like that so much. You have me so wet."

"Slide your hand down your stomach, that soft flat stomach of yours. Don't stop until you can tell me just how wet you are."

She gasped when she reached her slick heat. He responded with a groan. "I'm so wet," she said. "And oh my God, I'm so swollen. My fingers. They...they slip in before I can stop them."

"How many?" His voice was strained. She was having the exact effect she wanted to have on him. Doing as much for him as he was for her.

"Two." She arched her back, pushing her breasts in the air, wishing he was there to take them, to take her.

"Are they in you now?" His breath was heavier than before.

"Uh hum. I wish it was you. I want you inside me."

"Make it three," he demanded.

"It's three," she responded, her breath in her throat.

"Go deeper." His voice was lower, so close to ear.

"Oooh..." she moaned. "Oh my God."

"I want to be in you," he said. "To feel how hot and wet you are."

"I feel you in me." She licked her lips, reaching deeper.

"Do you feel how hard I am?"

"You are so hard. So. So. Hard."

"I'm so far inside of you." His breath was heavier still. "Stroking so deep into you."

"I want more," she begged. "Please give me more." The phone nearly slipped from her hand.

"I'm as far as you want me to be. As deep as you want me to go."

"Don't stop," she whimpered, moving her hand to a rhythm that was soon going to take her over the edge.

"I'm not stopping," he promised. His breath was coming as fast as hers. "I won't stop."

"Harder," she begged. "Harder and don't stop. I'm going to..."

"Ohhh. Oh Rebecca. Ooh honey..." He lost it.

"Oh my God. God. My God…Gavin!" She followed him. Crying out as spasms shook her. One delicious tremor after another. It took all her strength to hold onto the phone to not miss a second of his breath coming together with hers, quieting slowly. She waited to see if he would speak first.

"I want to kiss you," he said. "You've got the sexiest mouth."

She closed her eyes and bit her lip. "I want you to kiss me," she whispered.

"If I come over there right now, I will. I'll kiss you, hold you all night long. Really make love to you."

Her body froze. She brought her hand to her stomach in response to the knot that suddenly clenched it. "Don't," she said louder than she meant to. "This is enough for now."

"It's definitely a start," he said softly. "So much more than I expected."

"Sweet dreams," she told him and closed the phone in her hand before he could say anything else.

Chapter 7

"You'd *druther* wait outside in the rain, than come inside my cabin where the coffee's ready and everything's all nice and dry?" Rebecca said, arching her brow and eyeing Gavin suspiciously.

He pulled her through the threshold and met her lips with a kiss that shot straight to her toes. "It doesn't matter what I'd druther do. After last night, I'd better wait out here," he said.

She would have completely melted into him right then and there if he had given her a chance to. Instead, he held her at arms length and handed her a bag used to keep her clean laundry dry in the downpour. Rebecca smiled. She wasn't sure what to expect after their phone rendezvous, but he was behaving perfectly. He wasn't pushing her, or expecting more and he wasn't running away either. He was taking it slowly, just as he said he would.

"You're beautiful," he said, pushing her hair away from her face. "I love your smile."

God, it sounded good when he said that.

"So you go for the phone sex thing?" she asked.

"It definitely beats the way I'd been having my way with you."

"You've been having your way with me?" Her heart pounded and her body flushed from the top of her head to the bottom of her feet.

His thumb traced the quiver in the corner of her mouth. "So many ways with you."

She leaned closer. "Kiss me one more time," she whispered. "Like you would have kissed me last night."

His arms slipped around her waist and his head dipped to her neck trailing kisses into the V of her robe. His mouth sank into the soft flesh of her breast and moved to her nipple. She cried out as he swirled his tongue over the sensitive knot of flesh. He stood replacing his mouth with his hand and led her tongue in a dance with his that left her seeping with need.

"I'll bet you're an amazing lover," she said as he stilled his lips but kept them at hers, barely touching.

"I hope you'll think so."

A shiver zipped up her spine. She wanted to find out. In the wake of what they'd shared, and the heat of his kiss, none of her reasons for holding back held an ounce of rationale. It was time. Past time. She took his hand to coax him into her room. "Show me," she said.

* * * *

Marge held the phone away from her ear as Chet swore.

"I need something concrete," he said. "Something that I can shove so far up their asses their lawyers can't pull it out."

She gripped the stem of her glass. Wine for breakfast. Again. Her bones jarred with every one of her nephew's words. "I don't think there's anything illegal going on here."

Chet snorted. "Let me do the thinking!" For the next few seconds she could almost hear the gears turning in his head. "Alright here's what you're going to do. Make sure that cowboy of yours is in your room tonight. Late. Do whatever you have to do to keep him there. I'll round up the whole ranch and have them locked up before sunrise."

"Clayton won't do anything. He wouldn't."

"He don't have to. If he's in your room I'll have enough probable cause to get a search warrant and confiscate the cabin surveillance videos, and you can bet your saggin' ass we'll find all the proof we need."

"But…"

"Just do what I told you to do. Make sure he's in your room. And don't forget who's footin' the bill for you to play like the rich and famous for a week."

* * * *

"The leather smith can put your name or initials on anything you want," Gavin said as he and Rebecca entered the barn.

"Like being branded." She made her way toward the rack of belts. "Just what a woman needs." She couldn't shake the weight of rejection. She didn't know much about casual sex, but she damn well knew she shouldn't have to beg for it. Not even from a hottie like Gavin.

"If you were being branded I'd have him put my initials on there." His fingers brushed her collarbone. "What's wrong? What'd I do? You liked me last night and even for a little while this morning. Now you don't." He leaned close enough to whisper in her ear. "I told you I want nothing more than to peel every stitch of clothing off your body and taste every square inch of you. But I can't. Not yet. For both our sakes."

The sound of his voice vibrated through her. Goose bumps rose on her skin and a flash of heat snatched them back. She hated herself for being too weak to control the effect he had on her, even now that she had slapped herself in the face with the reality of what he meant. She had started to believe his feelings for her were real, but there were definite lines he wouldn't cross. Rules he wouldn't break. He was just playing the game. He wouldn't even come into her room, like there was a sensor wired to his belt and he'd get shocked in the dick if he tried to cross the threshold.

She nudged him playfully and tried to act like she hadn't been a fool. "You'd brand me? You think I'm a cow?"

"You're the one who wanted a belt. There are some perfectly nice key chains over there." He pointed toward the rack of dangling leather patches like he was serious.

"Pick one out for me," she said, nodding toward the belts. And just that easily she was enjoying his company again. "Let's see if you have any taste or if you're just a smooth-tongued devil who'd wear socks with sandals."

He ran his hand through a line of belts and pulled out one with an antiqued finish and a running design of wavy vines with cowboy hats peeking from behind heart-shaped leaves.

"You think I'm twelve?" She narrowed her eyes at him. "A twelve-year-old cow?" He was so easy to play with, like Cowboy Ken with a brain and a voice box. Ranch and limousine sold separately.

He raked his teeth over his bottom lip, a glimmer of light flashed in his eyes. She caught her breath. There was something on his mind, and whatever it was, she was pretty sure she would like it. He could tease her anytime, as long as she didn't try wrapping her heart around anything he did.

He slid the belt around her waist and tugged both ends jerking her forward until she braced her hands against his chest.

"I think they'd all look good on you," he said, pulling just enough to keep steady tension between them.

Outside, rain fell like a curtain in front of the open barn door and several feet of the wood floor was stained with wetness. The overhead lights cast a dull yellow glow over the hay and the varying browns of the leather for sale. The rhythm of the rain and the muted colors surrounding them became the background she knew her memory would play anytime she thought back to her week at the ranch. And then she realized the most distinguishable beat of all was Gavin's heart beneath her hands.

"I'll take it." She gave into her smile. "Amazing how you can call a woman a cow and still get her to buy what you're selling. Harvard must have a darn good marketing program."

"Want your initials on it?" He pulled the belt a little more, but she held herself back.

"Nope." She squeezed his chest. "Yours."

He raised his brows. He hadn't expected that. Maybe he wasn't used to women who could play a game as well as he could.

"I always play fair," she said. "I roped you. I'll let you brand me."

The heat in his eyes warmed her. The steady pull of the belt against her back only fueled the fire. Another guest began working her way through the rack next to them. Gavin dropped one side of the belt releasing the tension so Rebecca could step back and lift the leather from his hand. Her fingers brushed his palm and his hand closed around hers. The barn suddenly felt very crowded. Cowboys and guests milling about shot glances in their direction.

"Let's get you branded, before we start a rumor." His voice was low, meant only for her, reminding her of how he'd sounded on the phone. The muscles in her thighs tightened and a frantic tingle danced between her legs. Why couldn't he be real?

A few minutes later the leather smith set Rebecca's belt and custom instructions on a stack of others at the end of the table then went right back to the one he was already working on.

"He'll take them all to the office when he's done, and I'll bring yours to you later," Gavin said, walking her toward the front of the barn.

"It's still raining. What are we going to do now?"

"I have some work I need to take care of before we go out tonight." He reached for her hand. "Would you mind if I got that out of the way for the next couple of hours?" This was the least convincing lie he had told all week. The tendon in his neck tensed and his jaw muscle jumped. Not a good liar. And he was opting out of spending time with her. Again. Men like Scott lied. Charmed. Then lied again.

"I thought I was your job." She didn't bother to temper her voice.

His breath was warm on her ear, his body closer than it should have been in front of the others. "It's pouring down rain. I don't think we should go back to your room, and I don't think of you as a job."

"But if I wasn't a job," she whispered back, "you'd take me back to my room?"

"No. I'd take you to mine." His hand burned into hers, his grip tightened.

"So I guess that settles it." The hair on the back of her neck bristled and she jerked her hand away.

"Settles what?"

"I'm a job." She threw the words at him. "I know that. I'm the one paying you. Don't keep lying to me to try and make me forget it. I'm not stupid enough to fall in love with you or to completely forget none of this is real. I just want to play the game."

Gavin closed his hand around her arm and led her to the back of the barn. A couple of women had to step out of the way for them to pass, but his gait never slowed. Horses snorted and stomped in the stalls they passed. The rain echoed off the roof, and the odor of animals lingered in the air. He didn't speak until they were well beyond earshot and completely out of sight of everyone else.

"What do you want me to do?" His voice was harsher than she'd ever heard it before. "Take you to my room, do what we both want, so I can hold you while you cry afterward. Or so you can jump on the next plane back home and wish you had never come here."

His breath was hot on her face, his body so close she could feel the tension in his muscles. Her lip trembled. Why did he have to be so right about it? And how had she managed to twist everything around between them?

"Look…" His voice softened. He ran the back of his hand along her cheek and traced her lips with his finger. "I want to take you out tonight. I want to spend time with you, and when you're ready - honestly ready to deal with what's happening between us - I want to do everything with you that you can imagine. But I'm not going to take you to bed just because I can, then be the man you wished you hadn't slept with. So, for the next couple of hours I think we need to find something to do away from your room and mine."

"You should have said that to begin with. I told you I don't like lies, even white ones." She took his hands in hers. "I want to trust you."

"Sometimes I don't think straight when it comes to you, but you can trust me." He raised her wrist to his lips. "And right now I'm going to go in my office and work, so I don't drive myself crazy thinking about you. I'll come get you for lunch. If the rain stops, I'll come back before then. Okay?"

"Okay." Why was this game so hard to play? All she had to do was remember that it wasn't real. It wasn't Gavin's job to make her remember that. It was his job to make her forget, and he was good at his job. Too good. But the game was hers to play as hard as she wanted to play it, and she hadn't come to Wyoming to fight with a cowboy.

"I think I'll take a bubble bath," she said, "and I'll keep my phone by the tub."

"Thanks for the visual." His lips spread across his face. "That ought to help me keep my mind off you."

"I'm sorry." She draped her arms over his shoulders and kissed his cheek. "For losing my temper. The bubble bath was a gift. And the phone was an invitation."

"You're relentless," he said, spreading his hands over her back and planting kisses along her ear.

"So I've been told." She shivered against him, but she definitely wasn't cold.

* * * *

Lighting crashed outside and thunder rattled the tin roof of the barn. The smell of hay and animals hung heavy in the air. Down the corridor, horses snorted and stamped in their stalls. Days ago, just the thought of being closed up in a building with that many dangerous animals would have sent her into a sweat, but she felt stronger here on the ranch, less confined with limitations. Marge fingered a black leather wallet with brown whip-stitched seams.

"Go ahead," Clayton whispered over her shoulder. "Buy it for him."

She set the wallet back on the display case and stepped away. "I can't."

"Why in the world not?"

"He wouldn't accept it." A familiar burn settled into her chest. "He'd have to explain where he got it. He'd think I was trying to cause trouble."

Clayton squeezed her arm. "After thirty years, I'd say you're entitled to a little trouble."

"His wife gets the entitlements." Heat crept up her temples and flamed the top of her head. Good lord, where had that come from.

"And you get the raw end of the deal." Clayton picked up the wallet and tucked it into her hand. "Give him a little hell."

She placed the wallet back on the rack just as Gavin and Rebecca made their way toward the open barn doors. Water sheeted off the roof. Gavin picked up an umbrella from the row of them leaning against the wall and took Rebecca's hand. She shook her head and mouthed something. The next second, he'd scooped her in his arms and she held the umbrella over them both as he carried her off into the storm.

"Fighting one minute..." Clayton whistled. "Maybe you're right about those two."

"My heart flips just watching them."

"Her fate's not any better than yours. Gavin's a player. Probably worth playing with though." He laughed. "Now tell me about old Harry. Is he old and hairy or still worth playing with?"

Marge giggled. "Old. Fat. And hairy. But still worth playing with." She nodded toward the door. This trip wasn't a freebie. She had a job to do. "Do you think they're *playing*? Be honest."

"Gavin would be stupid to let that happen. And he's not a stupid man. Looks like they're just having a little fun. Or getting a little frustrated with the rules around here."

She nudged his arm and lowered her voice. "Is Garrett worth playing with?"

"Oh my God, is it that obvious?" Clayton almost snorted trying to hold back his laugh. "I wish I knew, girlfriend. I wish I knew." He fanned himself with his hat sending a wave of cologne her way. "I'm in a worse boat than you are. He's in a relationship, and he's as committed as they come. Hell of a flirt though. You wouldn't believe how he toys with me."

Marge's heart dropped a notch and settled like a rock low in her chest. "You don't want to get started like that. Next thing you know you'll be old, fat and hairy and he'll still be dragging your heart at his heels." She blew a hard breath between them. "And you'll jump at the chance to let some little cowboy half your age make you feel special again. No matter what you had to do to make that happen."

"Let's go back to your cabin. I've got an idea." He escorted her to the open barn doors and chose an umbrella off the wall. "Stay close. Sugar melts."

* * * *

Gavin tapped his eraser on his desk. The damned rain was still pouring down. Rebecca was in her room alone probably doing exactly what she told him she'd do, and he didn't need another romp on the phone to make him any harder for her. If he could just take her in his arms the way he wanted to - the way he needed to - maybe that would be enough, but he couldn't afford to be wrong. Pushing too hard or doing anything she wasn't ready for wouldn't get him anywhere. He had never worried so much about what a woman would think the next day. He didn't want any of them hating him, never promised anything he didn't intend to deliver, but he wasn't one to send flowers either.

Rebecca wasn't any other woman, and he was committed to finding out where this attraction might lead. Probably not the best decision he'd ever made, but he'd made it. And he wasn't turning back.

"Nice weather," Garrett said as he stepped through the door. "The boys will be glad for the break."

Gavin dropped the eraser on his desk and stood to leave.

"About last night," Garrett began.

"Unless you're apologizing, I don't want to hear it."

"I'm not apologizing."

Gavin was out the door before Garrett finished. He was not going to play by the rules, and he wasn't about to ask Rebecca to leave. Or do anything else to screw up his chances with her. Period. The issue wasn't open for debate.

* * * *

Rebecca waited outside in the hall for Garrett to finish his phone call and then knocked lightly. Her hair was still damp from the bath, and the rain that had finally slowed to a drizzle.

"Hello, Ms. Ryder. Gavin's not here right now."

"I came to see you."

"Please come in." Garrett laid his pen down across the top of his desk. "Have a seat if you'd like."

Too bad Gavin wasn't in the office, but it was probably better this way. And probably better too that her phone hadn't rung while she was in the bath. She sat in the chair nearest to Garrett and smoothed her hands on her jeans. Maybe it hadn't been a good idea to wear Gavin's sweatshirt, but the temperature had dropped with the rain and she wanted to give her blouse a break before dinner.

"I should give you this while you're here." He lifted a belt from a stack of belts on his desk and checked the tag. He ran his finger over the initials stamped into the leather, and then handed it to her. "This one is yours right?" There were questions in his eyes, eyes so similar to Gavin's and so different at the same time. So unfamiliar.

"Yeah, that one's mine." She folded the belt across her lap and took a deep breath.

"Is there a problem?" he asked. Worry had carved lines across his forehead. He was handsome though, the resemblance to Gavin enough to make Rebecca want to like him. His hair was darker, shorter, more primped.

"I came to apologize," she said. "For a couple of things."

"You don't—"

"Please," she interrupted. "First, I wanted to say I'm sorry that my brother-in-law called. He has a tendency to be less than pleasant."

"It does concern me that he felt the need to call. Are you unhappy with anything here? Is this not what you expected?"

"It's definitely not what I expected," she said. "But I don't have any complaints."

"He implied that Gavin might have been too forward."

"Not at all!" Rebecca jumped to his defense. Scott could be such a bastard.

The lines in Garrett's forehead deepened.

"Scott's just trying to stay in my sister's good graces. She worries about me. He probably showed up this morning to take out the trash for her, too. When his girlfriend kicks him out he'll need my sister to take him back in. Don't worry about him. That phone call's all the energy he'll waste on me."

Garrett's face visibly relaxed and he restacked a perfectly straight stack of files. "We have to be careful here. Not everyone believes we run the kind of business we actually do."

"That kind of brings me to my next apology. I'm sorry about the movie thing last night. The ranch feels so much like home, and Gavin's so generous, it's easy to forget that this is a business. But I know what I signed on for, and I should've had more respect for your privacy."

"I'm sure you weren't uninvited." Garrett smoothed the back of his head. The lines in his forehead deepened again.

"Gavin's been really good to me." Rebecca smiled. "Probably too good, but I'm not blaming him."

"He plays this game better than anybody." Garrett's eyes held hers. There was more he wasn't saying, but she didn't know what that might be. She shifted in her seat, uncomfortable with his stare and the stone cold reminder of how well Gavin could play the game and manipulate women into feeling something for him that he didn't feel in return.

"About you and Gavin," Garrett began.

"What about us?" Gavin said from the doorway.

Her heart picked up its pace. She couldn't deny how much she liked having him around.

"I was just going to make the same suggestion to Ms. Ryder that I made to you last night," Garrett said.

"I've already told you what I thought of that." A warning flashed in his eyes.

"Thought of what?" Rebecca asked.

"Nothing," Gavin said quickly. "Nothing you need to worry about. I've handled it."

Rebecca turned to Garrett. Her brows creased in question.

"I shouldn't have brought it up," Garrett said.

"No, you shouldn't have." Color had risen in Gavin's neck, and his tendons were more pronounced than usual.

"There's a reason—" Garrett started.

"There's a reason for everything around here," Gavin snapped back at him. "I know all the reasons." He turned to Rebecca. "Have I tried to sleep with you?"

She shook her head unable to take her eyes from him. Obviously the movie business had been more serious than she imagined. At least between Garrett and Gavin, and she knew whose side she was on.

"Are you uncomfortable with me?" Gavin continued. "Afraid that I'll do anything beyond the boundaries of the contract you signed?"

"Not at all." Even in this state he didn't frighten her. As much as she knew she shouldn't, she trusted him more than she wanted to admit. Her ability to trust him so easily was what frightened her. But that made her afraid of herself, not him.

"That's not what I meant," Garrett said.

"You ready?" Gavin asked Rebecca without responding to his brother's last remark. She joined him at the door. He lifted the belt from her hand and tossed it on his desk. "I'll bring it to you later," he said.

* * * *

"Your days of being a doormat are over, my friend," Clayton plopped onto the loveseat in Marge's cabin with several sheets of ranch stationery and a pen in hand.

"I've never been very assertive." She sighed and took a seat next to him.

"That's why we're making you this little handbook. It'll be Marge's Rules of Empowerment, complete with relevant footnotes and infallibly wise antidotes provided by yours truly."

"This dog might be too old for new tricks."

"Honey, age is a number. And that's a totally different book. Now sit up and pay attention, Rome wasn't built in a day.

"Rule one. Refuse to play second fiddle. If you don't you'll always be making the music for somebody else's song."

"I'm going to need some wine." She pushed herself off the loveseat and crossed the room to the chiller.

"Rule two. Control your own destiny." Clayton kicked his boots up on the coffee table. The pencil scratched the page as he scribbled, and Marge's nerves kicked up a notch.

"I don't know." She placed two bottles on the baker's rack and searched for the corkscrew. "People around me tend to take charge."

"Because you let them. If you put your foot down hard enough, they'll stop yanking you along."

She reached for the glasses. "You want red or white?"

"None for me, thanks."

"I refuse to drink alone, and since I'm taking charge now you'll have a glass."

"Sorry. No wine for the cowboys until after ten thirty." He tapped his eraser on his knee then pointed the pencil back on the paper. "Rule three. No more unavailable men." He laughed. "Maybe I should make myself a copy of this page. Let's examine this. Why should we stay away from men we can't have, and why would we want them in the first place?"

"Harold made me feel like I was somebody he needed to love even when he shouldn't. Like I was worth more than he had to lose." She poured Pellegrino in one glass and merlot in the other.

"Ahhh...Grasshopper! The student has surpassed the teacher. But the teacher must remind you, you're only as valuable as the price you put on yourself." He reached for the water she offered. "Let's list your most stellar attributes. Give us something to gauge your worth by." He sipped the water and set the glass on the table. "I have a feeling that once we're done, Old, Fat and Harry won't be able to afford you."

* * * *

"Is that a tree fort?" Rebecca asked, staring up at a small log structure that stood a head above the ground. A pulley hung from the floor and a rope ladder led to an opening cut into the side. She circled the playhouse, craning her neck. Opposite sides had perfect Lincoln Log construction windows. "Can we go up?"

"If you don't mind the squirrels that live in it now," he said.

She grabbed hold of the rope ladder and climbed up. As soon as her eyes cleared the door, Rebecca stopped and looked back at Gavin, still on the ground.

"You did this?"

Lunch was spread on a thick blanket that covered the damp floor. The roof was too low for either of them to stand, and years of dirt and cobwebs had accumulated in the corners and on the window frames. She didn't have to ask. This place was not where he entertained guests.

"You like it?" he asked.

"I love it." She climbed the rest of the way in and hung her face over the side. "All that's missing is you."

"That was my line."

"I stole it." She smiled back at him. "And there's something else I want to steal."

"What's that?

"You'll have to come up here to find out."

He pulled himself up and crawled in beside her. One window opened to a view of the mountains and an old silver hubcap hung from a nail on the wall. Painted on the hubcap's smooth surface in two different hands was:

Rule #1 NO GIRLS

Rule #2 NO OTHER RULES

Rebecca laughed. "Who came up with the rules?"

"Garrett made the first one. I made the second."

"And let me guess, you kept breaking the first one and he kept breaking the second."

"Something like that." All the tension from the scene in the office had completely disappeared, at least from the surface.

"This is really nice," she said, plucking a grape off her plate. "You didn't have to go to so much trouble."

"It wasn't trouble." He opened a Diet Coke and offered it to her. "I'm just glad the squirrels didn't run off with our food before we got back."

As if on cue, feet scampered across the roof and Donald Duck chatter broke out in the trees overhead.

"So what did you play up here?" She sipped her drink and pictured the little boy with light blond hair and the broad grin she'd seen in the family room pictures.

"The usual. Outlaws. Cowboys and Indians."

"Were you the cowboy or the Indian?"

"Indian."

"You're not going to kill me are you?" She popped another grape in her mouth and laughed at the confusion that crossed his features. "Before I came here, one of my sister's theories was that Fantasy Ranch was a front for some serial killer's garage."

"What kind of serial killer goes after women who like cowboys?"

Rebecca laughed again. "Melinda's answer: the one who always had to be the Indian."

"Are you and your sister alike?" Gavin lay on his side and propped his head in his hand. He hadn't eaten much. Maybe he was more upset than he was letting on. From the smile on his face, he didn't appear to be.

"We look alike, but we're opposites in just about every other way. Kind of like you and Garrett from what I gather."

"Does she drive you as crazy?"

"We're family. She's supposed to drive me crazy, but I love her anyway." She offered him half her turkey and vegetable wrap. "Mine must taste better than yours," she said.

"What about your parents?" he asked, and took a bite.

"They're great. Still married and live about half an hour from Charleston. Now that my sister's pregnant, they'll probably try to move even closer."

He studied her for a couple of minutes before he asked, "Why didn't you and Todd have children?"

"He wanted to wait until he'd gotten more established in his career." She put the wrap down and pulled her hair back. "We had just started trying." She paused, she hadn't even told her family this. She and Todd were planning to surprise them. "The Lifetime Channel asked us to let them document the pregnancy because we had been part of a wedding documentary and they thought it would make a great follow-up piece for us to have a baby. A happily ever after kind of thing. I guess it's better I didn't get pregnant right away." The subject was bittersweet. If they'd had children she would still have a piece of him, but their kids wouldn't have known their father, and that was a tragedy she couldn't wish on anyone. "Do you have any kids?" she asked.

"No."

"Think you ever will?" With his easy manner and the patience he'd demonstrated in the lessons she'd taken from him, it wasn't difficult to imagine Gavin would make a wonderful father.

"I think it'd be great to have kids," he said, "if I had married the right woman. I'm not looking to do it half-ass, living under separate roofs, or waiting around for weekend visits."

Either he'd changed a lot since he was married, or his wife had missed something that seemed incredibly easy to see. Or maybe he had cheated on her. Just a more handsome, more polished version of Scott who talked a really good game. She resisted the urge to ask him. He'd made it clear he didn't want to talk about his marriage.

"It's kind of hard to have the kind of family you want without even having a girlfriend," she said. "You might want to change your attitude about dating."

"I'm working on that. Starting tonight." He reached over and pulled a grape from her plate.

"About tonight." She wrinkled her nose. "I won't exactly have to spend an hour trying to figure out what to wear."

"Don't worry about it. You knock me out every time I see you." He sounded so sincere a wave of warmth flowed through her.

"We've still got a few hours," she said. "Maybe my suitcase will get here."

"You're determined to worry about it." He reached for her waist, his fingers gripping her through the thickness of his sweatshirt. "Is that all that's bothering you?"

"I'm a little nervous about going out with you," she confessed.

"Why? We've been together non-stop since you got here."

"Yeah, but you just called it a 'date.'" She leaned into his shoulder, so he couldn't see the tears if they sprang to her eyes. She prayed they wouldn't. "I haven't been on a date yet."

"It's just dinner, hopefully at a place you'll like and with company you won't mind." His voice was reassuring. He made perfect sense and it was so much better this way, going out with someone she was so comfortable with. He was like a good set of training wheels on her first bicycle.

She squeezed his side. "I'm glad it's you I'm going out with. Any man who can make a tree fort romantic is definitely worth at least one date." The tears didn't come. She lay back and stared up at the log rafters. G.I. Joe hung in a parachute from one of them, a spider web stretched above him. "I like it here," she said, slipping her hands in the pocket of her sweatshirt.

Gavin lay next to her and folded his hands beneath his head. Outside the rain started to fall again, and the squirrels scampered for cover chattering to one another. This felt real. Nothing like a game at all. And that wasn't good. Not if she wanted to protect herself.

"Ever play five kisses?" Playing on her terms was so much easier. The games were uncomplicated, the objectives too simple to lose sight of.

He rocked his head from side to side, not meeting her eyes, giving her a pretty clear indication that elementary school party games didn't hold much appeal anymore. Not that she should expect them to, he was a grown man obviously used to getting a lot more from women than phone sex and lip action. Silence stretched between them.

"What are the rules?" he finally said.

"I ask you a question. If you get it right, you kiss me. But not on the mouth."

He propped himself on his elbow, studying her, obviously still uncertain. "Then what?"

"You get to ask me a question. Five questions total. Do you want to play?"

"I'm in. Ask me anything," he said, the easiness had returned to his voice. "Preferably something I know."

"What's my favorite color?"

He hesitated. "Green."

Close enough. This week it was. She'd never seen a more beautiful shade than the one that was staring at her right then, waiting for permission.

"Good guess. Where are you going to kiss me?"

He smiled and moved toward her. "Sit up and turn around." His voice was low, reminding her again how he had sounded on the phone, the muscles between her thighs contracted. She positioned herself the way he wanted her. Her body tingled with anticipation, wanting to feel his lips, to see which part of her he wanted to taste first. He brushed her hair to one side and draped it over her shoulder.

"Did I mention how sexy you were last night?" His breath was on her ear, his fingers slipped beneath the neck of her sweatshirt, pulling it down enough to expose the curve of her shoulder. "I loved hearing your voice in the dark, imagining how you looked." His lips were hot, barely grazing her. "How you felt." His tongue glanced lower. "How you tasted."

She completely lost her fleeting train of thought as his mouth came down on her shoulder. His hair brushed her face, filling her with the clean scent of his shampoo. His kiss moved up again toward her neck and the wet heat of his tongue struck a fire between her thighs.

"This isn't the way we played in fifth grade," she said, her voice betraying the power he had over her.

"Let's hope I've learned a little more about women since then." His laugh was low in his throat, his breath warm on her neck. "I think it's my turn to ask a question."

She licked her lips in anticipation and turned around to face him. He'd upped the game a notch higher than she'd planned on, but she wasn't about to complain.

"What is dendrochronology?" he asked.

"I thought you'd want to make this easy." She smiled at him. "Don't you want me to kiss you?"

"I do. Very much. Now, are you going to get this one right or not?"

"The method of using tree growth rings to determine the age of wood." Nothing screamed NERD louder than seventh grade vocabulary spouting out of a thirty-two year old woman as easily as if she'd just taken the quiz on it.

"Did I mention, it turns me on that you're smart?" He held his arms open in invitation. "Please make this interesting."

"You'd better be glad I carry a dictionary around in my head, or you wouldn't be getting a kiss at all right now." She took his hands in hers and trailed her fingers up his arms. "Now which part of this smokin' hot body am I going to pick?" She leaned in until her cheek grazed his. His hand heated her waist and slid beneath her shirt to the small of her back.

"Close your eyes," she whispered, her mouth at his ear. "I'm not wearing anything. Nothing but a smile. Do you like the feel of my skin?" His hand moved further up her back, urging her closer.

"I love the way you feel," he breathed.

She pulled his earlobe into her mouth with her tongue. His grip on her tightened, both hands covered her back, and his breath caught in his throat. She drew the kiss out, sucking gently, reveling in his response, in knowing one of his sweet spots. She sat back on her heels and smiled. "You have a good imagination, don't you?"

"Is that your question?" He shifted forward, ready to kiss her again.

"Not so fast," she said. "Are you good with numbers?"

"Yeah." His smile crept across his face. "Give me the best you've got."

"When's my birthday?" She raised her brows in a challenge.

"March twelfth." No hesitation.

"What else do you know about me?" she asked, surprised he'd paid such close attention to her application and taken note of such a personal detail.

"Not nearly enough," he said. "I think I'd like for you to lie down for this kiss."

She brought her legs around and lay back on the blanket.

"Raise your arms," he said.

She did as he instructed. He pushed the waistband of her sweatshirt above the top of her jeans, bent over her, and brought his mouth down in the valley above her hipbone. She dug her hands into his hair and squirmed beneath him. He steadied her with his hands on her hips, but didn't stop until she'd worked herself into a lather.

"You cheated," she gasped when he finally held his face above hers. "You can't lift my shirt up."

"You didn't mention that, and it's too late to start adding rules now. Especially when I have one kiss left. What state are you in?"

"Frenzy. This time you're naked." She tugged his wrist to her face and spread his hand with both of hers. He opened his mouth to say something, but before he could she closed her eyes and slipped his finger between her lips, sliding it in and out before tightening around the tip and plunging to the base again. His other hand moved over her breast, the thick sweatshirt buffering her skin from his grasp. His hair tickled her cheek, his nose touched hers.

"Wyoming was the correct answer," he said, exhaling sharply.

"My answer was correct too," she said. "What's your middle name?"

"How will you know if I give you the right answer?" His mouth was so close his lips brushed hers.

"I don't care." She didn't care about anything but his mouth on her, his body firing hers.

He reached for the bottom of her sweatshirt, bunched it in his hands and pushed it up. "Marshall," he said, lowering his head. "My mother's maiden name." His fingers slipped into the cup of her bra and slowly pulled it aside. She arched toward him willing him to take her in his mouth. He blew a breath so cool her nipple hardened with need. She lifted herself higher, silently begging him to taste her, to let her inside the warmth of his body. He answered in spectacular fashion, his tongue swirling and sucking the crest he'd created, feeding her need with an onslaught of sensations that rushed through her.

She clutched his hair in her hands holding him to her. His knee spread her thighs. She wrapped her leg around his back wanting a lot more than kisses from him. So much more.

"You better stop," she said as the urges of her body screamed louder. Too loud to ignore. "You have to stop. Please."

He took his time drawing away, gingerly placed her bra back in place and lowered her shirt. His eyes were on her lips, his mouth within inches of hers. "Why?"

"The game's over," she whispered, her voice shook with shackled emotion. She caught a strand of hair that hung near his cheek and tucked it behind his ear.

He lowered his mouth to hers, but took his time entering her slowly, giving her a chance to welcome him, to invite him further. His kiss didn't have the urgency or the raw need he spurred in her. She fought to not push for more, willing her pulse to match the unhurried tempo of his pace. He caught one arm and then the other, pinning her wrists above her head, dominating her gently. Even then he didn't hurry, didn't press for more, didn't even grind his hips into hers when his erection was more than evident through the layers of denim between them. He only responded to what she gave him with the control of a man who could savor her kiss. A man who wanted to make her fall in love. And if she hadn't signed on to play his game, she would have completely let herself go.

Chapter 8

Rebecca smoothed her blouse and glanced down at her jeans. "Are you sure I'm okay dressed like this?" she asked.

Gavin paused on the steps leading up to an old ranch house that had been converted into a restaurant. Lanterns flickered on the porch, and bushes loaded with white roses scented the air. Her shoulders relaxed beneath his hands but her lungs rebelled. Since the tree house, he had grabbed every opportunity to kiss her, and the slightest indication that he might do it again left her breathless.

"You're gorgeous," he said, moving closer, lowering his head to hers. His lips erased the worry from her mind and took every other rational thought from her.

"Gavin…" she said as he pulled away.

"Hmm?"

She wanted the heat of his body on her, all over her. Pretending wouldn't be enough anymore. She pressed her breasts into his chest and took his mouth again, demanding he let her set the pace this time.

"As nice as this is," he said steadily, "I'd better take you in."

"Before we go in there, I want to know, is this something you do with guests regularly? Or sometimes? Or is this really a date?" She didn't take her eyes off his, watching for the slightest indication of dishonesty.

"I've never left the ranch with a guest, unless I was taking her to the airport." He looked directly at her when he said it, and there was nothing in his gaze that reflected anything but truth. "Now, I want you to do something for me."

She raised her brows. Waiting.

"Don't think about the game. Just let me take you out. Forget all about the ranch. Pretend we met somewhere else, anywhere at all."

"So you want me to go on a real date with you and forget that it's your job to try and make me fall in love?"

"Tonight I'm not at work and I don't want to make you do anything," he said.

In the tree fort, her nerves had completely vanished, but now they were back with a vengeance. In theory, everything was perfect. Gavin was taking her out. She didn't know a single man she'd rather be going on a date with, but this was still very new territory. Frightening territory. Unless, of course, this was just part of the game and he was too good a player to admit it.

She laced her fingers through his. The feel of their body intertwined and his skin pressed so close to hers filled one desperate need and opened an even more desperate one. She loved his touch, and now that she had been reminded what companionship felt like, living without it would be that much harder.

She may as well enjoy the evening, she would be catching hell soon enough. Melinda had left a message, but she hadn't taken the time to return her call. Or more precisely, she didn't want to hear all the reasons she shouldn't leave the ranch with Gavin.

The lights inside the restaurant were dim, but beyond the hostess podium it was easy to see all the men wore jeans and the women were dressed considerably better. Rebecca glanced down at her jeans again. At least they were stylish, not standard issue cowgirl, but a pair of heels would have done a lot more for her than the boots she had on. Gavin wrapped his arm around her waist and kissed her temple.

His voice was low in her ear. "Not a woman in here looks half as good as you do."

"I should've worn my dress." The temperature had dropped even lower after the rain, and her cotton sundress hadn't seemed like a reasonable option at the ranch. They had stopped at a sporting goods store on the way to the restaurant, but the blouse she'd worn all week was far more suitable for dinner than anything Nike designed.

"You'd be freezing and I'd be forced to do all kinds of things to keep you warm."

"I definitely should have worn the dress." She winked at him and moved closer. Would she really be this comfortable with other men, or did she just feel safe with Gavin because he was temporary? Her time with him would expire before the milk in her refrigerator back home. Best of all, the end of what they shared had a predetermined date. There wouldn't be any surprises, no traumatic endings. No tears.

The maitre d' led them to a set of French doors at the back of the restaurant and escorted them onto a wide plank deck. Space heaters were tucked discreetly into the railing. Gas lamps flickered on all the tables and lanterns were strung along the back of the restaurant, but the most impressive light was the full moon reflected on the lake beyond the deck.

"Wow," Rebecca said. "For a man who doesn't date much, you know how to impress a lady. I was getting worried after you took me to the sporting goods store."

He pretended to be stung by her lack of confidence, but recovered with a smile. "I'm glad you like it. And I promise you'll thank me for taking the sporting goods detour when you tackle that rock face tomorrow. I don't think your boots would've gotten you very far, and shorts will work much better than jeans." He held her chair out, took a seat across the table and ordered a bottle of wine. The same kind they'd stolen from Garrett.

"Any of these cowboys here work at the ranch?" she asked.

"This place has nothing to do with the ranch. This isn't part of the game that we're not playing."

"Sorry. You've really never brought another guest here?"

"Never even considered it. What do I have to do to convince you this is a real date?" He held her hand across the table and ran his thumb over the ridges of her knuckles and the delicate skin in between.

"Club me over the head I guess."

An odd expression skewed his features and he laughed. Ripples on the lake lapped the moonlight as the server poured wine into their glasses. That first dinner in the loft seemed so long ago. Were women really so easy to manipulate that a week could have them thinking thoughts of forever, even when they were under contract and direct threat to walk away and never look back when the time was up?

"Have you ever had a woman not fall in love with you?"

"No more ranch questions."

"Just answer that one," she said, sipping her wine. "Please."

"Nobody really falls in love at the ranch. It's just a game."

"That we're not playing?"

"That we're not playing."

* * * *

"I don't want this to end," she said as he unlocked his truck outside the restaurant, their shadows stretching in front of them.

He reached for her again. "I don't either."

The driver's door was cold along her back, but his body against hers was more intoxicating than the wine and more breathtaking than the moonlight on the lake.

She held him, fighting tremors of pleasure every time his thigh brushed against hers or her breasts touched his chest. His gaze had an openness that completely rattled her. If this wasn't a real date, the man deserved an Oscar.

The heat of his body burned through his clothes, and Rebecca edged nearer still, craving his warmth, the movement of his muscles, everything about him. Neither of them spoke.

His heart thumped beneath her hand. She needed the familiarity of his touch deeper than she had felt it before. And now she knew for certain, what she had started to fear, she longed for him, Gavin Carter. Not just a man. One particular man.

"I'm not going to feel like this with anyone else am I?" Her emotions were thick on her voice and her heart pounded so loudly he could probably hear it.

His eyes were full of something Rebecca hadn't seen in them before. Not just lust. Not just need. Something that told her she wasn't the only one who didn't want to be with anyone else.

He moved closer, close enough that their hips pressed together. Rebecca closed the tiny gap between them and lifted her face to his, the current of his kiss raced through her, curling her toes inside her boots. If he felt what she was feeling they really weren't playing, and the implications that surfaced were better left buried. All she wanted to do right then was lose herself in Gavin, follow him as far as he'd let her go.

Their lips had barely parted when his mouth curled into a playful smile and he asked, "Does this mean you're going to fall in love with me?" Victory danced in his eyes.

"Do you give yourself a bonus if I do?" Her anger barreled out of her with as much force as every other emotion that had whipped through her. She was a fool. "Thanks for reminding me." She held her voice as even as she could, not leaving room for the slightest quiver to betray how weak she'd let herself become. "I'd forgotten how well you could lie. How not playing the game is how you play the game best." She gulped the cold air and clenched her hands at her sides before he could see how badly they were shaking. She was so angry at herself for believing so earnestly in something that was never meant to be real.

His jaw settled into a firm line and he pulled back putting enough distance between them to make room for a new kind of tension, one that had nothing to do with passion.

"I haven't lied to you, but trying to convince you of that's like banging my head against a brick wall." He opened the door. She climbed in and scooted to the window on the other side. The seat seemed to stretch a mile between them.

Neither spoke until he pulled to a stop in front of the Fantasy Ranch gates and turned to her before driving onto the property. She should let the anger fall away. It was better that he reminded her of the game. It would have been cruel to let her completely forget. But he had made her forget, so completely. Purposely.

She was exhausted from the emotional yo-yo she'd been playing all week. No matter how many times she reminded herself everything that happened at the ranch was part of a game, she'd let it all become real in her mind. And in her heart.

"I'm jealous of you," she said, reaching for her sharpest weapon. Painful truth. "I wish I could wear my emotions beneath a hat and pull them out when they suited me."

The glow of the dashboard lit his face, but masked his eyes, making it impossible to read the impact of her words. He stiffened in defense. She expected his retaliation. Readied for it. Anticipated her own cutting response. He passed his hat to her, bottom up. She stared into the empty black hole and then straight at Gavin.

"There's nothing in the hat," he said. "But keep it, maybe you'll find something in there I haven't." His words were hard.

She glared at the perfectly sized Stetson he held between them and realized he didn't hold onto much. He'd hand anything over, if it was easier to just let it go. His control of the game. His sweatshirt. His hat. This argument.

"I don't want it," she said, shoving the hat away. "Do you always give up this easily?" Even as she bit into him with the words, she knew they weren't true, or at least they hadn't always been true. He had accomplished too much, been too competitive when he was younger to walk away without a fight. He didn't grow up in Podunk, Wyoming and run off to Harvard on a whim. He didn't work his way through graduate studies at a top university without sticking out the tough times. He didn't take a ranch out of the hands of the bank and risk everything he had on a wild idea nobody would ever believe could work, only to prove them wrong. He didn't risk everything he'd worked for because he was attracted to her when there were undoubtedly countless women who would jump in bed with him. She was wrong about him. And she'd been a bitch.

"Some things aren't worth fighting for," he said. "And I can't…I won't even try to wrestle feelings out of you." Now he was angry and righteous. She had pushed his hot button without realizing how combustible the reaction would be, and it was too late to take back what she'd said. "Keep denying you don't know what goes on between us." His voice had an eerie guarded calm, but beneath it boiled a fury she could feel in the hot air that vibrated between them. "Act like you don't light up like the Fourth of July every time we touch. Pretend you can't handle it if we make love. Do whatever it is that allows you to sleep at night. But I'm out. I'm not doing this anymore. Garrett will make flight arrangements for you to leave tomorrow."

"Real love doesn't have a contract, and it doesn't cost a dime," she said evenly, her gaze fixed on the darkness surrounding them. A heavy weight descended on her chest. Games should have simple rules. The boundaries should be well drawn. The objectives clear and obtainable. This game had none of those things, and right now there was nothing fun about it.

* * * *

Sex didn't need strings. Gavin had had plenty of memorable sex with nothing attached to it but the moment. The trouble came when you got yourself tied up with someone before you got to the good part. Then, more than the sheets got tangled. The mess he'd made of things with Rebecca was wound so tight around him it was choking his ability to reason. Maybe if he just took her to bed, good and proper, they could unfuck the mess they were in. Wishful thinking. Good try, little brain.

He rounded the corral, his hand following the fence and his eyes on the late night sky. The smooth wood was familiar beneath his palm. He needed familiar, tangible. Life as he knew it had been slipping away all week. He couldn't seem to hold onto anything. And now the reason he couldn't keep a grip was leaving, too. Fine. It was better to let her go. There was only one way for something as strong as the attraction he had for her to end, and that was bad. Real bad. He didn't need it. And she sure as hell didn't either.

He turned the corner of the barn and heard her before he saw her. She was in the hot tub. Her eyes were closed, her head back, and though he couldn't see them, he guessed her hands were exactly where he'd have his if he was in there with her, slipping between slick folds of flesh and into her, so far into her the thought of it made his neck tighten and his teeth clamp down. There was only one place he had ever really needed to be and he couldn't get there fast enough. But he stopped short of climbing in with her.

She hadn't invited him. They weren't even speaking. It would have helped to remember that before he let his dick take control of his legs.

Her breasts rose up out of the swirling water. She arched her back, lifting herself higher before she dunked down again. He should have turned away, but he moved closer. He could barely breathe. There was no holding back now. He didn't have it in him. He was hard enough to break himself in half, and longing pulled at his gut with a firmer tug than he'd ever felt before. A second later he was sitting on the edge of the hot tub. Her eyes opened, but he couldn't tell if she'd seen him. She didn't stop what she was doing. She kept right on, taking herself closer to the place he wanted to take her. The place he wanted to go with her. The need to drive himself home bore into his core.

He should have said something, made sure she knew he was there, but his throat was clamped too tight to make a sound. He reached for her. Her moans entered him, ran through him like liquid fire, and pushed his erection further. His skin grew so tight, he burned from the stretch.

He was within an inch of making contact when she arched up out of the water again, cried out once and then sank beneath the surface, letting herself slip completely under.

She came up, her hair clinging to her head, and her eyes fell directly on him. His blood rushed through every vein, some more than others. The woman he needed more than any woman he'd ever known was all but within reach. His heart pounded in his chest. She had to be able to see how hard he was breathing, how much he wanted her. She had to believe he wasn't playing any lame ass game, and she had to admit she wanted him too.

Water coated her shoulders, her face. He couldn't move at first, unsure what his actions would be. He wanted nothing more than to take her in his hands, his mouth, push himself so far inside her he could feel her soul. Her skin glowed in the moonlight rosier across her chest and on her breasts, only slightly darker than her nipples. She was there for the taking, and yet he couldn't have her, couldn't touch her, not until she made it clear she wanted him to, not until she understood he couldn't play the game with her because he'd never hungered so bad for a woman before.

As if reading his mind, she reached for his hand and brought it down to her breast. She didn't say a word, and her eyes never left him while her chest rose and fell in a steady rhythm and slowly quieted. He leaned over her and took her mouth in his. He forced himself to take it slow, to drink in the taste of her, the feel of her.

She reached between his legs and squeezed leaving a dark wet print of her hand on the denim of his jeans. He could have exploded right then and there. She rose up on her knees and pressed both breasts into his hands.

"Are you going to show me what sex for the hell of it is?" Her tongue traced his ear. Her voice was breathy, trembling slightly, shaky from physical satisfaction or fear, he wasn't sure which.

"I can't do that." He barely recognized his own voice. It trembled more than hers.

"Too bad," she said and pushed herself out of the water. She reached around him for her towel and in a second she was walking away. He grabbed her wrist and pulled her back pressing her to him in a kiss he hoped would convey how deep his feelings ran. How he couldn't show her sex for the hell of it, because he couldn't invest that little in her. He couldn't need somebody for the hell of it, and he needed her.

Rebecca was the one who broke the embrace. She reached up to brush a strand of hair behind his ear. Her hand trembled. "I don't like this game," she said so softly he could barely make out the words. "It's too real for me."

"Rebecca," he breathed her name and reached for her, but she moved away from him, picked her robe off a hook on the wall and walked away. He didn't know which way to decipher what she meant. His mind was so rattled he probably couldn't remember his own name and there wasn't an ounce of blood left in his brain. She rounded the barn before he started after her.

"Gavin!" Garrett's voice shot down from the loft and stopped him in his tracks.

"What are you doing up there?" Every ounce of testosterone in him coiled, ready to spring. His protective instinct spooled to think someone else, even Garrett, had seen Rebecca so vulnerable and exposed. She was his, or she should be, and he wasn't about to share her with anybody.

"I just got here," Garrett said coolly. "What are *you* doing?"

Gavin pushed his fingers through his hair and exhaled. "What do you expect me to do?"

Garrett leaned on his elbow, looked down at him, and said, "Play the game."

"It's not a fucking game! And the reason I'm not making love to her right now has nothing to do with this ranch or anything else you think it should. Sue me. Put me in jail. I don't give a damn anymore."

Gavin took the deck in three strides, and jumped to the ground not bothering with the steps. If he went straight to her room nothing would stop him from taking her to bed unless she did. Then they'd be right back to where they started. He'd have a hell of a night and probably never see her again. She wasn't ready to face her feelings for him. He had accused her of pretending, but that caged look in her eye after the first time they kissed held real fear. Fear he couldn't comprehend, but fear that existed nonetheless.

Her responses to his touch and his kisses made him believe she knew exactly what he was feeling, and he wasn't the only one feeling it. And that's why he couldn't leave her alone, why he couldn't just walk away and let her tragedy cripple what could be their only chance to see where this undeniable attraction would take them.

He slowed his pace. If she wasn't ready to follow where those feelings would lead, she would run away thinking he was the biggest asshole in the world. And if he took advantage of her, she'd be right thinking that. For all her modern sensibilities and frankness with sex, she was an old-fashioned girl at heart. A woman who loved hard and forever. The exact opposite of his ex-wife. He couldn't screw this up. He wouldn't screw this up.

* * * *

Marge shivered as a breeze whipped through the porch of her cabin. "To friendship," she said, raising her glass to Clayton's. Their stemware glinted in the moonlight, but the merlot in the glasses was dark as blood. Thicker than water she told herself. Her loyalties didn't belong to this beautiful young man sitting next to her. Chet was family, and she'd agreed to come out to Wyoming for the sole purpose of doing a job for him.

"Friendship and self-respect," Clayton said, kissing his glass to hers.

She gulped the wine in hopes it would help her swallow some of the guilt that rose in her throat.

"Uh oh," Clayton said, sitting back in his rocker and pointing toward Rebecca as she ran to her cabin dripping wet and wrapped in a towel. "More trouble in paradise."

"Gavin's probably not far behind." Marge swallowed the last of her wine and reached for the bottle standing on the rail in front of them. She was going to need all the help she could get to convince Clayton to come inside her cabin.

"I should go," he said, standing. "If Gavin is behind her, I don't think he's going to be in the mood to see me here this late."

He opened the door for Marge, and held it while she stepped inside. "Thanks," he said, handing her his glass. "We'll get back to the business of whipping together the new you first thing in the morning."

Over his shoulder, Marge saw Gavin come around the barn. "Get in here," she said, grabbing Clayton by the arm and shutting the door behind him. Through the window they watched as Gavin shoved his hands through his hair and strode toward the cabins.

"Drink up, girlfriend," Clayton whispered. "We're about to see fireworks."

* * * *

Rebecca toweled off and pulled Gavin's sweatshirt over her head. She was trembling and could still feel the heat of his hands on her breasts, the way her wet skin had slipped in his grasp. Thank God he hadn't followed her. Wouldn't a man who wanted her as much as he said he did have chased her down? One more kiss and she would have given him every piece of her. She wouldn't have been able to stop herself. She'd regret it in the morning, but at least she would have him tonight. One night would be too much. Or not enough. Too much. Definitely. Too. Much.

She couldn't sleep, couldn't stay in the cabin. She just needed to move. She slipped on her jeans and headed out. The damp grass was cold beneath her feet and the night air blew through her wet hair sending a chill down her spine.

She didn't have a destination, only the need to move. She walked past the barn and the corral toward a long narrow building seated low on the first hill that rolled down from the big house. The closer she got, the clearer the voices became, men's voices loud and laughing.

At one end of the building two figures moved together. The taller one dropped to his knees and his head disappeared into the shadow of the other's body. She turned around. Gavin stood less than two feet away. She didn't know he'd been following her, the soft ground absorbing his steps, the wind covering his breath, but there he stood. Obviously still unsettled and as unable to go to bed and forget as she was.

"Are they all gay?" she asked.

"Yep."

"Are you?"

He cocked his head waiting for her to answer the question herself.

"Not even a little bit?" she asked.

"Not at all."

"And I turn you on?"

"You do more than turn me on." The catch in his voice made him very easy to believe. "A hell of a lot more than that."

She crossed her arms and brushed the softness of his old sweatshirt with her palms. She tried not to read into his words. He could be saying she pissed him off. He could be saying he had real feelings for her. He could be saying a lot of things. He was right about her. No matter what he said, she wouldn't believe him. She wouldn't let herself believe him.

He reached for her elbow and pulled her closer. Her knees almost buckled as the heat rose between her legs again. She didn't care anymore if she could believe him. She just had to have him. One night. If that was all she could have him for, she'd take it. No one had ever died from a one-night stand before. She wouldn't be the first.

She wound her arms around his neck and lifted her mouth to his. He responded with a hunger that shot straight through her. His hands moved from her hips, slid beneath the sweatshirt she wore. Waves of heat rolled through her as his palms slowly passed over each rib until they pressed against the sides of her breasts.

She kissed him deeper, opening her mouth to take more of him, moving her tongue with his. Why should anybody resist this? How bad would it be if she just gave in, let her heart feel what it wanted to feel. What made her think she'd meet another man that she'd want half as much? She could deal with the consequences tomorrow. On her flight back to South Carolina. Cry through a box of tissues. Battle the tears at home. She'd beaten them before.

He cupped her breasts rubbing his thumbs across her nipples, hard and alive. She pressed the front of her jeans against his, grabbed his ass, and pulled him to her. His desire was as obvious as it had been at the hot tub. His hips responded, pushing harder. His mouth fell to her neck and she gasped as he held her to him. His breath was unsteady, labored.

"I want you," he breathed. "My God, I want you."

"I want the real you," she said, fighting to find her voice. "Not the fantasy. Not anything I'm paying for. I want the man I think you are." She swallowed her pride. "But I'm willing to take whatever I can get."

"This is me." He took her head in his hands and leveled his eyes with hers. His pupils were dark, rimmed with the slimmest line the color of the pasture grass. "This is who I am. And I really am crazy about you."

"How do I know that?" she whispered. "You're supposed to tell me everything I want to hear."

"I'll find a way to prove it," he said, blowing a heavy breath between them. He lowered his mouth to hers and kissed her again, slower this time. He took his time, drawing her into him, unhurried and passionate in a way that held promises of what making love with him could be like. Just as slowly, he pulled away. "I will prove it to you," he said.

She trembled at what that could mean and reached for him again, but he held her back.

"In the hot tub." His chest rose and fell beneath his shirt and if he did half as much to her as his eyes said he wanted to, the consequences would be worth every minute of it. "Were you thinking about me?"

"Yeah." She stepped back but didn't look away. "I was thinking about you."

"Did he enter your mind at all?"

"There wasn't room for the both of you." She squeezed her arms tighter, hugging herself. The truth of what she said didn't bother her as much as it should have. It didn't come without pain though, and she hoped he couldn't see the pools blurring her eyes.

He held her as they crossed the property. At the door to her cabin he kissed her again. Brief tender kisses they could both walk away from, but as soon as one ended another began. Rebecca backed toward the door.

He traced the line of her jaw and pressed his thumb to her lips, then moved his thumb and pressed his lips once more to hers. Before he could pull away again, she kissed him the way she wanted to. His response was everything she hoped it would be and every ounce of her defense fell again.

"I'll go now," he said, still kissing her.

"I don't want you to." Her words were barely louder than her breath. Almost without doubt she didn't give a damn how real anything was beyond the feel of his skin and the way he lit her body on fire. There was that one stubborn part of her though. That damned teeny tiny part determined to dig its heels in and scream. That was the part she'd have to live with after the night was over.

He reached behind her and closed the door, then backed her against it. His kiss revived their earlier passion. She slid her hands beneath his shirt, around to the smooth muscles of his back and pulled him to her.

"Stay with me tonight," she whispered.

"Are you sure?" His breath was coming as fast as hers.

"Yes." An unexpected tear fell from her eye. He wiped it away. His brow creased and he kissed her again. Slowly. Tenderly. The tears rolling down her cheeks wet them both. He buried his lips in her hair.

"You don't have anything to feel guilty about," he said. "There's nothing wrong with this. Or with us."

She sobbed and hid her face in his shoulder. He relaxed against her. His hands moved across her back, reassuring her.

"I know." She pulled back so she could see his eyes. "I want you to stay."

He blew another heavy breath, dried her face with his hands and kissed her forehead. She could tell he was giving her a chance to back out, not wanting to push her for what he wanted if she didn't want it as much. Another reason he was the man to make this mistake with. Because as good as it would feel, it was a mistake. She had no doubt about that.

"What if you just spent the night?" She didn't want to let him go, didn't want to spend another night wishing she was in his arms. "What if we didn't take things any further than we already have?"

"That wouldn't happen." His hands slipped beneath her shirt, raising it above her breasts. He lowered his head, taking first one nipple and then the other with his well-versed tongue, proving his point beyond a doubt.

"Why do you always have to be right?" She leaned into him, loving the way he made every cell in her body dance, and knowing she wanted nothing more than to do the same thing for him. "And how can you turn me down?"

He lowered her shirt, but eased his hands beneath it, holding her breasts. "I don't ever want to be a regret," he said, his voice low, his eyes focused on hers. "Not with you."

"You'd be the best mistake I ever made." Her words poured into the shallow space between them.

"I'm going home now." He brought his hands down to her hips and rested his forehead against the door. "I'm going to try and fail miserably to sleep, and I'll see you first thing in the morning."

"Sweet dreams," she said, her lips on his neck.

He squeezed her hips, sending another wave of sweet agony through her. "I really have to leave now." He released her and walked away. She watched him go and trembled again in the cold night air.

* * * *

Marge released a long, slow breath as Gavin stepped off Rebecca's porch. Next to her, Clayton let out a low chuckle.

"Damn." Clayton's voice was barely more than a whisper crossing the shadows between them.

Marge's blood pulsed hotter than she'd ever felt it. Old, Fat and Harry had never made her as weak as the kisses she'd just witnessed. No man had ever made her knees want to buckle with need or torched her chest with such heat. "I think…" She paused to gather her voice. "I like you, but I think I was robbed. Did she pay extra for that?"

Clayton frowned. "I don't think that's something you can pay for. It's definitely not anything we sell around here." He patted her arm, and set his glass on the table next to the window. "I need to go."

Marge bit her lip and tried to calm her racing heart. "Stay," she said. "Please."

* * * *

Gavin left his boots in the mudroom and walked through the kitchen. Garrett glanced over his shoulder but kept rinsing his wine glass in the sink as Gavin pulled a beer from the refrigerator and twisted the top off.

"We've got to talk about this," Garrett said.

"I'd still be there if anything happened." He opened the trash compactor and tossed the bottle top in.

"Maybe I was wrong about her leaving." Garrett dried the glass and set it on the counter. "Does she care as much for you as you do for her?"

"I don't know." He raised the bottle to his lips. He'd been wrong about her leaving too. There was no way in hell he was letting her get on a plane any sooner than she had to. "She feels something."

"Her brother-in-law said she came out here looking for a blow-up doll. Her words, according to him." Garrett folded the dishtowel into a perfect rectangle. Worry creased his brow.

"I'm sure she did," Gavin said, taking another drink. For the first day and a half he had been content to be just that.

"And you think she wants something different now?"

"She knows I'm not her husband, if that's what you're getting at." Gavin rubbed the tension from the back of his neck and raised his eyes to the exposed ceiling beams. "And I'm not going to let her do anything before she's ready."

"She looked ready to me." Garrett laughed. "I don't know how you kept it together as well as you did out there."

"She's not ready," Gavin said, relaxing a little even as his dick jumped at the memory of her wet body in his hands, her tongue hot against his. "She wants to be, but she's not." He sized Garrett up. "What were you doing in the loft anyway?"

"I needed to think. I'm not sure I'm going to see John after next week." He smoothed his hand over the back of his hair. "Probably why I've been on edge myself."

"Is there a number I can reach John at tonight?" Gavin asked. "Probably not the best timing, but I need to ask him for a favor." Finally his brain was working, fired up with possibilities. At least one possibility and he was going to grab it for everything it was worth. After all, he had something to prove.

Garrett unclipped the phone on his belt and tossed it to him. "Speed dial one. Go ahead and ask him. I think he and I are on the same page. There aren't any hard feelings between us." He lined the dishtowel up next to the sink and stored the glass in a cabinet. "You didn't turn in yours or Rebecca's menu requests for the farewell dinner."

"We won't be here tomorrow night. We'll be gone all day."

"I hope she's who you think she is," Garrett said. "I really do, but I'm going to bed and deal with my own problems."

Gavin leaned against the counter, dialed John and finished his beer.

When he'd taken care of the only thing he could think to do, and thanked his stars for the digital age, he threw the bottle in the trash and turned off the kitchen lights.

In his room, Gavin stepped out of his jeans and pulled his shirt over his head. His bed wouldn't ever get any emptier than it was tonight. He was reaching for the band of his boxer briefs when his phone rang.

"What are you calling for?" His words were softened by the smile on his face.

"You never brought me my belt," Rebecca said. Her voice made him want her all over again, even more than before.

"And you need it now?" His heart was slamming blood to every part of his body, his dick already standing at attention waiting for direction.

"Right now. I need it desperately." There was no mistaking the tone of her voice or what it was she needed.

"I thought we agreed I should come home." He couldn't turn her down. Not again. Not any more.

"I had an idea."

"Another game?" He was already pulling a t-shirt out of his drawer.

"No. No more games."

Screw the security cameras. There were ways around them, and they'd have more privacy in her cabin than across the hall from Garrett.

* * * *

Before the door of Rebecca's cabin clicked into place behind them, Gavin reached inside her robe, covered her bare bottom with his hands, and lifted her onto his hips. The effortless way he handled her churned something on a molecular level, struck her basic female craving for a man with brute strength. The rush of excitement emanated from her womb and hurried lower, hovering between her thighs. His body screamed *man* so loud, hers just wanted to wrap around him and tuck him inside. She wanted him to make her whole again, to take the emptiness away. To fill the cavity in her soul.

"I thought you'd never get here," she breathed into his ear. He was all soft fabrics and hard muscles, not looking anything like a cowboy, and if anything, that made her hotter for him. Made him more real. More exactly what she needed. She raked her fingers through his hair, loving that she could touch him the way she had wanted to the first time she saw him. That he wanted her hands on him, and wanted to touch her, too. For tonight that was enough.

His eyes were intent on hers. In the pale moonlight that slipped through the window she could see deep into him. And her every instinct rallied against the distrustful corner of her brain. Her feelings for Gavin Carter were rooted so much deeper than she was willing to examine.

"What do you want to do first?" she asked.

"Feel and taste every inch of you. Find out exactly what turns you on, and I want to hear how much you like it." His words echoed her plans for him to the letter, easing any niggling doubt that she was in the arms of the wrong person.

"Can you always read my mind?" she asked as he walked her over to the bed and followed her down, bracing his arms at either side of her head. She didn't expect him to understand how precious physical contact had become to her. How until this week, until she'd met him, the simple act of touching another person had been missing so completely from her life that she ached for it to the point of distraction. He had given her a gift without knowing what a treasure it was, one that she would hold onto long after she returned home. She grabbed the back of his t-shirt, bunching the fabric together as she worked the bottom of it up to her fingers. "I want to feel you against me, nothing between us," she told him.

He sat back on his knees and lifted the shirt over his head. He had been hiding something good under that cowboy getup. Something that turned her long pent-up desire to pure liquid heat. She pulled his shirt off his arms and threw it to the floor. A smarter woman would have left the lights on. Too late now. She wasn't leaving the bed for anything. She swallowed hard, salivating like one of Pavlov's dogs as he moved toward her, his knees between hers. She caught his hands and laced their fingers.

"Me first." She resisted the urge to press herself against him or pull him down on top of her, opting instead to hold him with her eyes. "Just let me look at you for a minute." Every muscle of his chest was defined and tense. His shoulders were strong and round. She traced every line, starting high and working her way down to his abs, shadowed in the semi-darkness. He let her take her time, but when she flattened her hands against his stomach and her fingertips edged beneath his waistband he straightened. She tried to follow but he gently pushed her back onto the mattress and reached for her ankle.

"My turn," he said.

Her legs trembled in anticipation as he raised her calf to his shoulder and her robe fell open to her thigh. His eyes followed the trail of skin and she bit down on her lip until the pinch of her teeth brought a tear to her eye. From his sharp intake of breath and the way his grip tightened around her ankle she guessed he liked what he saw.

He stroked her leg and kissed the inside of her ankle. She fought to memorize every movement, bank it in her memory for later, but it was hard to concentrate on anything beyond the smooth heat of his shoulder beneath her leg. Why had she waited so long for this? What had she been so afraid of? He obviously wasn't in the business of hurting her. She felt so safe, so secure.

Their ragged breaths were the only sounds until her leg slipped on his shoulder, damp from the heat between them, and a low needy moan crept from her throat. She was more desperate for him than she'd known. Her muscles tensed as he stroked from her ankle to her shin, his fingers brushing the bone, treating her as fragile as china. She sucked in her breath as he reached her knee and spread his hand across her thigh climbing higher still.

"Kiss me." She didn't ask. Her need was too urgent.

He ran his hand over her hip and up her side. His erection pressed into her thigh and his mouth found hers. Their lips and tongues met in a kiss there was no turning back from. She wound her other leg around his back and pulled him to her.

"Touch me," she breathed, bringing her knee higher.

"I'm going to touch you all over," he whispered in her ear, his hand followed the line of her body back down her thigh. "Everywhere."

The robe was still knotted at her waist, but the two sides were no longer overlapping. She lay beneath him, hot, wet, and completely exposed, but never more at ease with a man.

"I don't think I can wait another second," she said.

"Yes, you can," he promised. His mouth came down to her again. His tongue brushed her ear, traveled down her neck and joined his lips on her collarbone. He moved to gently suck the hollow of her throat. Then lower, his mouth met her breast and moved over the hardened peak, hungry. He was so hungry. She dug her hands into his hair and cried out.

"Please," she begged. "I need you."

His mouth found her other breast at the same time his hand slid between her legs. He dipped his fingers in her wetness and moved them over her in a rhythm that quickly became too much. Her breath came in shallow gasps and just when she thought she was going to slip over the edge, he entered her with those same sweet fingers and drove her to new heights.

"Don't stop. Please. Don't stop."

His mouth never left her breast, his fingers never stopped. She arched her back, throwing her head into the pillow. "Aaaahhhh. Oh my God!" she screamed, shocked by the suddenness of her orgasm. The spasms that tore through her trapped his hand between her legs. He moved his tongue over her breast until the last of the tremors subsided and he could retrieve his hand.

"You did need that." His breath was on her lips, and his eyes above hers were filled with his own need. "Feel better?"

"For a minute. But I should warn you, it doesn't do any good to make me come that fast. I won't be finished with you for a while." She lifted her mouth to his and pushed herself up, rolling him onto his back.

On her knees beside him she ran her hands over his chest, brushing his nipples with her palms. She brought her tongue to one of them. His body was so hard. So smooth. So warm. So alive. She wanted to lie on top of him, cover him like a blanket and have him wrap her in his arms so she could listen to his heart, feel his breath in her hair, breathe the intoxicating scent of him. She wanted to experience the realness of this man in her bed. She continued dragging her tongue across the tight knot of flesh on his chiseled chest, drawing circles around it and sucking it while her hands worked the sweatpants over his hips. A low groan rumbled in his throat. She kissed her way down his abdomen, pushing the pants down his legs and finally past his ankles. They fell to the floor.

In the darkness it was hard to see anything but the contours of his muscular thighs and the thick tip of his erection peeking from the elastic waistband of his boxer briefs.

"Where's my belt?" she asked, her heart racing.

"By the door."

"Don't move," she instructed.

"What are you doing?"

She kissed his chest again and trailed her fingers down his stomach. "Don't worry, I'll be nice. Very, very nice."

She found the belt on the floor where he had dropped it, hurried back to the bed and straddled him, her knees at either side of his hips. "You didn't miss me, did you?" she asked rubbing herself along the wide ridge of his erection while she looped the belt through the headboard above him. His hands on her waist guided her along his gloriously long length as he pressed for harder contact and awoke every need she'd ever known.

Her hands trembled as her muscles fought to catch the frenzy of signals sent through her nerves. After several fumbles, she drew the end of the belt through the buckle and reached for his hand.

"I can't let you do that," he said, resisting.

"Don't you trust me?"

His arm relaxed and he let her slip the belt around his wrist. He sat up, taking her breast into his mouth. His other hand circled her back. His cock moved beneath her, the bare tip slipping over the most sensitive part of her, making it hard to think. Hard to breathe. And nearly impossible to not invite him lower, welcome him into her body with a fully fevered joining. If she didn't take control fast, they'd be having unprotected sex and she wouldn't care enough to stop it.

"Lie down." Her voice was commanding as she reached back to take his other hand. She tugged it into place and tightened the belt. There was no simple way to secure the loop tight enough to keep him from getting loose, and she didn't really care to. She only wanted to relieve him of some of the control he had exercised all week, to remove some of the burden she had put on him with her constant teasing and ready tears.

Her lips trembled on his as he lowered himself to the bed and she moved over him, lifting herself above him, allowing only the slightest contact. "You're on the honor system," she said, her breath on his ear. "You're going to have to pretend you can't get out of this, and I'm going to trust you to stay where I put you." Her breasts pressed into his chest and she teased his earlobe with her tongue. "Can I trust you?"

"I'll try." His words staggered. "No promises."

She positioned herself between his legs and removed his boxer briefs. Just as she had suspected, he was perfect. Better than perfect. And so much more than she could resist. She gave him an animated cowboy wink and took him in her hand. He was stretched smoother than silk beneath her touch. Every curve and line reminded her of why she loved men. He groaned and threw his head back as she moved her palm up and down his shaft.

"Just tell me what you like," she said, but before he could answer, her lips closed around him forcing the breath from his lungs. Her tongue covered him, tasting him again and again. She drew a line with her lips from tip to base and back to where she started then took all of him in her mouth. Her hand closed around his sac, and she pulled just enough to make him reach for the back of her head.

"Oh, honey!" he cried. His fingers wound through her hair. Either he hadn't tried very hard to keep his hands in the belt, or she had a bigger effect on him than he had expected.

"Just like that," he said between heavy breaths. "Exactly like that."

She gave him what he wanted, loving it as much as he did, knowing there was no turning back, and that she was making him as crazy as he made her. She wanted to please him. To know the scents and tastes and textures of his body so well she could recall them automatically. There was nothing one-sided about this connection they had.

From the sounds he was making if she didn't stop soon she was going to taste a lot more of him. She had to stop. The ache inside her was growing. There was somewhere else he needed to be, and she needed him there desperately. But she wanted to give him all the pleasure she was capable of. She couldn't stop. He was enjoying the warmth of her mouth too much. She was enjoying the taste of him too much.

A tremor shook her hand and his skin strained against another swell. He shot up, grabbed her beneath the arms and crushed her against his chest while he came. His cock slid between the belt of her robe and the soft then wet skin of her stomach. He tensed against her. A smile stretched her lips as the tendons in his neck strained, and his face contorted in pleasure. She kissed him as his lungs fought to settle back to a normal pace.

He ran his hands up her back and rolled her over. His kisses were fevered, and full of desire for a deeper connection. She lost herself in his mouth, in him.

"There are so many ways I want to make love to you," he said. He untied the belt around her waist and lifted her up enough to drag the robe from beneath her. He wiped her stomach with it and tossed it to the floor.

"What have you got in mind?" she asked, ready for anything. Absolutely anything.

"I'll do whatever you want to do." He pushed her knees apart and slid his palms along the inside of her thighs as he gently pressed them toward the bed. "Let me know when you think of something." He lowered his head. His tongue found her, drove inside then burned a pleasure trail everywhere it touched. She squirmed beneath him, but he held her still, keeping her exactly where he wanted her. How could he so easily give her exactly what she needed never having touched her body before? She dug her fingers into the comforter and told him over and over how amazing he was, until her words became a series of incoherent sounds. His lips closed around her, his tongue never stopped moving. Her voice grew louder as she held on and every cell in her body bounced like a ping pong ball in an earthquake. Her legs quivered between his hands and the bed, until she couldn't stand for another second not to feel him deeper.

"I need you," she moaned. "I need you inside me." God, why had she let him come?

Gavin sat up, but kept his thumb against the center of her pleasure. Her blood pulsed beneath the pressure of his touch. Without taking his hand from her, he brought his lips down to hers and entered her again with his fingers, stretching deep, seeking the spot that would release everything spooled inside her.

"Come for me again," he said. "I love to make you come. I want to hear you scream my name."

She pushed his shoulder down until his mouth found her breast. "You got it right the first time," she said. "Don't change a thing."

"One thing," he said, taking his fingers from her. She bucked in frustration as the wave that was building at the base of her spine ebbed. His mouth never left her breast, but his hand patted the mattress and the sound of the condom package tearing open sent a shiver up her back.

Within seconds his nose was brushing hers, his lips urging hers. The broad tip of his erection slid between her folds. The instant their tongues met, he pushed himself into her. They cried into one another's mouths. His strong back trembled beneath her hands. Her body sang. She wanted to touch him everywhere at once. To feel him with every part of her. He pulled back and moved into her again slowly, seating himself so deep she moaned in unadulterated ecstasy.

"Rebecca," he breathed as their hips met and he drew away only to find her again. "I can't get enough of you."

She spread her legs wider, tilted her hips to give more access. He responded, lengthening his stroke, entering her fully, again and again. Their slick bodies glided over one another. The sounds of their desire filled the room, rang in her ears while her whole body danced with his, devoured him with an urgency she couldn't control. Didn't care to control. She felt him in her lungs, her mind, her heart, every part of her. The more he gave the more she wanted. Her breath became disjointed. Her muscles began to tighten around him. She wasn't ready to find her release. She didn't want this to end. Not yet, she begged, but the inevitable was on its way, and in a hurry to get there.

"Not yet," Gavin panted. She hadn't realized she had spoken. Maybe he read her mind. Or her body.

It didn't matter what either of them thought or said, when he pushed himself deep again she lost herself completely, screaming his name in the darkness, and closing more tightly around him than she had before. He followed her, shouting as he poured himself into her.

In the darkness they lay perfectly still, neither wanting to break the connection. He held himself on his elbows, his hair falling against her cheek, and when his breath resumed a normal pace he kissed her. A kiss meant to assure her she hadn't made a mistake, his tongue caressing hers, their bodies still joined, the weight of him pressing her into the mattress. No matter what happened next, this moment wasn't a mistake, this was salve to her deepest wound. He shifted, rolling her into his arms, holding her close.

"Whatever it was for you," she whispered, her lips brushing his neck, "that felt like making love to me." She didn't have to tell him how deep her feelings ran, but she was nothing in bed if not honest. And open. She didn't want to change that part of herself.

He shifted back enough to search her eyes. His chest moved against her as his thumb trailed her cheek possibly searching for the tears that weren't there. Even in the darkness she could see his eyes dart to the upper corner of the room where the air conditioner vent was and then settle on hers again.

He pressed his lips to her forehead and tightened his arms around her. "Sweet dreams," he murmured. She relaxed against him, content in his embrace. The sleep that took her was so consuming, she didn't hear him leave.

* * * *

The blue glare of Garrett's computer screen illuminated the dark office. Gavin dropped his clothes on the floor beneath the desk and settled into his brother's chair, the leather cold beneath his bare legs. He'd only bothered to put on his underwear when he left Rebecca's cabin. The night air had been welcome on his skin. He needed to cool off in the worst way. He could have kept her up all night, falling deeper into her every time, but he needed to get hold of the reins.

He keyed into the security program, isolated the recording of the Darlin' cabin and hit rewind. As images of the two of them jerked awkwardly across the screen, his boxer briefs tented and his ache for her came back in force. His hands already missed the soft curves of her body, the warm silkiness of her skin. He had known if he ever buried himself in her, he'd never come out. He would be lost to her. And he was lost. More and more, that sounded like a chance he wanted to take. He should know better, but none of that seemed to matter now.

He clicked play. Onscreen, her head was buried in his lap, her body stretched between his legs. He got harder, hotter. His muscles tensed. His heart pounded like a thoroughbred tearing across the prairie. His body remembered every sensation, the warmth and wetness of her mouth, the taste of her still on his lips, the way she clenched around him when she crossed the point of no return. He probably should have taken her to his room, but Garrett would have heard them. He might have heard them anyway. They had probably woken the dead.

He scrolled the recording back to where he walked through her door and lifted her in his hands, her ass filling each palm. He went back another few seconds to before he entered her cabin, slid a blank DVD into the drive and burned all of the images of the two of them onto the disc. Then he erased the last two hours of the surveillance records.

He moved his fingers over the keys preparing to shut down the computer, but paused not ready to let her go yet. He slid the disc in and played it back. His body responded with such need a groan rose from his throat as he watched the two of them together, remembering the sound of her voice, the scent of her perfume, the taste of her heated skin, everything the screen couldn't give him but his mind could. He'd have to tell her about the DVD at some point. Maybe she'd want to watch it with him. But not yet. Not until this week was over. It wouldn't do any good for her to worry that her private time was being recorded. Nobody else would ever see the video anyway.

Onscreen, she was spread beneath him, her eyes hooded, her hands locked in his hair. He licked his lips searching for another taste of her, wishing he could go back and make love to her until he was too spent to move a muscle. A reflection on the corner of the screen turned him to the window. Outside, Rebecca held her robe tight around her, and fury was drawing her face. She glared at him through the glass. He jostled the window, fumbled the latch and jerked it up. The cold air stung his skin, stealing the heat the video had poured into him.

"Honey, wait!" His voice was as loud as he dared, but she stormed toward her cabin without looking back. Shit! He shut the video down, ejected the disc and ran out of the house after her. The cold air took his erection down to a manageable level, but he wished like hell he'd had enough sense to put his pants on.

She had barricaded herself inside by the time he got there and pounded his fist against the door.

"Don't you dare come in here!"

"Let me explain." His words blew out on a breath of fog in the cold night air.

"You taped us, without telling me. I don't need an explanation. I saw it!" The volume of her voice rose with every word. "Are you going to sell it on the internet or keep it for your personal collection?"

"The only copy is right here in my hand. You can have it," he said. "Please open the door." He was freezing his ass off and if he didn't calm her down the whole damn place was going to be awake.

"How could you do that?" She wasn't any calmer or quieter.

"We have to, for security. I won't come in, but please open the door, so I don't have to shout."

The door crept open an inch. "Every cabin is taped round the clock," he said, grasping the opportunity to explain with his voice lower.

"And you sit in your office at night getting off on women without them knowing it?" Her eyes glared at him, acid shot off her words.

"We don't watch the video. We just have to keep it to cover our asses."

"I just saw you watching it."

She was still pissed, but at least she was willing to hear him out.

"I had to erase it," he explained. "What we did was enough to get me arrested and shut the ranch down. This is Wyoming, not Nevada."

She opened the door another couple of inches and eyed the disc in his hand.

"I made a copy," he admitted. "But it was for us. Both of us."

"Are you lying to me?" Her shoulders relaxed a little, but he could tell he still had a lot to prove.

He handed her the disc. "If I am, you have everything you need to put me in jail and sue the pants off of me."

"You trust me that much?" She turned the disc over in her hand and narrowed her dark eyes at him again. At least the fire in them had softened and her voice didn't hold the same bitterness.

"Yeah, I trust you," he said, stunned by the truth of those words. Did he really trust a woman enough to put his future in her hands again? Holy hell. "Do you trust me?"

She dropped the disc to her side and bit her bottom lip, opening the door wider. "Come in."

"I can't. Unless I want to be up all night erasing surveillance video."

She glanced down at his underwear, stepped outside and closed the door behind her. "Any cameras out here?"

He shook his head and ran his hand through her hair, still tousled from their love making. His groin tightened. He loved that he was responsible for the state of her hair. They were responsible for it. Together. If he had his way, she would get in a habit of waking up with that very look about her. He wanted all of her in a way that clouded his head, made him not give a damn that he'd just handed a woman he'd known for five days enough evidence to completely destroy his life and his brother's.

"What are you thinking?" she asked.

"That I can't get enough of you," he said, reaching for her waist.

She untied her robe and opened it for him. He slipped his arms around her and let the fabric cover his arms. Her breasts molded around his chest. The scent of her swam up his nose, made him want to drink her in, hold her all night and keep her in bed all day tomorrow and the day after that.

He lifted her against the cabin, settled her legs around his waist and moved his hips along hers, the thin cotton knit of his underwear the only barrier between his hardness and her slick heat. He was careful not to press her into the rough logs of the cabin, but every instinct he had screamed for him to push harder, to give this woman everything he had to give. To stay inside her until she understood that's where he belonged.

"Come to the house with me," he whispered. "Let me make love to you again. I've never needed anything more in my life."

"Any cameras up there?" Her lips curved in the slightest smile letting him know the video didn't bother her. Only that she hadn't known it was being made.

"Not unless you want me to set one up." He nibbled her ear. "You're very photogenic." Her skin heated him. He buried his face in her neck. She gasped, driving him harder. Rebecca was like a drug, the more he had, the more he wanted.

"Won't the cabin camera record that I'm not here?" she asked, tilting her head higher giving him more access.

"It's going to show that I tampered with the recording too," he said, his lips gliding along her smooth skin. "But as long as the records are never subpoenaed we'll be okay."

"Can't you just disconnect the camera? Make it look like a malfunction?"

She was thinking too hard, a sure sign he could stand to step up his game. He retraced his trail along her neck, listening for a sign that he hadn't taken her too far off track. She gasped again, giving him all the affirmation he needed. "That would take a little time," he said. "And I want you now."

Headlights bounced off the porch post next to them. The car making its way down the drive was plain government issue, blowing its cover from even this distance. Fuck. Another impromptu visit by Canyon Creek's finest. The light in the office was on. "Garrett. Shit."

"Looks like you'd better go," she said.

He squeezed her hips and kissed her quickly before setting her feet on the floor.

"Gavin," she whispered loudly, pausing his rapid retreat. "Call me when they leave."

* * * *

Marge trembled as she watched the scene unfold outside her window. Her hand clasped involuntarily at her heart, and warmth spread between her legs. The look on Rebecca's face as she watched Gavin leave could have melted an iceberg.

Marge stared down at the screen of her cell phone. "Is he there?" the text from Chet read. She glanced back at the empty room behind her. An empty bottle of wine sat on the coffee table next to the tablet of self-improvements she and Clayton had been drafting. A soft flush came from the bathroom and guilt tugged at her. No one had ever judged her less or made her feel more deserving, and now he was going to go to jail for trusting her, for teaching her to trust herself.

Her phone beeped again. The same text was repeated across the screen. Her fingers stumbled across the keys. She wasn't used to this texting business, and the words glowing up from the dark screen seemed accusing. *Is he there?*

"Y-e-s," she sent back. Regret tagged each letter. He was there because she begged him to stay. Because they'd shared a bottle of wine and more secrets than she'd ever told anyone before. Her ears hummed and her hands shook. Why should she let Chet use her to throw an innocent man behind bars?

Because Chet was family, the only family she had left. The only person in the world who would see to her needs when she was too old to look after herself. Because he was her sister's child, God rest her soul. And because Chet would be furious if she couldn't do what he had instructed.

Clayton lifted the tablet off the coffee table and his hat off the back of a chair. "Tomorrow, we'll continue."

"Let's work on it some more tonight." Her hands trembled as he shook his head.

"Can't do. It's way past pumpkin time."

The door shut behind him, and she peered through the window at Rebecca's cabin. Chet wasn't going to let her get away with delivering nothing. She'd have to appease him one way or another. He was more interested in Rebecca anyway.

* * * *

Two familiar uniformed officers stood next to the desk while Garrett guarded his computer.

"What now?" Gavin asked from the door without hiding the irritation in his voice. He'd pulled on the jeans that were still in the middle of his bedroom floor, but hadn't bothered with a shirt. Garrett shot him a look that didn't need interpretation. They'd have plenty to discuss later.

"Just thought we'd drop in and make sure all your lovely guests were safe and sound." Officer Chet Bening smirked at Gavin, the same cocky expression he'd been sporting since elementary school. Whatever had originally stirred the animosity between them was long forgotten. But for as long as the men had known one another, Chet had always had something to prove and never seemed to get around to proving it. Probably had a little dick and a response time that was too quick to satisfy anybody but his right hand. Served the asshole right.

"Our guests are always safe," Garrett responded.

"Tell us what you need, so we can get back to bed," Gavin demanded.

"Why don't you let us take a little look-see at those surveillance monitors," Chet's partner said, bowing his chest out just enough to look as stupid as he sounded.

"Settle down, Barney," Gavin snapped. "You got a search warrant?"

"We can get one if we need to, then we can go in and search every cabin. Talk to every guest here."

It wouldn't take much to knock the smug grin off Chet's face, but that would give him every excuse he'd ever need to make their lives hell. He was obviously still pissed he hadn't gotten the previous false accusation to stick. Now he'd have a case. If he ever found proof. Not that he would find any. And what had happened with Rebecca wasn't what it would look like to outside eyes.

"We don't have anything to hide," Garrett said. "But it's an invasion of privacy to let you spy on our guests. That's not what the cameras are for."

"We ain't spying," Chet drawled. "We just want to make sure they're all tucked in by themselves."

"Fuck this," Gavin said. "Get a damn warrant if you can. You don't have any grounds to base this bullshit harassment on."

"We've got plenty of grounds." Chet sneered. "One of your guests has passed on enough information to warrant a full investigation. Seein's how we've barely closed the files on the last one, a search warrant won't be much of a problem."

Garrett scratched the back of his head. "We don't have anything to hide," he repeated. "I'll let you view the monitors, but only long enough to verify that none of our men are in any of the guest cabins."

Gavin stewed, but it was better to let Garrett handle these dipshits. He didn't have the patience. Especially tonight. Garrett keyed up the surveillance software and shifted his computer monitor over enough to give the officers a better view. Gavin leaned over the desk, ready to protect Rebecca from any leering eyes. Twelve gray boxes filled the screen.

"Make them bigger, so we can see what we're looking at," Chet said.

Garrett clicked the mouse and brought a single room onto the screen. The guest was sound asleep, sprawled beneath the covers and obviously alone. He clicked quickly to the next room and brought up a similar image. He continued through the next eight cabins with similar images in each. Then, something different. Everyone leaned closer.

One of the guests, the one who had arrived at the ranch with Rebecca, dropped a wine bottle in the trash and then pulled back her bedding before climbing in. Alone. Chet muttered a curse that would have filled Gavin with satisfaction if Rebecca's cabin wasn't the only one left. She wasn't asleep, and there was no telling what she was doing. Gavin knew her well enough to know there was a good chance she wasn't dressed. If he'd been a cartoon, steam would've shot out his ears and a train whistle would have sounded. He didn't so much as blink. His muscles were coiled, ready to spring himself across the desk and shove that monitor out of sight if he had to. These ass clowns weren't about to gawk at her.

The inside of the Darlin' cabin filled the screen. Rebecca was pacing the floor. The shadowy shape of the disc he'd given her showed dark against the light robe she wore. She held a phone to her ear. Who in the hell was she talking to at 3:00 a.m.? It was barely daylight in South Carolina, too early to be on the phone with anybody. Her lips moved. She was talking alright. She held the disc up and turned it in her hand. Her lips kept moving. Who was she telling? Gavin's chest gelled. What the fuck had he done?

Garrett clicked the mouse again and the screen went dark. "Satisfied, gentlemen?" he asked.

Chet's partner hid his chagrin behind a cocky smirk and chicken chest, but Chet's hands fisted in frustration. His knuckles were white, and anger lurked in his eyes. "You boys got lucky tonight," Chet said. "Better get some sleep. You've got another rough day of work ahead of you tomorrow."

Gavin followed them through the house and waited on the porch to make sure they got in their car and left without poking around anywhere they weren't supposed to.

Gavin stormed back into the office. "Lock the fucking gates, and don't open them for those assholes again unless they've got a search warrant."

Garrett stared hard at him. "Where were you when they got here?"

"I was talking to Rebecca." It wasn't completely a lie, but Garrett wasn't buying it.

"In her cabin?"

"On the porch of her cabin." Gavin felt the heat in his neck, and he didn't know who he was madder at the local donut-holes or himself.

"Who do you think she was on the phone with?" Garrett asked.

Gavin shrugged. "How the hell should I know? Probably her sister." He dropped into his chair and threw his feet up on his desk.

"You think her sister's concerned enough to call the police?"

"I don't know why she would be."

Chet and his lackey wouldn't have gotten there that fast unless Rebecca had talked to her sister before she caught him with the video. She could've done that. He had no idea how long she had been awake before she came to the office window. He knew he screwed up when he handed her the damn disc. He should've listened to his gut instead of his dick. He could go over there and snatch it back, but that wouldn't do anything but piss her off. He couldn't afford to piss her off now. What a fucking dumb ass. Pussy whipped dumb ass. He deserved to be in jail. Or shot.

"Anything you need to tell me?" Garrett asked.

Gavin shook his head. Sweat trickled from his armpits and nausea churned his stomach. Lying to Garrett was bad enough, throwing away everything they had worked for was just too stupid to believe.

Garrett stood up and slung Gavin's clothes across the desk. "I hope it's worth it," he said on his way out the door.

Gavin stared at the phone, the leg of his sweatpants covering the receiver. She wanted him to call her, to take her bed again. His little brain had done enough thinking.

Chapter 9

"You didn't call," Rebecca said, rubbing the remnants of sleep from her face. Fog hung low over the ranch, and the sun had just begun to color the sky when she answered Gavin's knock at the door.

"I'm sorry. And I know it's early," he said from the porch, "but if we're going rock climbing, we need to hit the road."

An apology was better than a lie. He looked tired, but his shorts revealed the muscles that carved lines in his thighs and ran along the outside of his shins beneath the sexiest curls of blond hair. The man continued to get hotter by the day. Unbelievable. Forgiving him for a phone call was easy. Too easy. An explanation would have been nice though.

"I'll wait out here until you're dressed," he said.

"Why would you want to do that?" She took his hand, pulled him inside and lifted her eyes to the corner of the room. The vent near the ceiling was covered with a hand towel. "Is that the only camera?" she asked.

"Yep." The tendons in his neck tightened, but other than that he didn't move. The door stood open at his back.

"Well what are you waiting for?" She stood on her toes to cover his mouth with hers. His response was cool, not an ounce of the heat they'd shared only a few hours ago.

Something heavy settled in her chest. He either had a hell of a night after he left her, or she had imagined something between them that had never really existed. Even her imagination wasn't that good.

"You want to tell me about it?" She positioned his hand on her breast and coaxed his lips until his response became more urgent, more in line with what she had come to expect from him, minus the tenderness.

"This isn't a good idea." Heat welled in his eyes. His voice was soft and low, moving through her, revving her right back up to where she'd been the night before, but the rest of his body language was more in line with his words. Whatever had happened with the police had him on edge. Or he had a problem with intimacy that only surfaced in the daylight.

"You're tense." She ran her hands down his chest, giving him one more chance, hoping her nagging doubt was wrong and his coldness didn't have anything to do with her or his attraction to her. "Tell me there's a condom in your wallet."

"There's one," he said, still holding his hands at his sides.

She steeled herself. "Is this what happens the morning after? I'm new at this, so please tell me how it works." Her lip trembled, but she bit down hard, clamping it motionless, refusing to show weakness.

Gavin closed the door behind him and tucked a strand of hair behind her ear. "I'm sorry," he said. "I didn't mean to." He blew a heavy breath between them. "That disc I made," he said. "I'm afraid if anyone ever found it. If anyone else ever knew…hell, we could lose the ranch over something like that."

"So destroy it." She motioned toward the table by the bed where the disc lay next to her phone. "Those kinds of things usually do come back to bite you." She tried a smile. So, he didn't trust her as much as he'd wanted to. She could live with that. Trust usually took more than a few days, and he had a lot riding on the gesture he'd made to calm her down last night.

He ran his hand through his hair and watched her. There was more to his angst.

"You're smart to be scared." She tried a compliment, not knowing what else he needed. "You look a whole lot better than Tommy Lee. The sharks on the internet would have a feeding frenzy."

If that's all that had him worked up they could still have a memorable morning. Without a word, she reached into his back pocket and offered his wallet to him.

"You can get it," he said.

"No regrets," she said, her heart pounding. "Not one." She waved the little foil package at him and licked the dryness from her lips. "Unless you're not being honest with me right now."

He bent his face to hers and took her mouth in a kiss so gentle it was like a drug, a toe-curling, womb-gripping drug whose hold she didn't ever want to break from. He could have thrown her across the bed and taken her like an animal and she would have been just as happy to join him, but this approach left her quivering with anticipation, anxious to see how long he was willing to let the build-up last, how much time he was willing to spend to take her back to where they had been.

His tongue seemed directly connected to the muscles behind her knees and the ones between her legs. Gripping the condom so hard the sharp corners of the package poked her palm, she pressed her mouth harder to his, forcing her hunger on him.

She stepped closer as he lifted the sweatshirt over her head. The muscle in his jaw tensed and his chest moved beneath his shirt. He hesitated, gripping her arms. She could practically see him changing his mind, debating whether or not he wanted to do this with her.

She shrugged free and crossed her arms over her chest, feeling too naked. "Just forget it," she said. He caught her wrist, stopping her as she darted away.

"Last night was my mistake," he said. "Not yours."

"Mistake?" She swallowed hard. She had been a fool to think last night had meant something to him.

She turned the condom package over in her hand. Her thumb dipped into the recessed center of the smooth plastic, rubbing hard. "I'm glad you cleared that up. I don't believe in repeating mistakes."

"That makes two of us. I'll meet you outside." He swept the disc off the night table and started for the door.

"Do you want to tell me what's going on here," she said, following him off the porch, her arms crossed over her bare breasts. The cold air drew her skin into bumps and shot chills through her. "Or are you just going to be plain mean about it?"

"I'm sorry." His response was automatic.

"The apology without explanation is old. Give me one reason I should go anywhere with you right now."

"Who'd you tell?" His neck tightened, and the anger and hurt in his eyes confused her

"Who'd I tell what?" She stared at him dumbfounded until her mind worked out what had to be the problem. "You think I told the police something?" His silence gave her the only answer she needed.

"Why would I do that? I wasn't feeling violated until now." Her arms tightened in a protective embrace. The condom wrapper bit into her hand again. She flung the little package at him. "I'm not going anywhere with you, and the last people I expect to protect me from sexual stupidity are the police!"

* * * *

"What did you say!" Chet's voice barreled through the phone with so much force, Marge's spine vibrated.

"I'm..." She breathed deep. "I'm not cooperating." Last night the wine had made it seem so easy to dish the dirt on Rebecca and Gavin. The harsh light of morning made that notion a lot harder to swallow. Love wasn't meant to be persecuted. If anyone knew that, she did.

"You will cooperate unless you want to sleep in your own piss and eat peanut butter when your teeth fall out! That married man you been messing around with ain't gonna have any use for you much longer."

"I don't need you to take care of me." She eyed the bottle of wine open on the baker's rack, but held firm. She could do this. Without alcohol.

Chet's laugh was full of condescension. "Yeah, that's right. You couldn't even pay your light bill last month."

"My rent went up." Her voice sounded too weak. She straightened her spine and swallowed hard. Clayton's number two rule echoed in her mind. Control your own destiny. There were mistakes she had made. Things she couldn't change, but the choices she made right this minute weren't any of those things. "I'm not going to help you put nice people in jail. They don't deserve it."

"Since when do you know anything about what people deserve? You think that old man's wife deserves having her husband's dick in you?"

Marge gasped, and her face flamed. "Chester Lamar Bening, your mother would roll over in her grave if she heard you speaking to me that way. And God bless her soul, I'm not giving you a chance to do it anymore!"

"You'll do what I say and you'll listen to whatever I feel like saying!" Chet yelled back. "And if you don't, I'll come out there and make you sorry you ever—" She clapped the phone closed, cutting off the last of his threat. Her legs wobbled as she crossed the room and lifted the wine bottle directly to her lips. Before she came up for air, her phone rang again.

* * * *

Gavin climbed into his truck and threw the condom on the seat. So much for not pissing Rebecca off. He'd already given her enough rope to hang him with, he should've just fucked her. His temple throbbed. Was he really such a jerk? Until last night he would have defended her dignity against anyone, and now he was acting like she didn't deserve to have any. He still didn't know who she was talking to in the middle of the night. Or if she had anything to do with the cops showing up. What if he'd just lost the best thing that could have happened to him because he was a dumb ass. Too dumb to find out if his suspicions had merit. He could've asked her, explained why they were watching her, but she could easily lie. He expected her to lie. The acknowledgement hit him like a hoof to the head. He didn't trust her. When push came to shove, he would never trust any woman.

The best thing he could do was book her on the next flight out of Wyoming. He clipped his cell phone onto the charger and saw the message envelope in the corner of the screen. Garrett had probably called last night when the cops showed up. He dialed into his messages.

"You have one message. Received at three oh seven a. m.," the electronic voice announced. He waited, expecting to catch another round of hell for the same crap, but it was Rebecca's voice that played in his ear. She had called him last night, when the cops were at the ranch.

"You've barely been gone and I'm already missing you in the worst way." She whimpered playfully. "Call me as soon as you get this and please tell me you have a DVD player in your room." Her voice shot straight through him erasing his anger in a flash of heated adrenalin. "I got my hands on a pretty hot movie tonight," she continued, "and I enjoy this kind even more than scary ones. I came up with some ideas. Lots and lots of ideas. I think you'll like them all."

There was no doubt which head was doing the thinking when he folded the phone in his hand and snatched the keys out of the ignition. They both were, and it didn't take a man with two brains to figure out he was a bigger dumb ass than he'd thought.

"I just got your message. I'm an idiot," he said almost before she had the cabin door open, his breath still heavy from sprinting across the yard.

"You're such an idiot." She smiled wiping a tear from her cheek. "We could still be in bed right now. Making mistake after mistake. And I could still be fool enough to think we were making love."

His chest pounded. He didn't deserve her to let him off easily. "You're a lot of things to me, but you're not a mistake. The cops had to check the monitors. You were on the phone. With the disc." He kissed the damp trails on her face and sank into her eyes. "I thought..."

"You thought I slept with you and then called the police?"

He could see how he had hurt her, and he wanted to give her the honesty she deserved.

"No. I thought your sister called the police."

"But you thought I slept with you and told my sister I had the disc?"

"I have an issue with trust," he said, bending his face to hers. "But it's not your fault, and I won't pawn it off on you again. Please give me another chance."

"I haven't talked to anybody but you since we..." She frowned. "Did what we did."

He believed her and he wanted to trust her more than any woman he'd ever known. "Can you forgive me for being such a dick?"

"Are you going to make a habit of it?"

"God, I hope not," he said before taking her lips with his. Her response filled him. The sweetness of her tongue pulled him into a place that was too deep to climb out of. His instinct was to run, get as far away from her as he could, but there was nothing he wanted more than to stand there and love her, to try and be a bigger man than he was.

Her tongue swirled his, her hands held the back of his neck like she was as desperate for him as he was for her. Like this week wouldn't be enough. Forever might not be enough. He was thinking crazy thoughts, and he didn't care, she rattled his brain until every one of them made sense.

* * * *

"You didn't meet me for breakfast. Are you okay?" Clayton peered at Marge through the cracked door of her cabin.

"I'm fine." The lie rolled off her tongue, but she closed her eyes and her chest shook with sobs.

"Let me in there," he said softly as she moved aside. "My lord, what happened to you?" He wrapped his arms around her, and every tear she'd ever held in threatened to pour out of her eyes.

He walked her over to the loveseat and lifted the almost empty bottle of wine sitting on the coffee table. "Girlfriend, this is not what we were drinking last night." He eased her down, but the motion tipped her stomach.

She gestured toward the trashcan, and Clayton set it at her feet without a second to spare. She vomited, retching everything she could and knowing it would never be enough.

He held her hair and fanned the back of her neck with his hat. When the worst had subsided, he helped her sit back then brought two washcloths. One he cleaned her face with, the other he folded across his thigh. "Lucy, you got some splainin' to do," he said in his best Desi Arnaz.

Despite the nausea that still churned her stomach and crept like a hot glove up her throat, she smiled. And then she laughed, until the tears came again and it took all she could do not to choke on self-disappointment.

She had caved. Chet had played his trump card, and she had folded completely, giving him everything he'd ever need. She had to. If Chet phoned Harry's wife, Harry would never forgive her. She wouldn't even exist in his world. All those years of giving herself only to him, would end in nothing. She would be totally and completely alone. She dragged in a jagged breath and clutched her chest before the sobs took her again. Her eyes were too heavy to open, and even in the cool morning the room was suffocating.

"We're going to talk," Clayton said, helping her to her feet and over to her bed. "But first you need to sleep this off." He pulled the covers back, then tucked her in like a child once she'd settled between them. "Leave the door unlocked." He folded the clean washcloth and laid it across her forehead. "I'll come back to check on you, and I'll bring you something for your stomach."

"You're taking care of me?" she murmured, sinking into the pillow. No matter what she owed Chet, she couldn't let Clayton fall into the trap. He was too good to her, better than anyone had ever been.

He turned to go, but she grabbed his wrist. "He's coming back," she said.

"Who?"

"My nephew."

Clayton clasped her hand in his and gave it a squeeze. "Sleep now. You can tell me all about your nephew when you feel better."

She wanted to argue, but her lips didn't cooperate. The bed swayed slightly beneath her, and sleep crept in from the corners of her mind.

* * * *

"This is so good," Rebecca said, holding a cheeseburger in one hand and a grease-spotted napkin in the other. "Climbing rocks makes me hungry." About a mile outside downtown Canyon Creek, beneath the roadside marquee for Mike's Burger Joint, she sat on the open tailgate of Gavin's truck swinging her legs. The shorts and shoes she'd bought at the sporting goods store were dusted with red clay, but her new dark jersey top hid the dirt well.

"Best in Wyoming. The place is a dive, but you can't find a better burger."

"I'm starting to think I can believe all these things you tell me," she said, raking her gaze over him from head to toe. Her mind was still wrestling with the hint of a future he had thrown at her after they had scaled the rock face earlier. *Next time we'll climb the Tetons. They're good for beginners and they'll give you some bragging rights.* She smiled. *Next time.* She played with the possibilities caught in those words, twisting them like putty. Turning them over and over. Front to back. Side to side. Corners stretched taunt and rolled together again. *Next time.*

Gavin wadded his wrapper and tossed it back in the bag. He squeezed her thigh and his eyes grew earnest. "I never imagined I'd meet you like this."

"What do you mean?"

"I never thought the woman I couldn't live without would sign up for a week at our hokey ranch."

"Now you're really laying it on thick." Her heart skipped. She could sell the connotations to Parker Brothers as a mind game. *Next time. Can't live without.* The ball of energy that spun in her chest grew more frantic and she swallowed hard. Hints of a possible future together had unlocked what she had clamped down so tightly, not dared to let herself imagine.

Everything she had been holding back flooded her. It was too late to go home now, too late to save her heart. She had gotten everything she paid for, even the stuff she hadn't banked on. Gavin really could make a woman fall in love with him in only a week, less than a week. There was still a day to go.

"I like you like this." She wrapped the last of her burger, dropped it in the bag and stretched. Above, an eagle loop-d-looped in the pale blue sky. She would ride this as long as it lasted, ride it into the dirt, and figure out how to dust herself off when the time came.

"Like how?" His features softened and he cradled her neck in his hand.

"Without the hat." She ran her palm up his thigh until she was leaning close enough to brush his lips with hers when she spoke. "Tell me why your marriage didn't work." This was it, either he was a man who could be trusted or he wasn't. If he wasn't, at least she would know who she was climbing into bed with.

"I guess she needed something she couldn't get from me." He caressed her back. "But back then I thought everything was working fine right up until she left me for my best friend and business partner."

Rebecca smiled inside. The woman must have been an idiot. Thank God for stupid people. "Did you ever cheat on her?"

"No. I thought I had everything I wanted."

"I should thank her."

"Why would you do that?" He smiled and twisted her hair in his hand.

"If she hadn't screwed up I probably never would've tasted the best burger in Wyoming."

He kissed the grease from her lips. "She didn't screw up. I've heard they have a couple of kids now, and seem happy. And now that you're here, I can see things worked out the way they were supposed to."

"Everything always works out the way it's supposed to," Rebecca said. Her voice was barely a whisper. She met his mouth again. He responded with desire as deep as hers. His skin grew hot beneath her hands, his body firm against hers.

"You rock me." He nuzzled her neck. "Everything about you. And that's the truth."

"You don't know all of me yet. There are so many ways I can rock you."

"I'm sure you can, and I plan on getting to know every single part of you." His voice was low and suggestive, a tone that struck a chord deep inside her. A chord she wanted him to play again and again and again.

She eased closer. The paper sack crinkled as it crushed between them. She closed her hand around his wrist and brought his finger up to her neck.

"Like you could get to know me right here," she said, "and then I could tell you how much I hate pistachio ice cream?"

He ran his finger down to her collarbone and then back up to where she had placed it. Goose bumps rose beneath his touch.

"Right here?"

"Uh huh," she whispered, her body already trembling with anticipation. "That's a very good place to start."

He bent his head toward hers and tasted where his finger had been. She gasped as the heat of his tongue connected with her skin.

"I like knowing you there." His voice was almost a growl.

"I've got a few other places you might like." She ran her hands beneath his shirt, over the ridges of muscles that covered his ribs and onto his chest.

"You've got lots of places I like." He lifted her hips and brought her onto his lap, then buried his head against her neck again. His breath was warm against her skin, his mouth stirring her up inside. She pressed her body against his, feeling how hard he was and hating the layers of clothes between them.

"Hey, get a room!"

Rebecca blew a frustrated breath through her nose and looked over her shoulder. The young man issuing the command held a long pole in one hand and a stack of plastic letters in the other. Grease from the kitchen clung to his hair and skin, and he didn't look any too pleased to have them making out on his turf.

Gavin made a sound deep in his throat. "I guess we should be going."

"Back to your place? So I can rock you?"

"I want you to see something first."

"I want to see you naked."

He brought her wrist to his lips. "This is important. More important to me than taking your clothes off right now." He smiled. "So you know it ranks up there above oxygen."

* * * *

"We're here," Gavin said. Rebecca could have sworn there was a note of hesitation in his voice and her nerves went on alert.

They were standing on mosaic floor tiles that flowed out to the cement sidewalk in front of the Wapiti Palace, a well-preserved theatre and movie palace that according to the brass plate imbedded into the exterior building was built in 1926. Playbills for local performances and encore films lined the walls.

"You want to see a movie?" She screwed her face at him, hoping this was more than a stall tactic designed to keep from going back to the ranch. "I'm questioning your priorities in a very big way."

"My priorities are in line." He rapped his knuckles against the glass. "Although I have to admit I'm a little nervous."

"It's not even open," she said, reading the hours posted on the box office window.

"I have connections." He blew an unsteady breath and knocked again. His impatience was new.

"You really are nervous," she said, "What's—"

Before she could finish, a lock rattled on the other side of the door and a young man dressed in a black satin vest and crisp white shirt let them in. He flipped a row of lights behind a recessed panel in the wall, and the wide hall behind him came to life. Gargoyles peered over the concession area and well-worn tapestries hung on the Venetian plaster walls.

"Wow. This is impressive." She looped her arm through his. "What are we going to see?"

"I promised I'd prove I wasn't playing the game with you." He pulled her in close and the muscle in his jaw jumped again. A feeling of unease tensed Rebecca's shoulders. He was obviously not comfortable, that didn't leave her much confidence she should feel any differently.

"You don't have to prove anything to me."

"This was meant to be for you," he said. "But now I think it's for both of us. So we know where we stand. Without doubt."

Beyond the concession area a gracious double staircase wound its way to the second floor. The man who had unlocked the door took the stairs, but Gavin led Rebecca to a theatre on main floor. Chandeliers hung from the ceiling, a Mighty Wurlitzer organ sat to one side of the stage and thick velvet curtains hung floor to ceiling.

They took cushioned seats in the center of the auditorium about six rows from the stage. The house lights and chandeliers dimmed, and the ceiling came to life with drifting clouds and twinkling stars. Above the mezzanine, a light flashed in the window of the projection room. Gavin reached for her hand, his thumb traced erratic circles into her skin.

"I need you to trust me," he said. The way his eyes pleaded, tensed her stomach into a tight knot. "I'm not doing this to upset you. Promise me you'll believe that."

A rectangle of light and jumping black squiggles hit the screen at the back of the stage. The lead images panned a broad Charleston street lined with blossoming trees and cut to the façade of an ornate church. Rebecca's breath stuck in her throat and before the opening credits began to roll, she dropped Gavin's hand and gripped the padded arms of her chair. Her fingernails sank into the broad chenille weave and a tear slipped from the corner of her eye.

"How did you do this?" she asked without turning from the screen.

"Garrett's on the theatre board and his boyfriend, John, is an executive with The Hearst Corporation that owns half the Lifetime Network." He placed his hand over her arm. "Are you okay?"

Rebecca didn't answer, but caught her breath as the camera focused on people inside the church. Todd was unbelievably handsome in his black tuxedo, shaking hands with his groomsmen and hugging his mother. She smiled and choked back a laugh as he hammed it up for the camera responding to the interviewer's joke about cold feet by lifting his pants leg to reveal a double layer of socks.

The edit jumped to her father lowering her veil before leading her to the petal-strewn aisle. At the front of the church Todd waited for her. His jacket lay across his broad shoulders and draped down to his hips, tailored to fit him to a tee. As the music flooded from the speakers in the auditorium, the camera lingered on his face, capturing the tears that shimmered in his eyes and the moment his chest heaved and his jaw fell slack.

Rebecca swallowed hard. He had loved her so much. She had never seen a man so unbridled in the expression of his love before, and as she had placed one foot in front of the other, she had known beyond doubt she was the luckiest woman in the world. She never imagined she would have to let him go without having a chance to say goodbye.

She gripped the arms of her chair harder, and her chest trembled with the sadness that sat deep in her soul. Gavin's hand covered hers, but she couldn't look away from the film.

The camera angle changed and she stood facing Todd. She read his lips as he whispered to her the same thing he said every time they made love. "Promise me you'll never change." Her heart clenched so tight she thought it would stop beating forever when she saw herself mouth back. "Not ever."

She had changed. She had changed what he loved most about her. Her passionate abandon. Her ability to let her heart soar and trust it would never come crashing down. She had lied. To Todd.

The minister held his Bible in front of them and led them through their vows. She watched herself promise her love, the words echoing in her ears. "I, Rebecca, take you, Todd, for richer for poorer, in sickness and in health, forsaking all others, until death do us part."

She covered her face and wept into her hands. The vows were complete. She had fulfilled them. They both had, but the marriage bond was broken by that last little clause. Until death do us part. And the private vow she had made to him was broken along with her heart the day he died.

Gavin raised the armrest between them and took her in his arms. Her body stiffened. Todd was larger than life in front of her, sealing their commitment with a kiss, but Gavin's voice was in her ear whispering words of comfort. Telling her she would be okay. He would make sure of it. He would never let her hurt again. She crumbled, falling into the man who was holding her, the only one who wasn't a fantasy anymore.

He held her until the tears subsided and her lungs could fill without stuttering.

"Why did you do this?" she asked when she was strong enough to look him in the eye.

"Love does have a contract," he said evenly, cautiously, "and you already know it costs a lot more than we charge at the ranch." He handed her a slip of paper folded in half.

She unfolded the paper in her hand. The business's name and address were in the upper left corner of the check, Garrett's signature was at the bottom, and the tender amount was exactly what she had paid to spend the week at Fantasy Ranch.

"I should have given it to you days ago, probably the second I met you," he said. "You're not a guest anymore. You never really were. I want you in my room, in my house, in every way that matters for as long as you want to stay." His fingers trembled against her cheeks. "Please tell me you want that, too."

She held her breath at what his words could mean. She couldn't afford to read more into them than he had meant to put there. "You could've kept taking me to bed without going to all this trouble," she said. The screen went dark and the light from the projection room disappeared.

The man who had let them in called down from the balcony, "Gavin, you gonna lock up?"

"Yeah. We'll go out the back," Gavin answered him. "Thanks again."

The man disappeared into a wing and then his footsteps carried down the marble stairs.

"I definitely want to keep taking you to bed." Gavin smiled. "But I want you to be there for the same reason I am."

"And what would that be?"

"Because there's nothing I need to do more than make love to you. I thought I'd never take this chance again, but you're every part of me that was missing. I need you in my life."

Her heart curled around what those words meant. A tear slipped from her eye and rolled down her cheek. He kissed it, taking it from her. She tasted the salt on his tongue until the tear dissolved between them and all that was left was the rawness of her need for him. Her heart drummed in her chest to an ancient rhythm, the dance of life, of love, and the promise of tomorrow.

"Let's go take care of those *needs* we have," she said.

"There's nobody here but us. Unless you count Maynard. The ghost."

"There's a ghost?"

"Uh huh. He might want to watch. He's a horny old devil. Been known to blow skirts up. Touches women in all sorts of places that send chills up their spines."

"You sure you're not a ghost?"

"I want you," he said, slipping his hand beneath the hem of her shirt and planting kisses down her neck. "Over and over. Here. Now. Everywhere. All the time."

"And you plan on doing this for longer than a week?"

"I don't ever want to stop." He unbuttoned her shorts and slid the zipper down.

"I can't help but feel..." She caught her breath as his fingers found the silk of her panties. "...a little robbed."

"What am I robbing you of, except maybe your movie palace virginity?"

She could feel his smile against her neck as the clouds floated overhead and the stars twinkled.

"I won't ever get to have sex for the hell of it." Her smile was rooted in the center of her soul.

"I'll try to make sure you don't miss it."

Chapter 10

"You're undercover?" Clayton placed his napkin next to his plate and sat back in his chair. Early afternoon light poured in through the picture window next to the small dining table in the Honey cabin.

Marge pushed her food around with her fork. She had managed a few bites, but her stomach wasn't up for much more. Her head felt like someone was using it as a trampoline and even her bunions were throbbing.

"Please don't tell anyone." Her eyes were too raw to cry, and her swollen throat forced a rasp into her voice. "I just don't want you to get caught in the middle of this. You haven't done anything to deserve it."

"No one else has either. Your nephew can't arrest anyone here."

She shook her head and wiped her nose on her napkin. "I told him I saw Gavin leaving Rebecca's room in his underwear." She focused on the mountain of potatoes in front of her. "He'll use my statement to get a warrant for the cameras."

"And then we'll all be cleared anyway." Clayton leaned forward on his elbows. "I told you, the cowboys don't have sex with the guests. None of them."

She lifted her eyes to his. "Not even the young pretty ones?"

"None of them," he repeated. He came around the table and walked her over to the mirror above the vanity. Standing behind her, he tucked her hair behind her ears and ran his fingers through the loose tangles at the back of her head. "Look in that mirror. Look past the hangover." He laughed gently. "And the snotty nose."

She smiled in spite of herself.

"Look at that beautiful woman. Men could drown in those eyes." He traced the hollow of her face with his fingers. "My grandmother would have called yours a Queen's complexion. Cream and roses. Don't tell me you've never seen yourself this way."

She lowered her eyes to the countertop. He was filling her full of compliments a handsome young man would never mean. He tilted her chin up again and stared at her through the mirror.

"You are an incredibly attractive woman, Marge. And Old, Fat and Harry needs a good swift kick in the knee if he's never let you believe that." Clayton leaned closer. With his mouth close to her ear he whispered, "You deserve better than a married man who doesn't know how much you're worth. And that's not a secret."

He squeezed her shoulders and stepped away. "Now, beautiful Miss Marge, how are we going to spend your last day on the ranch?"

Without pretense or forethought, the tingle started at the base of her spine and traveled higher, gaining momentum, puffing her lungs with courage, and pouring out of her lips in a rush. "I want to ride a horse."

He looked at her for a long minute. "Is this a new you, I'm sensing?"

"I don't like the old me."

"Let's go, then!"

"Wait. Maybe I should tell Gavin what I did."

Clayton brought the backs of her fingers to his lips. "You focus on leaving old Marge in the dust, and don't worry about Gavin. I told you, he's a smart man. He can take of himself and the ranch."

* * * *

The late afternoon light filled Gavin's bedroom. There was no darkness to hide in, nothing to mask the fear, or any lingering doubt. Not that there was any doubt in Rebecca's mind. He lifted her shirt over her head and dropped it to the floor. The ride from the theatre was no more than half an hour, but already she wanted him again so badly she could barely pull air into her lungs.

"I've never craved a woman like this before," he said, reaching behind her back to release her bra. "Not this bad." His voice vibrated between them as he slid the straps from her shoulders and lowered his mouth to hers. She melted into him, already so familiar with his taste, his scent, and the heat that flowed through him, that the essence of him filled her as naturally as the blood that pumped through her veins. His thumbs traveled the vertical line that divided her abdomen, his hands covered her ribs, pushed her shorts below her hips, down her thighs. He undressed her as if he was unwrapping a package, unhurried at first then driven with anticipation.

She pushed his shirt up over his chest. He helped her pull it off. "If you turn this place into a nudist resort," she whispered as she reached for the button on his shorts, "we could just run around naked." The zipper jammed and she tugged at it.

"You're brilliant." His hands dipped into the curve of her waist and he lowered his lips to her neck. "We'll convert this room first. No clothes allowed, and I'm not letting you out of here."

Her hands fumbled on the front of his shorts, her muscle control hindered by his tongue.

"Rip it," he said.

Fueled by the need that rode his words, she jerked the stubborn zipper, with enough force to unhinge it. She had him undressed in seconds and stepped closer to press her body to his. Her mind spun, overloaded with the sensations shooting through her, the increasing pressure of his hands, the heat flaring between them. She raised her fingers to his neck, the tendons defined and tense beneath her touch. "There's not a single part of you that doesn't turn me on," she said. Her voice was weak, he made her that way, but that no longer frightened her.

His mouth moved lower along her neck and she moaned as her thighs flooded with prickling desire. He cupped her bottom, lifting her off the floor and settling her legs around his hips. She hooked her ankles behind his back and raised herself higher, frantically guiding the most sensitive part of her body, the part of her that hungered for him more than the others, along the length of his erection. The perfect long length of it.

Every movement brought more pleasure than the last, made her even weaker than before. There in the middle of the room there was nothing to fall back on, nothing to hold her but him, his strength. She slowed, afraid of losing herself, her balance, of getting hurt.

"I've got you," he said, interpreting her hesitation. "I won't let you go." He lifted her higher, dangerously high, before edging her down again. The slightest miscalculation and he would be inside her without any protection. Not that she cared. She was too close to the edge to care about anything at all. Her nipples tightened. The ridge of his erection was wet from the pleasure pouring out of her. She braced her arms across his shoulders and moved against him as one mind-bending sensation after another coursed through her, rocked her within a centimeter of consciousness and left her helpless in his arms. He guided her until a series of spasms filled the room with her cries.

Gavin walked Rebecca to the bed, a million thoughts running through his head. Her body still quivered against his. She was such a responsive and passionate lover, eager to please and be pleased. It was easy to see why she couldn't separate sex from emotion, she poured every ounce of herself into their lovemaking. She gave herself to him without hesitation, without restraint. There was no doubt in his mind, she was his as much as he was hers. She had given herself over to him. She wanted to be with him, and while every man she bumped into would be more than willing to take her off his hands, he knew that once he had her heart she wouldn't give it to anyone else. Another tremor shook her, lighter than the previous ones, just an aftershock that brought a wide smile to her mouth.

"Have I mentioned you make me crazy when you come?" He didn't wait for an answer. His lips found hers, his cock skimmed her hot swollen clit, shooting vibrations up to his chest. He already knew how right they were together, how her body would embrace his and all the pleasure she could spill from him. Still, she was like a wonderland he was driven to explore, to memorize every nuance, every hidden way he could please her. She squirmed beneath him, demanding harder contact, trying to position herself higher, inviting him into the only place he belonged beyond reason. He had known the first time he kissed her, every time he held himself back, and during every failed attempt at rationalization, she gave a reason to his life. And now every minute he had denied his body had to be compensated tenfold.

"Please." She whimpered carving light lines up his back with her nails.

A barrage of emotions was connected to that single word. He needed to protect her, to claim her, to give her everything she needed and to take everything she had to give. He needed to be closer to her than he could physically get. He needed to hold on tight, but give her room to breathe. He needed everything at once, but more than anything he needed to love her. To make love to her. To open his soul to her with a prayer she would step inside, stay with him. Only him. That he would be enough, all that she would ever need.

He leaned over and opened the nightstand drawer. She followed him with her eyes, her breath coming hard as he brought the little square package up to his mouth and tore it open with his teeth. His eyes never left her, the way she wanted him softened every last edge his broken marriage had left behind. Rebecca wasn't a woman who walked away. She held tight, so tight she didn't know when to let go. And he wanted her to hold him.

Her lips curved slightly as she sat up and rolled the condom onto him. Holding his stiff cock in one hand, she tugged his earlobe through the smile on her lips. "The more I have you, the worse I want you," she breathed curling her fingers around his shaft. "What kind of drug have you got in this thing?"

Her hair draped his chest, fell in soft tendrils over his shoulder then caressed his forearm as she bent to kiss his chest while she stroked him. He hadn't known what to expect when he arranged to have her wedding shown at the theatre. She could have run crying all the way back to South Carolina. She could have hated him for bringing the pain back to the surface. She could have fiercely protected those special moments she shared with her husband. She could have responded a million different ways, but she had found comfort in his arms. She had given herself to him on the thick chenille seats the ranch's donation had purchased during the last phase of the theatre's renovation. And now as she lay back on his bed, she was luminous, her cheeks tinted a subtle rose, her hair spread in dark silky strands across his pillow, her chest and shoulders damp. "You're so beautiful," he told her.

"Admire me from down here." She pulled him toward her.

He held himself back and slid his arm under her thigh, raising her calf to his shoulder, opening her to him even more. He entered in a long steady thrust that sent another cry erupting from her, louder than the ones before.

"I think we were made to do this together," he said, sinking as far into her as he could go, his voice heavy in his throat. His only focus was the fit of his body with hers, the way they responded to one another, and the sounds that filled the room. Notes of pure pleasure and undeniable need. Not a single string of sounds that formed anything coherent. Her eyes drifted closed.

"Look at me," he coaxed, his lips close enough to brush her cheek.

Rebecca forced her eyes open, though the intensity of sensations surging through her body made it difficult to keep them from shutting again. What she saw in Gavin's gaze was as intense as the waves he was sending through her. His rhythm was just as she expected when she first fantasized about him, slow and controlled. But like his gait, it gave her more time to enjoy what his body had to offer. And he had so much to offer.

"Talk to me," he urged. "You have no idea what your voice does to me."

His mouth met her neck, his tongue and the way he moved within her drove her too crazy to answer him with anything more than another string of broken syllables.

"You...oh my God. You...You're so...aahhh! I can't." She couldn't give him what he wanted. He left her unable to speak, unable to think. All she could do was feel. "Don't. Ever. Stop."

He answered her with a heavy groan and a soul-melding, continual joining of his body with hers. Each time he made the steady climb away from her she ached where he had been, but before the emptiness had a chance to settle, he filled her again, and again and again, telling her how much he wanted her, how much he needed her. She answered him with more words she couldn't string together. Thoughts she couldn't finish. His lips found hers. Their tongues met, and he continued, one long solid stroke after another until neither of them could breathe.

"I'm so close." She panted, moving her hips to meet his, keeping her eyes open with ever-increasing effort. She didn't want it to end, but she couldn't hold on. Her body screamed as it careened toward the finale. "Harder."

His thrust responded to her command, loud primordial grunts erupted from both of them. He lost every ounce of his well-conditioned restraint until they sang out in simultaneous release. Her body splintered beneath his, finally sated, and so limp she couldn't even bring her hand to his back. Their chests heaved together, their skin slick with sweat and covered with the scent of one another.

"I'm never going to get enough of you." He shifted to his side and brought her with him, letting her legs settle around his.

"I'm ready for more when you are," she said into his neck.

He laughed, a sound that rumbled low in his throat. He slid his arm from beneath her and sat up to get rid of the condom. She mustered enough strength to run her finger up his spine, and her hand along his back. Even this brief separation was more than she wanted.

When he lay back and pulled her to him again, she rolled into his kiss, holding her body against his. Todd wasn't the only man who could make her feel so completely content. Maybe that was okay. Maybe it wasn't, but what she did with Gavin didn't feel wrong, even if what she had done to Todd did. The guilt crept up on her, but she concentrated on the man lying next to her instead, and these feelings for him that expanded her heart.

"You are exactly what I needed," she said.

In the comforting calm that followed, she traced the curve of his chest, the contour of his abdomen and the palm of his hand. Her body quieted and she remembered what she had so blissfully forgotten. She had to leave. In the morning. She had a job, a home, a life on the other side of the country. "What am I going to do without you?" she asked.

"We're going to have to figure that out." He trailed his fingers through her hair. His hand traveled down her back and he lifted her more fully onto him. He was stiffening again already.

She rubbed herself over him, from the base of his cock to the tip and back to where she'd started, each time he grew harder until he steadied her hips.

"Hold on," he said, reaching for his nightstand. The shift of his body put him in a position that scrambled her senses, and before he could pull the drawer open she seated herself on him, stretching to accommodate the girth of him again. His entrance into her jolted every neuron of her body and ripped a growl from his throat. His hands gripped her hips as he disregarded the need for a condom and pushed himself up to meet her fully.

There was nothing between them, nothing at all but reckless intimacy that overrode all sensibilities.

"Are you sure?" he asked before giving her the freedom to move.

Her response was a kiss that dissolved the tension in his arms and sent every ounce of caution sailing. She lifted herself high enough to find a rhythm that she could easily maintain but threatened to end this joining far too quickly. Probably much too fast for him. When her muscles stuttered, he slowed her down.

"Take all of me," he said, guiding her down to his lap. "I need to be as far inside you as I can go." His voice was rough, his grip on her harder than before. His hands dug into her as he buried himself to the hilt and pulled her knees close to his ribs. She had never been filled so completely. Her hair fell around them both as she collapsed against him, surrendering to his power over her.

She moved slowly at first, testing her angle, relishing the sensations of having him so deep. "Deep enough?" she asked, arching her back and rocking against him, barely able to swallow the breath lodged in her throat.

"Never enough." He groaned as his head bent to her shoulder and they moved together taking what they both needed and giving everything they had.

She wrapped her arms around his neck and clung to him while her body answered his with one debilitating tremor after another and her screams echoed off the walls. If she had ever come that hard, she couldn't remember it. She couldn't remember anything at all.

He raised his head to watch her, but as soon as she tightened around him a familiar expression clenched his face. He was as loud as she had been, crushing her in his arms as he poured himself into her, filled her, spilled out of her. He held her as close to him as he could while his breath steadied against her throat. His hands moved along her back, down to her bottom and up again, covering her, branding her as his. And she couldn't imagine ever needing to be more than that.

The cool air dried the dampness from their skin, and they climbed between the covers. The rest of the night they drifted in and out of sleep and kisses and caresses. And in moments of lucidity they made love. Slowly. Tenderly. As if every second together had to be held before it shattered and slipped away. She couldn't have more fully appreciated his tendency to never hurry or his insatiable need to connect with her.

As the morning light filtered into the room, Gavin woke Rebecca with the full of his lips on hers, his hand moving down her body. He shifted, pinning her beneath his hips. She opened herself to him and he entered her slowly, letting her feel his journey into her inch by inch.

Every time he withdrew and sank into her again, she needed him more. Her body responded naturally, her hips meeting his. She moved to the edge of consciousness, slipped away and came back again. Not sure at times if she was dreaming or if she had actually found nirvana. She forced her eyes open, not wanting to miss a second of the tenderness and desire in his eyes.

They were sharing so much more than their bodies and the power of the emotions that swirled in her chest was overwhelming. She grabbed the back of his arms, his muscles tight beneath her grasp. The wave started slowly, built, then crashed over her with such intensity she could do nothing but completely let herself go.

His body tensed. She glimpsed the look of desperation in his eyes and her lids fell shut. There were too many senses at work, one had to go. As much as she wanted to see him, she couldn't field all the stimuli at once. In the darkness of her mind she completely lost hold. She traveled back through every minute they'd shared. The first kiss. The tree fort. Dinner in the barn. The theatre with her wedding playing out on screen.

"You're the most amazing woman," he breathed, his voice hoarse. "Promise me you'll never change."

She closed around him as her body found its release. "Oh my..." His back stiffened. Her fingers sank into his skin. A loud groan fought free from his throat. "Oh my..." she screamed.

"I love you so much, please don't ever change," he said as his body trembled and a warm liquid tide surged into her.

"Todd." She could only whisper his name as the final waves of orgasm rolled through her.

Gavin's breath poured into the pillow next to her head. The weight of his body on hers was so right. Everything she could have wanted. She opened her eyes and bit her lip. Oh shit. Shit. Shit. Shit. She didn't mean that, didn't even know where it came from. He had rocked her senseless, unlocked something so deep inside she couldn't wrap her mind around it. Gavin brought his face to hers. The pain she saw in his eyes scared her.

"Gavin," she whispered. "I'm...I'm sorry. I don't..." But she did know. It was the words he chose. Why at that moment did he use Todd's words? It was too much to make love, to feel love, after all this time and hear the echo of her husband's voice when she was too wrapped up in the throes of orgasm to be more than marginally coherent.

"I'm not Todd," he said. In one movement the weight of him was gone. The cool air of the room evaporated the heat from her skin and left her shaking. He grabbed his clothes off the floor and carried them out of the room.

"Gavin wait! Please!" Her body flinched as the door slammed into its frame.

Rebecca pulled the covers over her head. Todd wasn't coming back, and she lay there long enough to realize Gavin probably wasn't either.

Chapter 11

Gavin threw the tennis ball against the wall of his office and caught it when it ricocheted back. His shorts and shirt were wrinkled, dirty, and still held onto a hint of Rebecca's perfume. Her suitcase stood beneath the window. The irony of timing wasn't lost on him. Her flight out was early and she'd be on it. Going back to South Carolina. Back to her life. Ready to move forward. Or wallow in her memories. How the hell was he supposed to know which?

She had played the game. Outplayed him. But it was his own damn fault. She had told him everything about herself he needed to know. He was just too full of himself to think he needed a book to understand women. Cowboy expectation number one: Listen. Really listen.

If he had gone by the book for a single minute, he would have heard what she had really come to the ranch for. She wanted someone to hold her. She told him that. But she didn't want someone real to hold her. She could have found that closer to home. She needed someone like him, a warm body that she could hold onto, so she could close her eyes and have her husband back for a little while. Just like she had done at the gorge when she first arrived. She wanted a blow-up doll. Her words. He hadn't listened to those either.

She'd gotten what she needed. Another satisfied customer. Another woman he'd given a week of his life to. He threw the ball again. Harder this time. Hard enough to burn his hand when he caught it. A second's distraction from the ache that had settled deep in his chest.

She had him the minute he laid eyes on her at the airport. The game was over before it ever began. The more he learned about her, the more time he spent with her the more he wanted to. Dumb ass.

He let the ball shoot past his head and dribble on the floor behind him. He dragged his fingers through his hair, and closed his eyes.

"What did you do with Rebecca yesterday?" Garrett asked from the door.

"Doesn't matter." Gavin released an unsteady breath and focused on the wall in front of him. He didn't want to get into this yet. He'd really fucked up this time. Really been wrong about something he felt so sure about.

"Anything you want to tell me?" Garrett took a sip from his mug and dropped the ball he'd picked up from the floor into Gavin's lap.

"No. There's not," Gavin said, winging the ball against the wall again.

"I heard you last night." Garrett seated himself at his side of the desk. "The both of you."

Gavin shrugged. "So you heard. I gave her money back. Save the lecture."

"You don't look like you need a lecture."

"I've got everything I need right here," he said. The ranch. Enough women to ease his conscience. Enough women to warm his bed. Enough work to keep his mind occupied enough to believe those women were enough. Almost.

"Alright," Garrett said, setting his mug down. "Let's pretend the cops aren't already on our asses, and I'm just your brother who cares about what happens in your life. You've been in here all morning trying to knock a hole in the wall and pretend nothing's wrong. Everything's just 'business as usual.'"

"Nothing is wrong." The tennis ball landed in the trash bin with a thud.

"You should be escorting her to the limo in a little while."

Gavin shook his head but didn't make eye contact. "You take her. And don't forget her suitcase."

"This isn't the way you treat a woman." Garrett folded his arms across his chest and stared hard at his brother.

"Don't try telling me how to treat women." He didn't have enough fire left in him to yell. Outside the bedroom, he didn't know what in the hell to do with a woman. That much was obvious. He damn sure didn't need to be reminded of it.

"I'm saying this isn't the way *you* treat a woman," Garrett said. "Not even one you don't care about. And John told me what you did for her yesterday."

"How many times have you told me, it's just a game?" Gavin surrendered. Obviously people around him had a lot more figured out than he did. It was time he started listening to more of what was said, and worrying less about his own opinions.

"You haven't played the game all week," Garrett said.

Gavin rubbed his face. What was he supposed to do, go let her see what she'd done to him? Let her see what an idiot he was? He'd done enough of that already when he told her he loved her. How in the hell had he ever let himself fall in love again with a woman he knew he couldn't have? A woman who told him right off the bat that lust was all she could manage.

* * * *

Rebecca rolled over to face the wall closest to Gavin's bed. The pillow smelled of him, a clean outdoor scent with a hint of warmth, sandalwood, and something all at once new and familiar to her, the subtle musk of his passion. She pressed her face into the soft down and blinked away her tears.

On the wall next to a highboy, a framed picture of a Harvard track team hung next to a couple of high school track photos. Gavin stood to the left of the Harvard group, younger but not very different than he looked now. He really did go to Harvard. He really was real. She knew that. She didn't have a single doubt. And he'd said he loved her. Her heart was aching too bad to not be loving him back.

She shivered beneath the covers. She was so cold. Her blood was like ice in her veins. She had to leave Gavin's room, even if it meant she could never come back into it again. She had to find him, but she didn't know what she could possibly say that would make a difference in what he must think of her now. She had already said one word too many. He didn't want to be Todd, and he hadn't been, but she didn't know how to convince him of that. She only knew she couldn't cling to Todd as an excuse anymore, and Todd wouldn't want her to. He had loved her because she wasn't afraid to love. And Gavin deserved all that she could give him.

Her stomach tensed. If she had thrown away her second chance would she get a third? She didn't want another chance with anyone but Gavin. She had no doubt of that.

Rebecca wiped her palms across both sides of her face and lifted herself out of his bed. She had to find him. She picked her clothes up from the floor and pulled them on. Tangles strew her hair in every direction and her eyes were raw, but she didn't care. She took one look back at the bed and closed the door behind her.

Her bare feet padded soundlessly down the stairs. Sounds of the staff came from the kitchen. The smell of bacon and sweet breads was already wafting through the house. She wrapped her arms around herself. People would be coming through the door soon for breakfast. The big house seemed so foreign to her, a place she didn't have the right to be alone in. She'd only been in a handful of the rooms, if Gavin wasn't in any of those she was familiar with, she didn't know where to begin to look. And what if he had left the ranch? What if she wouldn't even get to see him again before she had to get on a plane?

She started for the office. Garrett would be there, and as much as she didn't want to have to explain anything to him, he would know where Gavin was or how to find him. She crossed the foyer. Voices met her in the hall. Her heart jumped into her throat and she swallowed it back down. Gavin was in the office. With Garrett. She was torn with whether she should interrupt them, let Garrett read on her face everything that had happened between them, or if she should slip out the back, return to the cabin and hope that Gavin would come find her.

He wouldn't. She had hurt him. Her heart made the decision for her. She had to go to him. She needed to convince him she didn't want him to be Todd. She wanted him to be with her. She just needed to tell him anything that would bring him into her arms again. Do whatever it took to make him believe.

The hall couldn't have been more than fifteen feet, but it would have been easier to walk a mile. Her heart pounded with every step. Her nails bit into her palms. Tears stung her eyes.

The voices became clearer. The words easy to discern. They were talking business.

"Get anywhere with that new marketing plan?" Garrett asked.

"No. We should keep the cowboy." Gavin sounded tired. "I need a shower, is there anything else?"

"Tomorrow you've got Erica Hirsh, 41, paralegal, from Florida, divorced."

"Great," Gavin responded. If he said anything more than that, Rebecca couldn't hear it over the pounding of her heartbeat. Could he really get up in the morning and try to make another woman fall in love with him? The room started to spin. She wrapped her arms around her stomach and held on until she could calm herself enough to listen some more.

"And Rebecca?" Garrett asked.

"Business as usual." His voice was so cold, so different than she had ever heard it before.

She braced herself against the wall for support. He didn't care about her. He hadn't meant any of it. Not the date. Not the stupid peas. Not the 'I love yous' he whispered in the dark. She was just an assignment and her week was up. He was better than she had imagined him to be. He had her believing it all, every word. He made her fall in love. Just like he was supposed to.

She swallowed the acid that rose in her throat and pushed herself off the wall. He might be used to getting away with all his lies, but not this time. She wasn't a woman who put up with men like him.

"I thought you entertained every other week," she said from the doorway of the office. Her heart hammered in her chest, pushing the blood through her veins with so much force it roared in her ears.

Garrett looked up but Gavin kept his back to her.

"You can't even look at me?" Her words had never contained such fire.

Garrett stood and started toward the door she was blocking. Gavin didn't answer, didn't turn around. She curled her fingers to keep them from shaking. Her fury built in his silence.

"Do you tell them all you love them?" She would make him face what he'd done, what a complete and utter ass he was. He wouldn't just sweep her under the rug without at least coming face to face with what he was capable of. Not that he would have heart enough to care.

Garrett shifted his weight trying to get by her. He obviously wanted to give them the room to themselves. She ignored him and focused on the back of Gavin's head.

"Do you make all of them wait until the end of the week to get in bed with you? Is that the way this game is played?"

"Excuse me," Garrett said, he couldn't get past her without physically pushing her aside and his discomfort was obvious.

"Why would you leave?" she asked him. "There aren't any secrets here, except from the guests. Except from stupid, vulnerable women like me. Right, Gavin?"

He stood up then, facing her, his neck tense and just as much fire in his eyes as she had raging inside her. "No, that's not right," he said. "You played the game better than I did. Congratulations. You won. I'm sorry but we don't give out trophies."

"That's okay. I got a belt. That's a cowboy trophy, right? But I hope you don't expect a tip for last night." Then to Garrett, she said, "You don't have to leave. I am. And I can find the limo by myself. Please send my bag."

The tears were about to fall, and she wasn't going to give Gavin the satisfaction of seeing any more of those. He may have made a fool of her, but he'd be the only man to do that. Ever.

She plowed through the front door nearly nailing a guest and her cowboy. The grass had never been colder, but the fire in her veins was gone and she was already freezing before her feet touched it. She didn't know if she'd ever be warm again. She hurried past the office window and kept her eyes in front of her, chin level. She approached the Honey cabin, hers was next. Darlin'. She never wanted to be called that again.

Inside, her phone was ringing. The screen said she had eight missed calls. She ignored this one from Melinda too, ripped her clothes off and stuffed them in the wastebasket by the sink. She caught her reflection in the mirror and turned away. She didn't need a picture of what he'd done to her. None of it had been real, and it was time to go home.

She showered and put on the sundress she'd worn on the flight out to Wyoming. She had a suitcase full of clean clothes in the office, but Garrett hadn't sent it and she wasn't going back over there to pick it up.

The car would be waiting out front to take her to the airport at 9:30, in ten minutes. Her cowboy was supposed to escort her, but she had no intention of waiting around for the send off. She packed her cosmetics bag, rolled her jeans into her carry-on, and lifted Gavin's sweatshirt off the bed. She put it back down. Picked it up again and pushed it into the bag. She should leave the damn thing, but it would be a good reminder. A reminder to never be stupid again.

She took everything that belonged to her except her trophy - the belt she would never be able to wear still looped through the headboard - and the check he'd given her. She tucked the check into the belt, it was probably worthless anyway. Another prop, like the hat.

A hard knock came at the door. Not Gavin's usual tempo. Obviously, he was still furious. She swung the door open ready to tear into him again.

"I don't have anything—" Her voice broke off. The officer Gavin had exchanged words with at the stream stood in front of her. Lieutenant Bening, his nameplate said.

"Ms. Rebecca Ryder?" he asked.

"Yes." Was he going to have her arrested now for sleeping with him? He broke the law as much as she did. More probably.

"Are you okay?" the Lieutenant asked.

"Never better."

"Do you mind if I ask you some questions?" His eyes swept the room, and settled on the hand towel that covered the air conditioning vent.

"Can you make this fast?" She lifted her carry-on bag off the bed and adjusted the strap over her shoulder. "I have a plane to catch."

"We've received a call concerning your safety and additional information about the type of business being operated here."

Rebecca slid the schedule of events off the night table and placed it in the officer's hand. "As you can see, I'm fine. And this is what goes on here. Now, if you'll excuse me."

"I can't do that. I'm going to have to ask you to come down to the station and issue a statement."

"Am I under arrest?" Her head was throbbing and she was ready to go another round with anybody who decided to piss her off, including this stupid cop.

"No, ma'am. You're not under arrest."

"Then I'm not going anywhere but the airport." She grabbed her purse and took a step toward him, daring him to keep standing in her way.

"I could cite you with solicitation, but I don't want to have to do that." His eyes traveled over to the bed where the dark brown leather of her trophy belt glared against the white birch headboard.

"I haven't solicited anything."

"We've taken Gavin Carter in already." A smirk settled over the cop's face. "Once we have a statement from him, we can issue a warrant for you. It'll be easier if you come now."

"He's under arrest?" Her heart constricted at the thought of Gavin in handcuffs, paying such a price for giving her what she wanted. What she needed. What she'd all but begged for. Even if he was a lying asshole who deserved to have a jailhouse dropped on his heartless chest.

"He hasn't been charged. Yet," Lieutenant Bening said with a look of smug satisfaction, "but he is a key person of interest in this investigation. Your brother-in-law has pulled a lot of strings to make sure you're okay. You really should be grateful."

Fucking Scott. All she wanted to do was go home and forget this week had ever happened and now he had his cronies hauling her off to some Podunk police station.

Chapter 12

Rebecca stepped out of the Canyon Creek police station, set her bag on the ground and flipped open her cell phone. The only thing left to do was call a cab to take her to the airport. Hopefully there were more flights back to South Carolina at some time today and she could get on one of them.

A familiar stretched-out Dodge Ram was parked along the curb. Garrett stepped down from the driver's side. She averted her eyes and dialed information. He was probably furious with her, ready to throw the contract in her face. He'd have to talk to her attorney. She was done talking about Fantasy Ranch, and after sitting in a tiny room fielding a barrage of questions from Officer Bening and another Barney Fife clone she was too drained to fight Garrett or anybody else.

"I got you on another flight and I'm here to take you to the airport," he said, picking up her bag.

"Why would you do that?"

"It's what we do." The lines on his forehead were more pronounced than usual, but his manner was polite enough. Either there was more to this than she could decipher or he was a heck of a nice guy.

"City and state please," the computerized operator chimed in her ear.

Rebecca snapped the phone closed and followed Garrett over to the truck. "Thank you," she said as he held the door open for her and handed her the bag. "Is Gavin still in there?" She nodded toward the police station.

"Yeah. Our attorney just got here." Garrett closed the door before she could ask him anything else. Unless Gavin was stupid he wouldn't say a word before he had his attorney by his side. And he definitely wasn't stupid. She'd told her story first. Now the case hinged on how much he trusted her.

She settled into the seat and closed her eyes. Her intentions for coming on this trip had been so simple, so naïve. A tear slid from beneath her lid. The road to Hell is paved with good intentions. She'd heard her father say that a hundred times. Smart man, but she was still waiting for the laughter to follow the tears. Obviously the tears weren't finished yet.

Her cell phone rang. She turned it off, didn't even check to make sure it was Melinda. There wasn't a soul she wanted to talk to. Not one. Garrett glanced back at her in the mirror. The glass divider was down between them. She averted her eyes as the tears kept falling. She had never been such an idiot. There was no telling what she had been exposed to making love to him without a condom. What if she'd gotten pregnant? God, she was worse than Melinda. She wasn't married to the liar. She didn't even have an excuse for being stupid. How could she have fantasized hard enough to think a week would extend beyond the foreseeable future?

Miles blurred past the windows. She pulled a small package of tissues from her purse and fingered the plastic, but didn't take one out. The tears were still coming too freely. It wouldn't do any good to wipe them away yet.

Right now Gavin was telling the police what? That he'd taken her to bed. That he hadn't. Would he keep lying? How many rounds did this game have?

And he had the nerve to tell her she won. Why? Because she'd bruised his ego, called him the wrong name? How much of what he told her had been true? Some of it had to be, didn't it? No, it didn't. Stupid, stupid girl. Idiot!

She'd gotten lucky with Todd, and she couldn't expect to ever get that lucky again. At least she knew that now.

Garrett turned into the airport terminal. Rebecca blew her nose and dried her face. The pity party was over. Time to go back to where she belonged and pull herself together. And never be stupid again.

Garrett opened the door and helped her out onto the curb. He studied her, but didn't say anything. She should be just as mad at him, but at least he had done what he could to keep her in her place, to remind her of what was really going on. Or maybe that was part of the game too, just the good cop/bad cop routine they had worked out. God, they had every angle covered. At least she could believe one thing Gavin said. He hadn't lied when he told her how fabricated the whole ranch experience was. Selective hearing. Must be innate to stupid women. That's how they choose so easily which lies to believe.

"I've checked your luggage," Garrett said. "Here are your boarding passes."

Rebecca took her tickets in silence and shivered in the cool Wyoming air. The straps of her sundress did nothing to ward off the chill. Gavin's sweatshirt was in her shoulder bag, but she couldn't bring herself to put it on. She didn't need a reminder of how stupid she was yet. Or probably ever. She should have left it on the bed next to the belt and check.

Garrett opened the front passenger side of the truck as Rebecca started making her way toward the double doors.

"Ms. Ryder," he called after her. He caught up to her before she'd gone more than ten steps. "You're cold, take this." He draped a large denim jacket around her shoulders.

"Thank you, but I can't take your clothes." Maybe she'd been wrong about which one was the nicer of the two. They should switch roles for the next guest.

"It's Gavin's," Garrett said, adjusting the collar.

Rebecca pulled the jacket off and shoved it back to him. "No thank you. I've had enough of his generosity to last me a lifetime."

"He wouldn't want you to be cold."

"He wouldn't care," she said, pushing the jacket toward him again. Her eyes brimmed with tears. "I'm sure he doesn't give his clothes away to every woman he entertains. If he did, he wouldn't have any left."

Garrett's face drew up into another series of concerned lines. "Why don't you come back to the ranch with me? We'll get you on a later flight."

She shook her head. "It's time for me to leave, but don't worry. My brother-in-law won't be sending in any more troops. I'm ready to put this week behind me. I don't ever want to hear or speak the words 'Fantasy Ranch' again."

"I think you and Gavin need to talk. Maybe you can work this out," he said softly, placing his hand on her arm. "Come back with me, please."

"Believe me, Gavin and I don't need to do anything else," she said. "But you can tell him something for me." She squared her shoulders and sniffed.

The cold air burned her lungs. "Tell him he played a good game. I believed every word. And nothing I said trumps that. I left the victory belt for him."

"Ms. Ryder." Garrett paused. "Rebecca." Lines burrowed deeper into his brow. "If my brother told you he loves you, you can believe it."

"I did believe it." Tears welled in her eyes and her heart became a suffocating weight. "But I'm not going to be stupid anymore." She left him standing there. He called her name again, but she didn't look back. The doors slid open and she didn't breathe until her boots hit the carpet inside the terminal and Fantasy Ranch became a mistake she had safely put behind her.

* * * *

Marge twisted her hands in her lap. Across the desk from her, Chet scribbled out a statement.

"What time was it when you saw Gavin Carter enter the guest cabin next to yours?" he asked without looking up at her, his pen adding more details she hadn't given him.

"I didn't see him go into her cabin."

"What time?" Chet said through his teeth. "Do I need to remind you what's at stake here?"

Marge clamped her lips tight and refused to lie even as her entire body trembled. All around her, men in uniforms moved around official-looking desks. They had guns and handcuffs and the authority to lock people away. She swallowed hard. The old Marge would have cowed, signed anything Chet stuck in front of her, and gone back to Philadelphia to hide while the details played out. Her knees bumped the cool metal of the desk and she focused on her hands.

"I'm not going to sign any statement full of lies. Or any statement at all. I'll pay you back the money you spent to bring me out here. But I'm not doing this undercover farce." She summoned the nerve to face her nephew, but the instant her head lifted she froze.

The Marlboro man didn't have anything on the gentleman standing behind Chet. Even the scowl on his face and the imposing uniform he wore didn't distract from his rugged beauty. His graying hair still maintained a hint of the chocolate hue he'd sported in his youth, and his tall sturdy frame was enough to make a woman swoon. Marge drew in a sharp breath and was met with a set of kind eyes and a smile. Her heart skipped. The old Marge would have wanted to slink beneath the desk, but the new Marge lifted her chin and returned his smile full on. Without another thought she stuck out a hand.

"I'm Marge Owen, Chester's aunt. From Philadelphia."

"Detective Allen Murphy. Do you mind telling me about the undercover farce you don't want to be a part of?" His handshake was professional and warm, but the way he held her eyes made her heart flip.

Chet tapped a stack of paper on his desk. "I'll have a full report for you this afternoon, sir."

"I think I'd like that report now, Officer Bening."

"Sir. I'm still writing up a witness account, and Gavin Carter has insisted on waiting for his attorney."

"Why would Mr. Carter need an attorney?" Detective Murphy's scowl deepened, but if anything it made him more intriguing. Sexier. Marge restrained from fanning herself.

Instead she motioned for the report in Chet's hands and gave her nephew a tight smile. "Chet brought me out for a week on the ranch so I could gather information for him. Only there's not any information, except that novel he's writing there." Detective Murphy planted his large tanned hands on his hips. "You brought a civilian into an undercover investigation without getting authorization for the use of a civilian or the investigation itself?"

Marge reached for a tablet on the corner of Chet's desk and waved it in front of her face. With each flick of her wrist the breeze was enough to lift her hair, but did absolutely nothing to cool her down.

"Sir, I..." Chet recovered quickly. "A poor judgment call doesn't change the facts."

"A novel is fiction, isn't it, Ms. Owen?" The detective lifted the report out of Chet's hands and skimmed through the pages of scribble.

"One big lie after another, with just enough truth sprinkled in to make you believe it," Marge said.

Detective Murphy laughed. "Ms. Owen, do you mind telling me what this report *should* say, starting with when you decided to visit our little town?"

"I'd love to. Could I trouble you for a little water first?"

Chapter 13

Rebecca's mattress dipped beneath Melinda's weight. "Hey sleepyhead," Melinda said.

Rebecca sat up and plumped a pillow beneath her throbbing head. "How're you feeling?" She was determined to focus on something besides the pain that refused to subside.

"I haven't thrown up this morning," Melinda said. "So I'll take that as a good sign."

Rebecca wiped the sting from her eyes and hugged her sister. "Congratulations. I can't believe you're going to be a mom. And I get to be an aunt."

"I can't either." Melinda's smile spread across her face. "I'm really happy about it now."

"So I take it Scott's back again?" At least she finally understood Melinda's weakness. Not that she would ever accept it for herself, but she understood. No matter how much she wanted to hate Gavin, she couldn't.

"I know you don't believe him." Melinda bit her lip. "And I probably shouldn't either, but he swears he's back for good, and no more women. He's so excited about the baby, he's already bought clothes and toys and every other word out of his mouth is about what we're going to name it."

"I'm happy for you about the baby, and I hope he really has changed. That's all I'll say."

"Fair enough." Melinda brushed Rebecca's hair off her face. "You look terrible."

"Thanks. I feel great." She rolled her eyes and forced a smile.

"Want to tell me what happened out there?"

"I don't know where to start." The tears threatened again, but she held them at bay. She would not let this break her. Losing Todd hadn't. Losing a man she never really had wouldn't either.

"Does this mean he really did go to Harvard?" Melinda tugged on the crimson sweatshirt Rebecca was wearing.

"He did." Rebecca took a steadying breath.

"And I take it you kind of really liked him."

Rebecca's chin trembled. Just because what she thought he felt for her was a crock, that didn't make her feelings for him any less real. She had a heart, and it still worked. At least he had shown her that.

"Oh, Becca." Melinda wrapped her arms around her. "What a jerk that guy is."

Rebecca pushed herself back against the headboard. "I won't die from it. I just need to figure out how to make it stop hurting."

"I have the perfect remedy," Melinda said. "Ice cream pancakes."

"Ice cream for breakfast?"

"Pregnancy gives you the best ideas. Trust me. I'll have it ready before you're out of the shower." She smiled and headed for the door. "And Becca, I really am sorry about what you had to go through with the police. I didn't know what else to do."

"I'll forgive you if make me some coffee." She probably would have called in the cavalry too if Melinda had lost her mind and run off with some make-believe cowboy then refused to answer her phone.

She lay there another fifteen minutes before she threw the covers off her legs and forced herself out of bed. The aroma of breakfast filled the house. Melinda had the television on and for a second the newscaster sounded like Gavin. She winced. It floored her how she could have been so totally and completely wrong about him. Is it that easy to misread someone? Boy did she have a lot to learn.

She pulled her hair into a ponytail and knotted it at the back of her head, just as her door began to open.

"I was just getting in—" Her sentence grinded to a halt.

"Have I told you how good you look in that shirt?" Gavin said from the doorway. He had a bag slung over his shoulder. His eyes were rimmed red, his polo and khakis wrinkled enough to have been slept in. He had never looked better.

Rebecca struggled to find her voice. "Not today."

He crossed the room and took her in his arms. She cried out, clinging to him, kissing him through her tears. Every bit of her anger dissolved with the feel of his body pressed to hers.

"I'm sorry," she said.

He responded with a kiss that traveled through her every nerve, then drew back, holding her face in hands. "Don't apologize. Just tell me who you were making love to."

"It was you. Only you. You said something he used to say. It rattled me. But I was making love with you. Every second."

"Am I the one you wanted it to be?" His pain was as obvious as it had been at the ranch. "Don't spare my feelings. I need the truth."

Eyes don't lie. She still believed that. She had to believe that.

"I loved him. I will always love him." She ran her hands down Gavin's chest, every curve of his body familiar beneath her touch. "But he's not here anymore, and when I was with you I was with the man I wanted to be with."

"Do you still want me?" His arms tightened around her sending an urgent need coursing through her body.

"Did you fly across the country in the middle of the night to ask me that?" Her shattered heart fused itself back together and beat victoriously in her chest.

"Yeah. And I'm really hoping you say yes."

"Yes," she said, "And I don't care how stupid that makes me."

"You're not stupid."

"Come to bed with me." Her voice was desperate, but she didn't care about that either. She was even more desperate than she sounded. "And don't ever leave."

He dropped his bag on the floor and walked her across the room. The back of her knees hit the edge of the mattress, and he followed her down, his thigh between hers. The weight of his body was so right. His mouth tasted like the only answer to her hunger.

Above her, his breath was ragged, his eyes searched hers. The need she saw in him echoed her own. But there was still one thing that bothered her. One thing she couldn't just ignore, no matter how much she wanted him.

"I thought you had another guest to entertain today," she whispered. A tear rolled from the corner of her eye before she could stop it.

"I was supposed to cover for Garrett this week, but I fired myself from that part of the job." He brought his lips to hers, barely brushing them this time.

"Why would you do that?" She moved her mouth against his unable to hide her smile.

"I realized I'm not very good at it."

"You're very…very…good at it," she told him between kisses.

He balanced his elbow beside her and rested his head in his hand. "I really screwed up this time. I don't know how to tell you how sorry I am."

"And you didn't even bring peas?" She ran her hand down his arm, needing to touch him, to know he was there, he was hers to touch. She looked into his eyes. "Just tell me what parts were real."

"From the minute I met you, I meant every word," he said. "I swear."

She raked her fingers through his hair and covered his mouth with hers. There was nothing else she needed to hear.

He pulled away from her, traced her ear and followed the line of her face, before bringing his finger to her lips. "Have you fallen in love with me yet?"

Her eyes never left his when she answered: "I'm in so deep, I couldn't stop loving you if I wanted to." She smiled. "Believe me, I tried."

She shivered as he ran his fingers along her neck, then brought his lips down in exactly the right spot. She gasped and dug her hands into his back, pulling him to her, wanting nothing more than to connect with him again, to forget everything but the feel of their bodies together.

"You lied to the police," he said.

She slipped her hands beneath his shirt, warming herself with his heat. "They asked me if we had sex. They didn't ask if we made love."

"And you want to do that some more?" His voice was low, vibrating in the tone that drove her crazy.

"Right now," she said, holding herself as close to him as she could.

"We've got forever," he whispered. "There's no rush."

When their mouths met, she closed her eyes and let herself go, and the only person in the world she could think of was Gavin Carter.

Epilogue

"Daddy will you draw a picture of me?"

Gavin laid his pencil down on his desk and lifted his daughter into his arms. She was as beautiful as her mother, the same dark mane of hair and matching eyes.

"You want to help?" he asked.

"I can't. Uncle Garrett's gonna let me ride Pilgrim." She wrapped her arms around his neck for a quick hug, then squirmed to get down. "I'll look at it when I get back."

He pressed his lips to her temple and let her jump to the floor. She ran out of the room ponytail flying as the phone rang.

"Fantasy Ranch, Gavin speaking."

"Yes, Ms. Boucher, we're looking forward to your visit. We do take requests, although we can't always accommodate— Which cowboy? That one's booked. For the rest of his life."

Rebecca smiled from the doorway. Gavin seated the phone, and held open his arms.

"What are you waiting out there for Mrs. Carter?"

She settled into his lap. "You really need to print new brochures. You're disappointing guests before they get here."

"Am I disappointing you?" He nuzzled into the hair above her ear.

"No, but if you don't come upstairs right now while we have a babysitter you will."

He ran his hand beneath the hem of her blouse and over her swollen belly. Their child responded to his touch, moving beneath Rebecca's skin. "We've got to get this one out here before we can make another one," he said.

"I just want to practice." She kissed his bottom lip with both of hers. "I need a lot of practice."

His heart hammered in his chest. He still thanked his stars every day she was his. Forever. "You are the sexiest woman in the world."

"Then why aren't you upstairs yet?" she asked with a twinkle in her eye.

He stood, and lifted her with him. Rebecca wrapped her arms around his neck and kissed him with as much passion as she had the very first time.

"You ever gonna get enough of me?" he breathed.

"Never."

"That's exactly what I want to hear," he said as he carried her into their room and locked the door.

COWBOY GAMES

THE END

WWW.WENDIDARLIN.COM

ABOUT THE AUTHOR

Wendi Darlin grew up twenty miles from the nearest stoplight, minutes to the Gulf of Mexico, and steps from an open pasture. Like any native of the South, she can tell you there is nothing more sultry than a Southern setting, whether it's at the beach or on a rural rolling hill. Warm nights, sweet scented air, and a lazy drawl can absolutely melt a girl.

She writes from the home she shares with her husband, son, their two shelties, and Sparky, the little wiener dog. When it is time to take a break, you'll find her near the water, usually not far from a white sand beach.

Siren Publishing, Inc.
www.SirenPublishing.com